C000281573

Producer & International Distributor
eBookPro Publishing
www.ebook-pro.com

Mission Rocket Man
Charlie Wolfe

Copyright © 2019 Charlie Wolfe

All rights reserved; No parts of this book may be reproduced or transmitted in any form or by any means, electronic or mechanical, including photocopying, recording, taping, or by any information retrieval system, without the permission, in writing, of the author.

Contact: Charlie.Wolfe.Author@gmail.com
ISBN: 9789655751055

MISSION
ROCKET MAN

CHARLIE WOLFE

PREFACE

A blast from an Improvised Nuclear Device, an IND, is no longer a question of 'if' only a question of 'when.' There is also little doubt about 'who,' 'why,' and 'where.' The simple answers are 'radical Islamists,' 'in the name of Allah' and 'Israel or the West.' This series of thrillers looks at some of the unlikely scenarios, or perhaps frighteningly realistic ones, that may occur. How can these dastardly conspiracies be foiled and by whom?

The author, a nuclear scientist and aficionado of suspense stories, has allowed his imagination to run wild while staying within the realm of technically feasible deeds. The villains are always dreadful (an alchemist, a renegade, a misled patriot, and a Rocket Man) and our protectors are agents of intelligence organizations vowed to defend our way of life. The battles between 'good and evil' are fought all over the Middle East, Europe, and the United States.

Some readers have commented that the plots scared them so much they suffered from sleepless nights. Others asked if it was scientifically possible to build a nuclear device as outlined in the books. A particularly paranoid friend worried I may be giving the 'dreadful enemy' ideas for action. The author assured him, and all other readers, he has been careful not to expose details that are not readily available in published sources.

PROLOGUE

The standard forty-foot shipping container was secured to a flatbed trailer being towed by a powerful tractor. All three items were purchased for ridiculously low prices on the net from a large Chinese vendor and assembled in the Syrian port city of Tartus.

Three things that would have looked odd to anyone observing the truck. First, the color of the container and tractor appeared to be rusty but were in fact a camouflage pattern that would have been difficult to spot in the daytime, even by a satellite with advanced imaging software. Second, there was no port nearby, or even a large city to where such a container would normally be shipped. Third, the contents of the container were the harbinger of death on such a grand scale it would surpass all acts of terror of the last 100 years, combined.

However, only a few stray camels that had escaped from their owners, and perhaps a jackal or two, looked curiously at the strange truck, and then got back to their daily business, finding something to eat and survive in the desert.

Dr. Raymond Mashal, known only as the 'Rocket Man' to the organization that had hired him, sat next to Selim, the young driver. Murad, the man in charge of the mission, wearing a nondescript uniform and brandishing an automatic rifle, sat near the other door.

Raymond kept fussing and telling the driver to slow down and mind the irregular surface of the track they were following. It wasn't even a dirt road but more like an imaginary line drawn between the two most prominent features in the landscape. Behind them was a cliff of red-colored sandstone and a lone tree stood ahead of them.

As opposed to outdated common wisdom, they travelled by day and stopped an hour before sunset for a meal. This was done to allow the engine to cool down to avoid leaving a thermal signature that would be easily spotted by satellites equipped with infrared cameras.

That is why they didn't even light a fire to make coffee or warm food after dark. The trip was a long one and they were getting on each other's nerves. They slept through the night without even bothering to stand guard – the area was so remote and unpopulated they had no fear of being attacked by nomads or terrorists.

Raymond was the only one who was told what the deadly cargo could do, but even he wasn't confident he knew its true nature. After all, his task was to make sure it reached its intended target – he was the 'Rocket Man' – and to do that the truck had to travel as far west as possible and passable. The range of the rocket he had designed and built was limited because of the large payload it had to carry, so every mile increased the probability of reaching the target. The exact distance depended on his location, but it was about 275 miles at an azimuth of 265 degrees.

Their destination was the desolate area called Umm

Chamain depression in western Iraq, near the border triangle with Jordan and with Saudi Arabia. They had avoided the busy highway that led to the official border crossing. Raymond's instructions were to go as far west as he could but not cross into Jordanian or Saudi territory. The Jordanians had increased the number of patrols along their border with Iraq and supplemented their ground forces with aerial reconnaissance drones. Ever since the disintegration of the central government of Iraq the greatest fear in the Hashemite Kingdom of Jordan was from Islamic State supporters infiltrating into Jordan.

Murad checked his GPS navigation system and said something to the driver. The truck stopped and Raymond and Murad got out of the air-conditioned cabin and gingerly set foot on the hot desert soil that was badly eroded. Raymond examined the smooth surface and tested it first with his foot and then with a sharp metal rod. He nodded to Murad and together they opened the double doors of the shipping container. They used the truck's crane to unload the cargo and started setting up the launcher. Then they climbed to the container's roof and patiently watched the large ball of orange turn to red as the sun set in the west.

Raymond couldn't help but wonder if there would be two balls of fire the following morning – one on the east, known as Sol or simply the sun, and a new sun, a manmade creation on the west.

CHAPTER 1

Outskirts of Baghdad, 2013

The small meeting was attended by three of the senior Al Qaeda people in Iraq. Colonel Saad Husseini had been the commander of an elite paratrooper unit in the Iraqi army and Major Taleb Aswadi was his executive officer. They were professional soldiers and quite good at their chosen trade, but their unit was no match to the American superiority in weapon systems.

After the defeat to US forces in 2003, the unit had been disbanded by the Shiite-led puppet government that had been set up by the American occupation forces. This was part of the plan to establish a democracy in Iraq and to remove Sunni Muslims from positions of influence. Thus, the Colonel and major found themselves, as did many other Sunni officers and soldiers, out of a job, without a livelihood, and in a constant risk of being arrested by the Shiite regime.

Colonel Husseini was a distant cousin of Saddam Hussein the former ruler, or dictator as the Western press called him, and, therefore, was lucky to escape prosecution by the Americans or the Shiite government.

Major Aswadi, as his name implied (aswad is black in

Arabic) was a descendent of dark-skinned Bedouins that lived near the border with Jordan on the western end of Iraq. Despite the discrimination against people of his skin color, Aswadi excelled in battle during the First Gulf War in 1991 and rose through the ranks.

Both men were in their mid-forties and had been soldiers for most of their lives. When they were discharged from the Iraqi army, they slowly drifted toward extreme Islamic movements until they became key figures in Al Qaeda.

The true-identity of the third participant in the small meeting was known only to a handful of people. He was known simply as the Yemenite or Al Yamani in Arabic, an obvious indication of his country of origin. In fact, he was a religious leader and the most powerful man in northern Iraq.

The Shiite government had tried to capture him, or preferably kill him, numerous times but he always managed to get away, usually leaving behind piles of bodies of the people who were pursuing him, as well as innocent by-standers deemed as collateral damage. After so many attempts on his life the Yemenite had gone underground, figuratively and literally, and had met only with the very few people he trusted.

He recorded weekly sermons on audio tapes, and monthly messages on video. These were distributed by a network of faithful followers to all Sunni mosques in Iraq. In his sermons, he reiterated the sins of the Crusaders, or Messianics as he called the Christians, and vowed he would fight them until the last Crusader was either expelled from all the lands of Islam or buried in their sacred soil.

The Shiites and all other Muslims would fare no better, but

they would be given the choice of joining the true religion (as he saw it) or forfeiting their lives. The Jews were not usually mentioned in his sermons, but he persisted in mentioning the need to destroy the Zionist Entity, the name Israel was anathema and avoided, and vowed to remove this stronghold of infidels from the heart of the future Islamic Caliphate.

After praying to Allah, the Yemenite stated, "We have managed to make the life of the Crusaders intolerable thanks to the valor and sacrifices of our *Shahids*. Our young people are willing to give their lives for the cause of Islam and the grandeur of Allah by blowing themselves up and taking many infidels with them. Allah will receive them in heaven and reward them with seventy-two virgins while our enemies will rot in hell. These heroic acts have forced the Christian pigs and their Shiite dogs to quarantine themselves in closed enclaves. These ghettos they willingly built for themselves are like jails and their occupants are like prisoners on death-row that know they will be executed but don't know when. This is a great achievement for Allah and his true followers, but it is not enough. The number of troops that are our targets has decreased since their coward president started withdrawing them from Iraq. The Shiite dogs are keeping out of areas where our supporters rule. In effect, we have control of most of the country from around Baghdad up to the north where the Kurds resist us. The Shiites still control the south of the country with the help of the treacherous Mullahs' regime in Iran and the bayonets of the British and American soldiers that are still in Iraq. However, we need to demonstrate to the world that the infidels are not safe anywhere, even in their homeland. And we need to do this on a grand scale, not by blowing up a railway station here or bombing a plane there. Do you have any suggestions?"

Colonel Husseini responded, "Our great leader Saddam Hussein used chemical weapons against the Kurds and against the Iranian Shiite mongrels. The results were disappointing. We had expected tens of thousands of casualties and that they would lose the will to resist. The effect was not as impressive as we had hoped for. There were only a few thousand dead Kurds that died a terrible death they fully deserved but their will to fight us did not go away. The Kurds published photos that shocked the world for a few days, but the attacks did not break their spirit or diminish their resistance. With the Iranians, the outcome was even less impressive. The Mullahs just threw more and more people, including teenagers, into the battlefield and stopped the advance of our brave warriors. A group in Japan had tried to use a combination of chemical and biological agents in an underground train station but only a dozen or so people died there. More recently, in the internal conflict in Syria, Bashar Al Assad's Syrian army forces allegedly used full-fledged chemical weapons or other poisonous gases like chlorine, but without achieving a breakthrough on the battleground. The rebel forces tried to do the same, on a smaller scale, but didn't fare any better. Once again, the world press managed to get a few photos of the victims but no one cared for some dead Arabs, especially if they were killed by other Arabs. Therefore, I think that we need something much more powerful, to cause many more casualties, and collateral damage to property. This must be something that would shock the world and convince them the Muslims are a rising power, something that would instill the fear of Allah in their dark hearts. What comes to mind is to renew the plan that Saddam had to manufacture nuclear weapons."

The Major cleared his throat and when the Yemenite signaled for him to speak he said, "Colonel Husseini, with all due respect, if Saddam couldn't do this when he had complete control of the country, how can we achieve the goal and manufacture atomic weapons secretly, when the Shiite government and its collaborators are harassing us? I think we need to acquire them, or a good substitute, by other means."

The Yemenite listened patiently and then smiled. "I had expected these answers and the conclusion. I believe we have a solution. It will require a lot of money, considerable time, enlistment of volunteers willing to sacrifice their lives, cooperation by experts, and a lot of luck with the mercy of Allah."

Noticing the skeptical looks on the faces of his underlings he added, "I have made a plan to obtain fissionable material from a source that is so badly guarded it would be like taking candy from a baby, as the Americans are fond of saying."

The Colonel and the Major looked expectantly at the Yemenite. He was in no hurry to satisfy their curiosity. He clapped his hands twice and when his servant, Ibrahim al-Hinnawi, appeared at the door he asked him to bring coffee. A few moments later, when Ibrahim returned with a tray, he picked up the small cup of thick, bitter coffee brought it up to his mouth and took a sip of the dark brew, smacking his lips appreciatively.

After a long pause he said, "I have been briefed by my scientific advisor, Dr. Kasim Walid, a former nuclear scientist at Osiraq, the reactor that was bombed in 1981, by the Israeli Air Force. He said that while the stocks of 'classic' fissionable materials, plutonium, and enriched uranium, are closely supervised and guarded there is another source."

The Yemenite waited, for dramatic effect, before continuing, "He told me that few people understand that irradiated nuclear fuel, called 'spent fuel' contains large amounts of plutonium." When he saw the look on the faces of the two officers, he added, "This means the fuel elements removed from electricity-producing nuclear power plants, they contain enough plutonium to make an atomic bomb."

The Colonel interjected, "But this plutonium is of very low grade and the spent fuel is highly radioactive. How can this be of any help to our plan?"

The Yemenite smiled benignly. "Dear Colonel, once again your comment is predictable. In some nuclear reactors, the fuel is removed after a shorter than normal period. These fuel rods contain plutonium of a higher quality, perhaps not ideal for making atomic weapons but not totally useless. True, the radiation hazard is very serious, but we have enough dedicated people willing to die, even a painful death, knowing that their sacrifice was in the name of Allah."

The Major cleared his throat with a cough and said, "I have many questions. How do we know where to find this type of higher-grade material? And once we find it, how can we get our hands on it? I know very little about nuclear materials, but I understand there is only a small amount of plutonium in each fuel element and small factories or large laboratories are needed to extract it. They are called reprocessing plants. Even if we can construct a suitable facility, I wonder who has the necessary knowledge to carry out the work? And..."

The Yemenite gave him a look that could stop a raging bull elephant and raised his hand slightly. The Major stopped talking and mumbled an apology for his outburst.

The Yemenite calmed down and said, "It is up to the two of you, my most trustworthy and best men, to prepare an action plan. The nuclear scientist I mentioned is waiting outside. He is determined to avenge the obliteration of Osiraq, the Iraqi nuclear reactor that was supposed to manufacture an atomic weapon for Saddam Hussein. He is sure, as are all patriotic Arabs, that the United States and its cursed allies wouldn't have dared invade Iraq and humiliate it if our country was in possession of a nuclear bomb. He blames the Israeli snakes for the annihilation of Osiraq and the damn Americans for providing the F-16 planes that did the damage. He is willing to do anything to help prevent another dastardly act against the Arab people, the Ummah. Dr. Kasim Walid also lost some of his best friends in that Israeli attack, including his fiancée, who was a technician in his laboratory. He has never formed another serious relationship with a woman since. If you need to prompt him into action just mention the name of the girl, Fatma, and see how enraged he becomes."

The Colonel and the Major exchanged a glance and rose to leave the room when the Yemenite said, "Go with Allah and keep this plan a secret."

***

Colonel Husseini and Major Aswadi entered the hallway adjacent to the room where they met with the Yemenite. After passing the two bodyguards posted at the door they reached a small room and found a man seated on a divan.

Dr. Walid stood up and shook hands with them. He was a tall man in his late fifties or early sixties and appeared to be in good physical shape. His eyes sparkled with intelligence and some degree of mischief in his voice as he said, "Colonel Husseini and Major Aswadi, I am honored to meet you. I have heard a lot about your bravery and the successful operations the two of you led against the invading infidels and their treacherous allies in Iraq."

The Colonel replied, "Dr. Walid, our esteemed leader, the Yemenite, has praised you for your total dedication and ingenuity. Please call me Saad, and my colleague, Taleb. We are no longer in the Iraqi army but fighters for the true cause of Islam so no need to refer to our previously held ranks."

The scientist smiled and responded, "Please call me Kasim. I am still a scientist, of course, but we are all working now for the same cause, so no formalities are necessary."

The Colonel asked, "Have you started to form a plan?" The scientist smiled and nodded. The Colonel continued, "Where can we sit quietly and discuss it? You probably need maps and diagrams to explain to us what we need to do."

Dr. Walid beckoned for them to follow him and the three of them went to his office, located in the basement of a nearby building. The scientist proudly pointed at a laptop that was his prize possession.

"This is my temporary quarters and although it doesn't look like the high-tech offices you see on TV, I do have a fast internet connection that allows me to follow the latest publications in my field. More importantly, I have, at the tips of my fingers, all the maps where the nuclear plants are clearly marked and access to police notifications of road closures near those plants, from which one can infer if hazardous materials are about to be transported. We don't need to rely on spies and informants as we did in the old days, although inside information is always useful and cooperation can simplify the job. And, let me add, even if this humble office is raided there is no incriminating evidence of any wrongdoing–"

The Major interjected, "But if your laptop is seized, they can follow the history of your internet searches and see what you were looking for."

The scientist replied, "I have my laptop ready. I can take it with me if I need to escape quickly, which I hope will never happen. But just in case, I have everything encrypted and made sure the search history is not retained. Fortunately, I have an exceptional visual memory so I can easily reconstruct all the relevant information I have found."

The Colonel was a very practical man and didn't care for the public relations one-man show Dr. Walid presented. He cut in rather rudely, "Kasim, this is fine, but we need to hear what you have in mind for our operation."

The scientist sighed quietly. "You military men are always in a hurry to kill someone or get killed yourselves. I needed to show you how we can use this 'freedom of information' thing that our enemies are so proud of to undermine their infrastructure and lives."

He switched on his laptop and brought up a map on which all the nuclear power plants were marked. "Look at this and tell me what you think." He found a website that was run by a British newspaper, The Guardian, and presented a map of the nuclear power plants in the world and said, "Last year there were close to 100 nuclear power plants that had a license to operate in the United States, mostly on and near the crowded East Coast, and quite a few on the West Coast. But look at Europe – the clatter of markers shows that there are many more there, mostly in France and Germany. But we have taken a special interest in smaller countries, where we believe security is more relaxed."

The Colonel and the Major scrutinized the map as Kasim zoomed in to the area that included Belgium and Holland. The Colonel asked, "What are the different colored dots?"

The scientist explained, "The green dots represent operating plants and the red dots show the plants that were shut down. We are not interested in the other dots that depict planned plants or those that are still under construction nor those that are not yet operational. We need to focus on the green and red dots because that is where we can hope to find spent fuel elements." He looked at the faces of the gentlemen and was glad to see they were impressed by the map and his logical approach.

The Major pointed at a red dot and asked what it referred to and Kasim said, "Wait a minute and I'll zoom in on it. This is called BR-3 meaning Belgian Reactor number 3 and is a test PWR which is short for a Pressurized Water Reactor that was started in 1957 and is now shut down. It had a very low power output so I doubt if there ever could be a large stock of plutonium in it. Anything else that looks interesting?"

The Colonel pointed at another red dot near a place called Julich, but before he could ask about it, the scientist said, "This is in Germany and we don't want to mess with the Germans because their security around nuclear power plants is very high. Do you have any other ideas?"

When the two officers didn't reply, Kasim said, "Well, I think that Holland is more promising than Belgium. Look at this power plant just across the border from Belgium. It is an old PWR that is still operational and has probably accumulated a large stock of irradiated fuel elements. I am not sure whether they store these spent fuel elements on-site indefinitely or ship them away for reprocessing. If they do, it is probably to France by rail or truck or possibly by ship across the channel to Dounreay, Scotland. But even if they do ship the spent fuel elements to some other place, they must first be placed in a cooling pool to allow the radioactivity to abate. These cooling pools do two things: first, they literally allow the hot fuel rods to cool to a lower temperature, and secondly, the short-lived radioactive fission products decay and the total radioactivity decreases rapidly to a lower level. The fuel elements are still very dangerous but can be handled by special equipment and moved from the cooling pools to special casks that are used for transportation. These casks are heavy and those that weigh about twenty-five tons are commonly used in Europe, so it is impossible to simply load them on a truck by a group of people."

The Colonel thought about this bit of information for a moment and commented, "So, Dr. Walid, are you implying that it cannot be done?"

The scientist responded, "On the contrary, I am saying that everyone thinks that the heavy cask ensures it cannot be hijacked and, therefore, security is quite lax. I propose that we hit the target when it is most vulnerable – during transportation. This would be a real military operation and your expertise is vital. We'll have to make out a list of the equipment needed for such an operation, but my basic idea is to hijack the truck with its load and drive it to a hiding place, preferably a ranch in a rural area, where we can establish a clandestine laboratory and carry out the reprocessing we need to isolate the plutonium from the irradiated fuel elements and then turn it into a form that is suitable for a weapon."

The two former officers exchanged a long glance, smiled, and nodded approvingly. The Colonel spoke, "It seems as if you have thought of everything, Dr. Walid."

But the scientist shook his head. "Far from it. There so many points that must be clarified first, so much planning to do, so many preparations and, of course, we must obtain all the operational intelligence required for such a project, not to mention the funds and manpower we need."

The Colonel bowed his head. "So, let's go back to our leader, the Yemenite, and present the plan. He certainly will approve and make sure we receive everything we need."

***

The Yemenite saw that the three men were jubilant and assumed they had devised a plan. He looked at them expectantly and Colonel Husseini, who was the senior among them spoke first, "Our esteemed Leader, Dr. Walid has outlined his proposal for getting our hands on a cask with spent nuclear fuel from which a batch of plutonium may be extracted. It is a daring plan and will require funds and skilled manpower as well as some of our best fighters to carry out the job and provide security. We still need to work out the details, but I believe it is so bold and daring it has a chance..."

The Yemenite intervened, "Have you thought about the target, and more importantly about the means of delivery?" The Colonel and the scientist looked at each other and shrugged, so the Leader continued, "The target is Tel-Aviv. A nuclear bomb there would destroy the infrastructure and commercial and cultural center of the Zionist Entity and force the Jews to return as refugees to the countries from which they came to our lands. Hopefully, there will not be too many of them after the atomic strike to their black hearts."

He saw his small audience swallowing his every word and added, "I have located the very man who will develop the delivery system for the weapon. You know him, as do all Iraqis as, the 'Rocket Man.' Dr. Raymond Mashal has been involved with Saddam's rocket plan almost from its inception. He is now not a young man but is dedicated and skillful."

The Colonel said, "Of course, we have all heard of him. I thought he had escaped from Iraq or had passed away. I will take it upon myself to locate him and persuade him to join our grand project."

CHAPTER 2

Amsterdam, Holland, May , Three years later

Dr. Kasim Walid stood up from the uncomfortable arm-chair and started pacing about the small hotel room. He had checked-in the previous evening, as instructed by phone, and impatiently waited to meet his local contact.

Colonel Husseini's voice on the phone had sounded relaxed when he told Kasim to resign from his job at the research laboratory where he had been employed as an experimental physicist for the last three years.

This laboratory, in the north of Holland, worked under contract with European nuclear agencies and provided support for universities that could not afford to purchase and maintain the facilities needed for studies in nuclear physics. The main reason he had spent these years in a position that did not suit his true abilities and was below his skill level was to familiarize himself with laboratory work in the West and acquaint himself with the firms that supplied equipment and chemicals to research laboratories.

He also learned all about the modern safety regulations required for working with radioactive materials – things that were ignored at the time he had worked as a junior scientist at the Osiraq reactor until its annihilation by the Israeli air force. Safety regulations were of secondary concern at Saddam's nuclear research centers in Iraq as the objective of obtaining a nuclear device took precedence over the health of the employees.

Kasim didn't understand why Saddam rushed to invade and occupy Kuwait in August 1990, rather than wait another year or two and do so as a country with a small nuclear arsenal. If necessary, a demonstration could be arranged – as did India and Pakistan a decade later, and North Korea a few years after that.

No one messed with countries with a budding nuclear capability. He strongly believed that Desert Storm, the humiliating defeat of Saddam and his Iraqi army a few months after the occupation of Kuwait, would have never taken place against a country with atomic bombs.

Kasim recalled the surprise he had a few weeks earlier when the Colonel had informed him they had all sworn allegiance to the rising forces of the Islamic State and they were no longer members of Al Qaeda. The Islamic State of Iraq and Syria (ISIS), sometimes called the Islamic State of Iraq and the Levant (ISIL), also known as Daesh for its Arabic acronym ad-Dawlah al-Islamiyah fi'l Iraq wa sh-Sham. Its rise was so rapid that within one year after its founding in 2014, it gained control of an area the size of the United Kingdom in what used to be Iraq and Syria.

The amazed scientist asked the Colonel how that change of allegiance had come about and what implications this would have on their project. The Colonel said that Al Qaeda had gone soft and the grand future of Islam lay with ISIS and the execution of the grand project would continue as if nothing had happened. He said ISIS had already taken the first steps to establishing the New Caliphate in parts of Iraq and Syria and was sending its tentacles to North Africa, other Muslim countries, and even to Europe where the influence of Islam was rapidly growing.

***

Three years earlier, Walid had left Iraq shortly after the meeting with Colonel Husseini and Major Aswadi and after receiving the blessing of the Yemenite himself. Once again, he lamented the untimely death of the Yemenite at the hands of the traitor, Ibrahim al-Hinnawi, who managed to enter the inner circle of the Leader's entourage and served him faithfully for several months. Although Al Hinnawi had never risen above the rank of a servant, whose main responsibility was to serve tea and lay out the rug on which the Yemenite prayed five times a day, he had gained the Leader's confidence.

When the servant received news that his entire family was murdered, and, in fact, the entire village in which they had lived was destroyed by the advancing Iraqi army, he was enraged and swore to avenge their death. He asked the Yemenite's permission to go to the ruined village and, at least, offer his family a proper burial ceremony. The Yemenite gave him three days to pay his respects to his family.

When Al Hinnawi reached the village, he saw the bloated human corpses in the streets, lying amidst dead and similarly bloated carcasses of farm animals. He was surprised to see that none of the bodies appeared to have bullet holes or limbs torn off by shrapnel but judging by their distorted features they all looked as if they had suffered a terrible, agonizingly painful death. He looked around and saw almost no buildings were destroyed but there was not a living soul around. A strange odor permeated his nostrils and he wrapped his *keffiyeh* around his face making sure the thin cloth covered his nose. It was an odor even stronger than the stench emitted by the dead carcasses of humans and animals.

He saw none of the signs he had expected from an armed offensive by the Iraqi army. Suddenly he had a terrible insight – the village was attacked by some dreadful chemical weapon.

He then recalled pieces of a conversation he had overheard while serving tea to the Yemenite and a mysterious guest. This guest had stopped talking mid-sentence when Al Hinnawi entered with the tray, but he could distinguish the words, "…this will be a test of our new…" The Yemenite had motioned irritably for Ibrahim to place the tray with the tea on a small table and leave the room. The servant left the room hastily and was slightly offended by the gesture of his boss but thought nothing further of it.

However, now at the lifeless village everything seemed to fall in place. Clearly, the Yemenite had not realized the village that served as the test site for the new chemical weapon was Al Hinnawi's ancestral home or he never would have allowed him to return.

The servant reached the dirt road where his family had lived and found the bodies of his parents and siblings. He dragged them to backyard of the house in which he had grown up, and with great difficulty dug a shallow grave in the rocky soil and gently placed the bodies in it. He placed an old blanket over the bloated bodies and covered the grave with the soil he had dug out earlier, placed wooden planks and some large rocks on the grave. He stood at the grave site for a long moment as tears dripped down his dust-covered face beneath his *keffiyeh*.

When he returned to the Yemenite's hiding place, he took a tray, placed a cup of sweet tea on it, and held a dagger underneath the tray. He entered the room in which the Leader was just finishing the sunset prayer, Duluk ash-shams. The servant threw the tray on the floor and the noise startled the Yemenite, who was about to rise from his prostrate position.

The two bodyguards standing outside the door also heard the unexpected loud noise and rushed in to see what was going on. They heard the servant shouting, *Allahu Akbar* and witnessed him grabbing the Yemenite by the hair and pulling a sharp dagger across his throat, severing the leader's head, just as seen on video clips released by ISIS.

In an instant, they shot the servant but could not wipe the smile off the traitor's face as he died at their feet. The grotesque head of the Yemenite remained clasped in the lifeless hand of the dead traitor and one of the bodyguard's needed to exert all his strength to pry it loose and place it near the leader's body.

***

The gentle knock on the door alarmed the scientist and woke him up from his memories and daydreaming. He looked through the peephole and saw a young woman standing at the door. He opened it and noted the woman was wearing a *hijab* and *niqab* that covered her head and body per the Islamic dress code for women.

In Amsterdam, it was a common sight to see Muslim women wearing these clothes, although covering the entire face with a *burqa* was banned in public places. Kasim tried to estimate her age, a difficult task when her face was partially covered by the *niqab* and her body made completely shapeless by the flowing robe of her *hijab*.

In a quiet voice she said, "I am Afrin and was sent to you by the Colonel."

Kasim smiled and replied, "I hope that you bring us luck, as your name means. I was not expecting a woman to be my contact."

Afrin removed the scarf from her face and when she saw Kasim's reaction to her beauty she smiled. "Dr. Walid, please close your mouth. I am a graduate student of chemistry at the University of Amsterdam sent to assist you in the grand project."

Seeing her face now, Kasim could figure out she was in her late twenties, or perhaps early thirties.

Kasim overcame his surprise, managed to finally close his mouth and asked her, "Have you been briefed by the Colonel?" When she nodded, he added, "Let's go over the plan together."

Afrin replied, "I am not involved in the operational side of seizing the irradiated fuel elements. That is the responsibility of the Colonel and his men. I am here to help you construct the laboratory and prepare it for extraction of the plutonium. Once we receive the spent fuel cask, I will oversee the chemical processing and purification of the plutonium, under your guidance, of course."

The scientist asked, "Did Colonel Husseini give you the funds for establishing the laboratory?"

Afrin reached into the *hijab*, hesitated for a moment and said, "Dr. Walid, please turn around for a moment while I remove the *hijab*."

When Kasim turned his head and looked out the window, she quickly took off her *hijab*. Underneath, she was wearing a top with short sleeves and tight, blue jeans. Kasim had turned his head as requested but could see her reflection in the window.

When Afrin realized he had seen her reflection, she smiled shyly and said, "Okay, Doctor, I only put on the *hijab* and *niqab* for the sake of appearance. I usually dress like every other young Dutch woman in comfortable clothes."

By now he knew his initial guess of her age was correct – she was a good-looking young woman in her early thirties. Afrin drew a large padded brown envelope from the folds of the *hijab*. "I didn't want everybody to see this envelope." She opened it and showed Kasim that it was stuffed with green 100 Euro notes.

Kasim tried to estimate how much money was in the envelope but had no idea where to begin, so he said, "I hope this is enough to start with." When he saw that Afrin was smiling, he continued, "Let's go and spend some of it on a good dinner."

***

They decided to go to one of the many restaurants in Amsterdam that specialized in Indonesian dishes. Afrin, who had lived in Amsterdam for over two years, told Kasim she knew of a small place that had the most amazing *rijsttafel* with an assortment of 20 different dishes.

Kasim said he liked the spicier dishes and Afrin laughed and said he could choose any degree of piquancy he fancied. He let Afrin lead the way, walking a couple steps behind her and enjoying the sight of her trim, athletic body in her tight jeans. She had left the *hijab* and *niqab* in his hotel room saying she didn't want to stand out in the crowd, and she would return after dinner to retrieve them.

Dinner included marinated chicken skewers of Satay – making sure none of the skewers consisted of pork – and beef *Rendang*, some raw vegetables, in peanut sauce; they amused themselves repeating, like children, the name of this delicious dish – *Gado-gado*.

Kasim smacked his lips with pleasure when *Telur balado* was served with the hard-boiled eggs in very spicy, thick, chili sauce. Afrin couldn't restrain herself and despite the Colonel's warning pulled her cellphone out of her jeans pocket and took a photo of Kasim enjoying his dinner. They sampled a few other dishes until they felt they couldn't eat another bite and had to pass on some of the other dishes included in the menu.

The dinner was accompanied by a pitcher of beer that helped them wash down the food and alleviate the burning feeling of the spicier dishes. The first pitcher disappeared in no time and they ordered a second one and then a third pitcher to wash down the second one.

Kasim paid the bill with a couple of the crisp 100 Euro notes he got from Afrin, saying that after all it was a kind of business meeting and business expense. Afrin liked his sense of humor and enjoyed the small anecdotes he related to her over dinner. Once they had completed eating and drank the remaining beer in the third pitcher, they managed to rise from the table with great difficulty and head out of the restaurant.

She suggested they walk around the city for a while to allow the effects of the beer to be dispelled and Kasim readily agreed. As both were a little tipsy, Afrin took hold of Kasim's elbow and they supported each other as they strolled along the banks of the canals that crisscrossed the neighborhood. Finally, they reached the hotel and went up to Kasim's room.

Afrin looked at Kasim and thought of her father, who would have been just a few years older than the scientist had he not been killed by Iranian Shiites during the last year of the Iraq-Iran war. She was born a couple months after he died and grew up without a father and all her life yearned for a father figure.

Kasim seemed to fit the bill and throughout dinner she kept wondering what it would be like to become intimate with an older man. As a young student in Iraq, she never had an intimate relationship with a man, but after moving to Amsterdam for graduate studies she did develop a relationship with a Muslim fellow student and agreed to marry him.

She was disappointed when he started to treat her like a

sex-slave and made her shut up whenever she tried to express an opinion or describe her own needs. Eventually, she managed to get a divorce – no small feat for a Muslim woman, even in Holland – and continued to pursue her studies. She then decided that perhaps Dutch men would treat her as an equal and had an affair with one of her lecturers.

She was shocked when she found out he was married and had no intention of leaving his wife and two-year-old daughter. She then had a few short flings with some of her classmates but none of those lasted more than a couple weeks as they all appeared to be frivolous and superficial.

For his own part, Kasim had lived a life of celibacy in Iraq and after moving to Holland had paid occasional visits to the Red-Light district in Amsterdam whenever his business brought him to the city. A number of times he had managed to overcome his initial reservations about being seen entering the room of one of the more enticing women that displayed their merchandize in the window.

Each time he was disappointed by what followed – cold, mechanical sex with a woman that wanted him to finish his business quickly so she could return to her window and get the next customer. He almost felt like a laboratory specimen – a rat running at full speed on a treadmill without getting anywhere.

During dinner, he started having fantasies about Afrin and enjoyed her reaction to his stories. With each pitcher of beer, the age difference between them seemed to shrink a little and after three pitchers they were more like a couple of good friends enjoying their time together.

He deliberated how she would react if he made a move and showed her his affection, but before he could reach a decision she took the initiative. She held his hand and told him how much she enjoyed his company and was looking forward to working with him and then hugged him, putting her head on his shoulder. Kasim's body responded as if he were twenty years younger and when Afrin felt it, she smiled at him and said it was too late for her to return to her apartment at the other side of town and half-jokingly said he could sleep on the sofa.

They didn't get much sleep that night. After satiating their physical craving for some warmth and tenderness and their need for intimacy and closeness they talked about the project, the laboratory, and the necessary equipment and chemicals they needed to acquire. They didn't discuss the risks of working with highly radioactive materials or the future but the shadow of what they were about to do and its implications hung over their heads.

***

Afrin and Dr. Walid drew out their plan. The first order of the day was to find a suitable place for the clandestine laboratory. Per Kasim's estimation, they would need something in the order of 200 square feet that would include three main sections for the chemical operation and one for the metallurgical process.

In the first section, the irradiated, or 'spent,' fuel elements will be dissolved in a large reactor vessel that must be made of materials that are resistant to strong acids. In the second section, the plutonium will be separated from the acidic solution that contains mainly the uranium that remained in the fuel and the fission products, some of which are highly radioactive. In the third part, the plutonium will be purified and converted to a metal. Finally, the last section of the laboratory would be a metallurgical workshop where the plutonium metal will be shaped into the spherical form to fit the requirements for a nuclear weapon. For that part of the project, they would need to recruit someone with expertise in metallurgy of plutonium as they were not versed in that area.

They knew there would be many other items necessary to make a real atomic bomb and more professionals required to finish the construction of the device. The required items included a set of charges made of conventional explosives to compress the plutonium sphere into a supercritical configuration, a neutron source to initiate the nuclear chain reaction, and several other bits and pieces to make the device effective and ensure a big nuclear explosion.

They were also aware that plutonium extracted from spent fuel elements would not be as effective as weapon-grade plutonium produced for the sole purpose of making nuclear bombs. Furthermore, they realized the probability of failure was large but knew that even a partially successful atomic explosion in the heart of Tel Aviv would cause havoc and have a great psychological effect on the enemies of Islam.

They reckoned they would need a team of about half a dozen people with experience in laboratory work to perform the necessary chemical operations to separate the plutonium and purify it. They would also need to find two people versed in metallurgical processes to construct the core of the bomb. Then they needed to enlist several armed guards to provide security and keep away snooping neighbors and people who may accidentally wander into the area of the laboratory. In addition to the space required for the laboratory, they would have to put up the entire staff and arrange to feed them on the site.

Afrin had read about *The Dreadful Alchemist* and suggested they hide their operation in a busy urban area but Kasim rejected the proposal saying that in Holland and Germany this strategy would not work as it had so successfully in Padova, Italy. When Afrin questioned this statement, he told her the Italians were carefree people who believed in 'live and let live,' while the Dutch and Germans always looked around them with suspicion and were glad to report anyone breaking the rules to the authorities. Afrin wasn't totally convinced by this argument but accepted his judgment, so it was decided they would look for an isolated farm.

***

They rented a car and started to tour the countryside looking for a suitable farm. Considering the density of the population in Holland they focused on rural parts of Germany that were adjacent to the border with Holland. In the European Community, the concept of a real border in the old sense between these two countries was passé. One could cross back and forth between the two countries and the only noticeable differences would be the names of the villages and, of course, the language on the billboards advertising products or businesses.

Before setting out on their journey they spent an hour studying the area of northern Holland where the border with Germany was just an artificial line on the map. Google Earth provided an excellent view of that area. The region east of Haren attracted their attention and they decided to start their search for a suitable place in that area.

After a little more than two hours of driving from Amsterdam through Zwolle and Emmen in Holland they crossed into Germany and stopped for a snack in the center of the small village of Haren that had a population of about 24,000 and was off the beaten tourist track. They didn't find anything that captured their attention as a potential spot for their project so continued driving through the flat country-side until they reached the sparsely populated area of the Tinner und Staverner Dose area and the forest near Stavern.

They noticed several of the old farms were available for sale, but none were advertised for rent. Kasim was ready to give up and mentioned he would prefer to rent a place for a year or so because buying a suitable farm would probably be much too expensive. Afrin told him that unlike Al Qaeda that was funded mainly by donations, ISIS had acquired large sums of money by robbing banks in the cities and villages its fighters seized and by selling oil from captured distilleries and oil fields to greedy buyers who were willing to turn a blind-eye and not ask where the oil came from if the price was right. She added that she would contact Colonel Husseini and ask for additional funds if necessary. Kasim remained skeptical but agreed to continue the search.

They entered a real estate office in the small village of Stavern and were received by a middle-aged proprietor, Herr Gunther Winkler, who was rather surprised to see two people, who were obviously foreigners in his modest office.

"Good day," he said as he ogled the pretty woman, and barely nodded at the older man with her, whom he thought must be her father.

Afrin looked at the man and instantly read his thoughts. She said, "My father and I are artists and we are looking for a farm in a quiet place where we can have a studio to pursue our work."

Herr Winkler didn't want to appear to be rude, but curiosity got the better of him and he asked, "And what type of studio are you thinking of?"

Afrin replied, "I am a photographer and painter and my work involves combining these two disciplines. I take photographs of interesting looking objects and then focus on small details and create paintings that are inspired by the micro-details of the photograph. My art sells quite well in Amsterdam where I live, and a few galleries in London and Paris also display and occasionally sell my work. My father is a sculptor who works with wrought iron and needs quite a large space for his larger pieces. He uses scrap metal and combines it with other materials to create innovative art. Some people say his work reminds them of some of the greatest artists of the early Twentieth Century but with a whole new perspective on the use of modern materials."

Kasim didn't utter a single word but Herr Winkler didn't even notice the fact. The detailed description left Herr Winkler slightly in awe as he knew nothing about art or artists and in any case followed every gesture Afrin made and every movement of her lips allowing his imagination to work overtime. He turned on his computer and invited the young lady to sit next to him while he showed her more detailed photos of the farms displayed in his window.

Afrin managed to sneak a small smile in Kasim's direction and drew her chair close to Herr Winkler's chair, presumably to get a better view of the computer screen but making sure her arm lightly touched his. She could almost feel his heart pounding at an accelerated rate and his flushed face was clearly seen as she unintentionally allowed her fingers to brush against his thigh. Herr Winkler showed her pictures of the farms adding a short account on each.

One of the photos caught Afrin's attention and she asked, "How come this farm is so much cheaper than all the others?"

Herr Winkler cleared his throat. "This farm is owned by an elderly childless couple who can no longer work the fields. The husband is very ill and as far as I know may have already passed but, in any case, it is the wife who runs things there as she had done for decades."

Afrin looked inquisitively at him, so he added, "The owners have a long feud with their neighbors. They keep complaining neighbors poach on their land, so they want a buyer who is not from the area. One of the neighbors has offered to buy the farm for a higher price but the obstinate owners refuse to sell and see their hated neighbor prosper."

The real estate agent stuttered a little when he said this, and Afrin could feel he was probably hiding something about the farm from them. Finally, he added, "Please don't tell anybody what I told you about the motives of the owners. It will make me look like the town gossip, but I just wanted to explain to you why the asking price is so ridiculously low."

Kasim intervened for the first time since they entered the small office. "Can we look at the farm?"

Herr Winkler looked at him for a second and replied, "Sure, you can. I'll draw you a map showing you how to get there and I'll give the owners, Herr and Frau Brandt, a call that you are coming to see the place. Just remember what I have told you is discreet and don't repeat it to them."

Afrin rose from her chair and thanked him for his candidness and help. Herr Winkler didn't rise from his chair and she understood he was trying to conceal the response of his body to her closeness. So, she gave him her best smile and said they would be back shortly after seeing the farm.

***

Kasim could barely avoid laughing until they reached their rental car. Afrin got in the driver's seat and smiled at him. "I hope my flirting with Herr Winkler didn't make you jealous."

Kasim responded, "Wow, I didn't know you had the natural acting skills of a temptress. I, too, would have fallen for you head over heels." He burst out laughing and added, "I am so proud to be your father..."

They used the small hand drawn map Herr Winkler

had made, and after following a narrow road they reached an unpaved road blocked by a wooden gate with a sign in German warning trespassers to keep off and a photograph of a large dog displayed below the sign.

Afrin said, "I really hope Herr Winkler called ahead. I am afraid of dogs as they remind me of the wild beasts that fed on dead bodies in Iraq."

This was the first mention of the atrocities she had witnessed as a youngster in Iraq. Kasim refrained from saying he had seen those dogs preying on the wounded and eating their torn intestines while they were still alive. He got out and opened the gate and after she drove through closed it and got back in the car.

They said no more during the short drive up to the farmhouse. Unlike most of the area that consisted of large, flat cultivated fields there were many trees along this part of the small rural road. The farmhouse itself could not be seen from the road because it was hidden among a grove of tall trees.

They both noticed the large decrepit barn and the rusted tractor parked in front of it. The farmhouse looked as if it urgently needed to be repaired and cried for a thorough paint job. They got out of the car and walked up the three steps to the unkempt wooden door. The stairs creaked under their feet and for a moment Kasim thought the whole veranda would cave in under his weight.

They knocked on the door and could hear a dog growling from inside the house, but no one came to answer the door. Afrin banged on the door and worried it would fall apart but then she heard footsteps slowly approaching and it was opened by an old woman using a walking cane to support herself.

Afrin said, "Frau Brandt, Herr Winkler sent us to see the property."

The old lady placed her cupped hand near her left ear and shouted, "What is it? I can't hear you."

Afrin raised her voice and repeated, "Frau Brandt, Herr Winkler sent us to see the property."

This time the old lady nodded and motioned for them to follow her. They entered a living room and saw a padded couch that had seen better days half a century earlier and a couple of wooden chairs placed next to a wooden table. Kasim admired the craftsmanship of the wooden furniture – it was made by artisans who had been long gone but knew how to make truly rugged furniture that would last for many years.

The fearsome dog whose photo was displayed on the gate was now an old beast that could no longer rise on its legs and could only emit a low growl. Afrin noticeably relaxed when she saw it lying on an old rug in the corner of the room.

Frau Brandt offered them tea, but they politely declined. Afrin spoke very loudly, "Can we please see the house?"

Frau Brandt said, "Please. Walk around freely. I'll remain here."

The rest of the house was in no better shape than the part they had already seen from the outside. There were four small rooms placed along a narrow corridor that led from the living room to a bathroom with a bathtub made of heavy steel and stood on four short metal studs shaped like the paws of a lion. The bedrooms were practically devoid of furniture except for what passed as the master-bedroom that had a wooden bedframe with a mattress that was long passed its prime and looked like something that was sure to leave you with a contorted spine. A worn woolen blanket, outdating the mattress by a few good years was thrown over the mattress. The kitchen connected to the other side of the living room had a sink also made of the same type of heavy steel like the bathtub. They tried to open the tap and were surprised to see that the water looked clean and fresh.

There were no facilities for hot water either in the kitchen or the bathroom and they figured out that if the owners wanted to have a hot water bath they would need to heat a bucket of water on the wood stove that stood in the corner of the living room. They were glad to see the house was connected to the electrical power grid but when they took a closer look at the wiring Kasim realized it was more of a safety hazard than a reliable source of energy. He told Afrin that they would need to purchase a generator to fulfill the power needs of their laboratory.

Afrin whispered to Kasim, "Now I understand why the price of this place is so low. I think Herr Winkler's story about the owners' feud with the neighbors was complete fiction. Obviously, whoever buys this farm will need to erase the structure and rebuild it from scratch, which for our purposes is just fine. Let's go and see the barn and the yard."

They returned to Frau Brandt in the living room and told her they had seen the house and now wanted to take a look at the yard. From her seat on the sofa she nodded and stayed on the couch and they went outside through the kitchen back door. Kasim noticed a small door, about 5 feet high, on the side of the house.

He approached the house closer and examined the area trying to figure out how to open it, when he noticed a rusted handle at the top of door panel. Cautiously he tried to turn the handle, half expecting it to remain in his hand, but to his surprise he heard a bolt click and the door swerved silently on well-oiled hinges.

Afrin looked at him and raised an eyebrow in an unspoken question. He shrugged and looked at the open space now revealed by the open door and saw a few steps leading to what appeared to be a basement.

Gingerly, he descended the steps that were surprisingly solidly constructed. Kasim called to Afrin, "There are 14 steps and then there is a locked metal door."

She stated, "Who knows what's behind that metal door. The wooden door looks as if it hadn't been opened for decades but the door itself moved easily and now you find this metal door. I am sure someone was trying to hide something and keep the basement itself disguised. Let's go up and ask Frau Brandt about the mysterious basement she didn't mention and Herr Winkler probably doesn't even know about."

Kasim came back up and said, "No, let's check the barn and other structures and say nothing about the basement." He closed the wooden door and made sure the rusted handle was in the same position he had found it.

They continued the tour of the backyard and barn. The barn looked as if it too would crumble with any breeze or even under its own weight on a windy day. No mechanic in the world would be able to salvage the tractor they had spotted earlier parked in front of the barn.

Kasim commented, "No kindergarten in Iraq would accept this tractor even as a gift. It is a potential death trap and tetanus hazard for any five-year-old that dares to climb it."

After convincing themselves the two-car garage and storage shack were still standing only because of inertia, they returned to the farmhouse half expecting Frau Brandt to have passed away while they were outside.

"I hope you liked what you saw. Herr Winkler assured me you were honest people and not from around here. I need the money to spend the rest of my days in an institution that takes care of people like me," she stated.

Afrin assured her they would return to Herr Winkler and make him an offer for the property. Frau Brandt nodded and said, "Don't wait too long. My husband passed away two weeks ago, and I have nothing to stay her for."

***

Afrin and Kasim drove back to the real-estate office. They agreed that the place was ideal although it would need a serious renovation job. Afrin said the four bedrooms could easily accommodate the professional personnel and the barn could be sub-divided to make a reasonable living area for the security detail. Kasim consented and said their own people could take care of overhauling the electrical system including installing a powerful generator. He added that all the buildings could simply be given a facelift that would strengthen them enough for the duration of the project.

Herr Winkler greeted them with a broad smile, meant entirely for Afrin. "I hope you liked the farm and that Frau Brandt was as hospitable as ever."

Afrin laughed. "We were impressed that the buildings were still standing upright and no less by Frau Brandt. Frankly, before seeing the farm we thought the price was ridiculously low but now we think it is overpriced. We are willing to make you an offer for exactly half of what you initially asked for."

Herr Winkler was not used to Middle Eastern style nego-tiation tactics and looked offended. Before he could say any-thing about how bargaining was frowned upon in Germany, Kasim intervened, "We could go a little higher if you are will-ing to present yourself as the buyer without mentioning us in the paperwork. As you can obviously tell, we are foreigners and may have trouble getting quick approval for a formal pur-chase of property in Germany. We would really like to start our new studio and my daughter here," he nodded toward Afrin, "is anxious to prepare for a big exhibition of her work."

Afrin put on her best smile and pouted almost causing Herr Winkler to rush forward and hug her.

The real-estate agent who was not really as big a fool as he looked said, "Well, in that case I would need to receive a personal bonus for appearing as the buyer and manager of the property. This will increase the price by 50% above the original price."

Afrin was impressed by the quick study Herr Winkler turned out to be. She looked at Kasim, saw the glitter of con-sent in his eyes and said, "Herr Winkler, you are a tough and clever man. I hope to get to know you better after we move to the farm. My father will agree to your terms, but you must be very discreet and tell no one of our little arrangement."

The business deal was concluded, and they promised to deliver the funds in cash to Herr Winkler the next day by courier service. They insisted no written contract will be signed and Afrin repeated they had complete trust in him. Herr Winkler was also glad to keep this little private transaction off the books and receive a nice tax-free bonus. In any case, the deed will be in his name, so this was a win-win for him.

Afrin said they would return to the real estate office in Stavern in three weeks and take over the farm. Herr Winkler nodded and said that Frau Brandt and her dog will be out of the farm by then and he would gladly hand them the keys. Afrin exchanged a short glance with Kasim because there was no need for any key to get into the farmhouse.

***

During the drive back to Amsterdam Afrin and Kasim were in an elated mood – they had made the first practical step toward initiation of the grand project. They knew they would have to surmount many obstacles before it could be completed but felt this little step was actually a giant leap because it meant the time for theory and speculation were over and from now on the project had evolved into a series of many small rungs on a ladder that had to be cautiously climbed.

Kasim, seated in the passenger seat, said, with some concern in his voice, "Afrin, you now need to contact the Colonel and give him an update of our progress. Will you tell him about our special relationship?"

She gave him such a long look he started to worry the car would veer off the road. "No, there is no need for him to know about this. I am sure our new bond will be beneficial for the project."

She didn't tell him the Colonel had made rather crude advances to her when they had last met face-to-face and she'd had to forcefully ward off his unwelcome attention. She added, "I would like him to come to Amsterdam, where we can discuss the details of our plan. He would appreciate your professional input and will be more willing to help if the plan was outlined by a respectable scientist like yourself rather than by a female graduate student."

Kasim suppressed a small smile because he knew she was right. The traditional Arab society and ISIS in particular, still regarded women as lowly creatures whose strength lay below their shoulder level. Kasim said, "When we get back to Amsterdam, we'll work out the details. Meanwhile, let's stop somewhere along the way for a picnic to enjoy a few more moments of serenity and peacefulness before we are totally consumed by the project. Please stop at the next gas station to get some food and something to drink."

CHAPTER 3

The meeting with Colonel Husseini took place a few days later in a safe house maintained by ISIS in a suburb of Amsterdam. The neighborhood was heavily populated by Muslims and practically off limits to the local police that preferred to let the local residents run their own lives as they saw fit.

Afrin adorned her traditional *hijab* and *niqab* for the occasion and kept a respectable distance from her lover, Kasim. The Colonel was in a foul mood. "We have been suffering setbacks on the battlefield. The strong influx of supporters from all over the world has dwindled down to a trickle. The quality of the new volunteers has declined – most of them are either juvenile misfits or ex-cons. The young girls are especially pathetic – they want to serve the cause by marrying a martyr and having his children – and then they become sex slaves. The only thing that can save our cause is to strike such a blow at the enemy that will prove to the unbelievers that we mean business."

Kasim said, "I thought after the success of the heroic acts in Paris, Brussels, Istanbul, Nice, Germany, and the United States our ranks would be filled with volunteers who have given up any hope of being treated respectfully by the infidels.

The days of denouncing and offending Muslims and the true prophet Mohammed should be over because we have proven that punishment at the hands of Allah and his followers is swift and harsh."

The Colonel shook his head. "No, sadly the infidels refuse to learn the lesson. A few dozen victims here and there, or even over 130 in a single night in Paris, are quickly forgotten by the people who hurriedly return to their hedonistic pleasures. We need something of unprecedented proportions."

Afrin spoke up for the first time. "Dr. Walid has formed a plan and with your permission will present it to you. I am proud to be of assistance to such an outstanding man and brilliant scientist, but we'll need a lot of support and funding to implement this plan."

The Colonel frowned at Afrin's interruption and ignored her. He addressed Kasim and said, "Dr. Walid, please give me a short overview of your plan and prepare a list of the facilities and equipment you need. Money is not a problem, but you must take care of the acquisition of the more sensitive materials that may expose our project. ISIS has a lot of supporters in this part of Europe, especially from neighboring Belgium as well as in Germany. I am particularly interested in the timeframe because the laboratory must be ready in time to accept the hijacked shipment of the irradiated fuel, and as you understand we'll only have a narrow window of opportunity to get our hands on the shipment. The time between your receiving the shipment and the delivery of the device must be minimal because the risk of being exposed will be high if the theft is discovered. We hope to avoid an all-out search for a missing shipment of nuclear material by cleverly diverting the real shipment and replacing it with a fake substitute."

The scientist deliberated whether to say something about maltreatment of his partner and lover but decided that upsetting the Colonel in his foul state of mind would be counterproductive. He drew out the notebook he had prepared with Afrin and read from the handwritten notes. "We have located a farmhouse that is ideally located in a rural area of Germany close to the Dutch border. It is isolated and the neighbors make sure to keep far away from it because of ancient feuds. The farmhouse and yard need an overhaul to support the crumbling structures, but this can be done quickly and cheaply as all we need is to make sure it doesn't collapse on us while we are there."

The Colonel remained silent.

He then told the Colonel about their deal with Herr Winkler and how he presented Afrin as his daughter and told him they were both artists who wanted to set their studio in the farm.

The Colonel looked at the two of them and slyly commented that indeed they did look like an ugly father with a beautiful daughter. Kasim didn't appreciate this comment but continued, "We need to assemble a team of professionals that will include half a dozen or so engineers and technicians from various disciplines as I have written on this page."

He gave the Colonel a list of the people he needed for handling the spent fuel elements and separating the plutonium and to produce the sphere of the metal that will be at the core of the nuclear device. "I can supervise the work that involves the aspects of nuclear physics and Afrin will oversee the chemical processing." He smiled at her but was met with a stone face as she was still deeply offended by the way the Colonel had cut her short.

Kasim added, "I trust that you, or Major Aswadi will handle all the security issues and, of course, the acquisition of the spent fuel. The members of the security detail can do most of the renovations and construction of the laboratory under my supervision. I expect that setting up the laboratory will take about six-months. During that period we'll try to conduct a dry-run to test the chemical and physical procedures and train the personnel."

He looked at the reaction of Colonel Husseini and was gratified to see the expression on his face that meant he approved the plan.

The Colonel said, "I'll need some time to recruit the engineers and technicians you have asked for – perhaps you can help me a little with this."

Kasim considered the idea and said, "It is well known that the German nuclear industry has shrunk considerably due to public pressure, especially after the disaster at Fukushima. Until 2011, there were 17 reactors that provided about one quarter of Germany's electric power but after the government gave in to the rising public outcry against nuclear power, there are now only eight operating plants that provide about one sixth of the country's needs. This reduction was accompanied by dismissing many skilled workers. I am sure some of them are Muslims with a new grudge against the government, the public, the Western liberals, and tree huggers. I wouldn't be surprised if some have also reverted to their original religion and are now avid followers of Islam and ISIS."

The Colonel agreed. "Good idea. I'll get my contacts in Germany to consider this and try and find suitable candidates. Now, regarding the security issue: Two members of the security detail are already in Amsterdam and two more can be summoned from Brussels tomorrow so they can start the renovations you have described. We also have on hand a woman who is the widow of one of our martyrs and she can be the housekeeper and cook. She is originally French and does not look like someone from the Middle East, so will raise no suspicion if she presents herself as your wife when she goes shopping." He saw that Afrin blushed and began to understand that her relationship with Kasim was not purely professional.

Colonel Husseini was disappointed as he had hoped Afrin would be available to fulfill his desires.

**

Afrin was simmering with rage due to the denigrating treatment she had received, and she took it out on Kasim. "Why didn't you say anything when he humiliated me? I thought we were equal partners in this project. What kind of man are you to sit quietly when your woman is demeaned?"

The scientist thought it best to absorb her anger and not provoke her further by trying to defend his impassiveness in the meeting with Colonel Husseini. He just hugged her and promised to make it up to her. Eventually she was placated, and they decided to return to the Indonesian restaurant where they had their first dinner together. The excellent food and the two bottles of wine they shared improved Afrin's mood and they returned to Kasim's hotel feeling closer than ever.

In the morning, after a night of mutual pleasure and a good breakfast, she was in a conciliatory mood. When Colonel Husseini called, they were a bit surprised to hear his cheerful tone. He said, "I paid close attention to what you said about the nuclear power industry in Germany. One of the remaining operating power plants is in Emsland, not far from your farm. The plant was temporarily taken offline when a tiny leak was discovered. Unofficial reports stated that the investigation found a couple of culprits that were summarily fired. I was told that one of them is a former Palestinian and with his reputation as a troublemaker could not get a job in his profession and is now working as a delivery boy in a minimarket that is run by his brother-in-law. He may be ready for recruitment. Kasim, could you contact him and see if he is suitable for the task and willing to participate?"

Kasim looked at Afrin and she nodded her approval, so he said, "Colonel, thanks for the information. We'll set up a meeting and interview him. We would like to move to the farm and start setting up the laboratory as soon as possible. It would be of great help if the security people you mentioned would be on call."

He proceeded to give Kasim all the contact details.

CHAPTER 4

Al-Raqqah, Syria, June

'The Rocket Man,' Dr. Raymond Mashal, was led by two large men wearing black uniforms with his hands tightly bound behind his back and a filthy sack over his head.

Three decades earlier he had been in charge of developing rockets for Saddam Hussein's army and due to his accomplishments had rightfully earned his nickname. During the Iraq-Iran war that went on unremittingly throughout most of the 1980s, the Iraqis were the first to use rockets and launch strikes at the civilian population in Iranian towns.

The Iranians retaliated and their own Scud rockets hit Baghdad. Saddam was furious when he realized his capital suffered from the onslaught of rocket strikes but Tehran was beyond the range of his old Scud B rockets and he was on the losing end of the "Scud duel."

He initiated a program to extend the range of the Scud B beyond 200 miles and the result was known as Al-Hussein rockets, named in his honor. According to some sources, 189 rockets were launched at Iranian cities resulting in about 2000 dead, 6000 injured, and most effectively causing millions of Tehran residents to flee the city. This development was Raymond's greatest achievement and his claim to fame, especially since the level of maintenance of the Scud B rockets supplied by the USSR had been close to zero because newer and better rockets were produced to replace the old ones. At the height of the Iraq-Iran war they were used almost as soon as they arrived in Iraq so not many were left in the stocks of the Iraqi army.

After the Iraq-Iran war ended the Iraqis continued to develop their rocket force and had some improved models that were used against Saudi Arabia troops and American bases in Dhahran quite successfully during the 1991 Gulf War. Raymond had worked day and night to enable the old Scud B rockets to reach Israel after being launched from the western border of Iraq. To his great disappointment the 40 or so rockets that were fired at cities in Israel caused more psychological havoc than real damage and only one Israeli citizen was reportedly killed by a direct hit from one of these rockets.

Raymond's largest setback was when he learned that one of the rockets launched at the Israeli nuclear research center near Dimona fell several miles short of its target, and for some reason its warhead contained nothing but solid concrete. This had made him the laughingstock of everybody that heard of this useless warhead. His life was spared after this incident only because the invading American forces captured him before Saddam's frightened troops could execute him publicly. After the Americans left Iraq without removing Saddam from power, Raymond was pardoned on condition he continued to work on improving Iraq's rocket capabilities.

The routing of Saddam's forces in the Second Gulf War in 2003, led to the disbandment of the Iraqi army, the dispersion of its rocket units, as well as curtailing all related research and development. Raymond was out of a job but managed to survive by becoming a high school science teacher in a small village in the north of Iraq. He stayed away from the fighting between the Kurds, the Iraqi army (or what it had become), and the different Islamic groups, but he knew that sooner or later his past would catch up with him.

Raymond figured out the only reason he was still alive was because his captors, who were obviously from the Islamic State, needed his skills. Although he was a Sunni Muslim like his captors, and a person who had lost his job after the American invasion like some of the leaders of Al Qaeda and ISIS, he feared his life would come to an end prematurely. He knew that if he wanted to live, he would have to cooperate.

Raymond thought about the irony of history – the Scud, based on the Nazi V-2 rocket, was designed by Nazi scientists and engineers that were captured and taken as prisoners of war in the aftermath of World War II. They were given the choice of working for their Communist enemy or being executed as Nazis and naturally chose to live. Their colleagues that were captured by the American forces were given the same choice – although they would have faced a prison sentence rather than a firing squad – and were glad to serve their new masters in the "Capitalist heaven" rather than in the "Workers' paradise."

The foul-smelling sack was removed from Raymond's head and he blinked a few times in the strong light that shone in his eyes. He heard someone speaking. "I am Colonel Husseini, chief of the Islamic State special missions' unit. Are you Dr. Raymond Mashal 'the Rocket Man'?"

Raymond tried to see the speaker but was blinded by the light, so he nodded at the silhouette and mumbled something inaudible.

The Colonel looked at the pitiful figure in front of him and said, "Speak up. If you cooperate no harm will befall you. Are you Dr. Mashal?"

Raymond found his voice. "Yes. I am the 'Rocket Man' and am willing to help the cause of true Islam." He knew that if he wanted to live, he would need to be very cooperative.

The Colonel saw that further intimidation was not required. He said softly, "We want you to direct a special project in which your unique skills are needed. You will have practically unlimited resources – as many men as necessary and all the funding you ask for. You will need to deliver a rocket that will reach the heart of the hateful enemy with a payload that will leave its mark. None of your concrete warheads." The Colonel laughed and the people in the room, who to Raymond were just shadows in the dark, joined him. "Dr. Mashal, I am only joking, we know that some of your frightened lackeys were scared shitless and responsible for the stupid concrete warhead. No, seriously, you'll have to work quickly and in secret, because this will be our ultimate weapon that will bring our enemies to their knees. Are you up to the task?"

Raymond was now emboldened, and his answer was loud and clear. "I would gladly do the impossible, if needed."

The Colonel was impressed, although both knew the

scientist had little choice but to obey. He added, "You know that the Imperialist border between Iraq and Syria has been erased from the map by our brave fighters. You will be taken to the missile bases, or what's left of them, that are now under our control, and will be given a free hand to take whatever you think will help. You will then establish your workshop, or manufacturing plant if you prefer to use that term, in a well-protected location, and build the rocket that will fit our specifications. You have exactly 12 months to complete the project and deliver the first rocket."

Raymond was about to protest the tight schedule but thought better of it. He knew that modifying a rocket and testing its performance in a place where skilled labor and proper facilities were available is one thing but operating under constant threat of aerial attacks with limited access to resources was something else. He adopted the strategy of all true survivors – get through one day at a time and hope to do the same the next day.

***

Raymond was taken to one of the former rocket depots of the Iraqi army that was now under the control of ISIS. He was given a crew of 10 technicians and engineers from the former rocket units of the Iraqi army. All with operational experience in launching rockets but with only limited knowledge on the actual production and testing. Most important was the fact that he had a free hand in gathering rocket components, pieces of equipment, guidance systems, rocket engines, and almost intact Scud B and Al Hussein rockets.

He toured the base and looked at main parts of the rockets – the engine, the tanks with the fuel and oxidizer, the nozzle, airfoils, fins, gyroscopes, and, of course, nose cones in which the warhead (or payload) is held. He knew that the key to extending the range was to increase the amount of propellant (fuel and oxidizer) and thus get a longer burning time.

Alternatively, he could try to improve the efficiency of the engine (combustion chamber, pressure and velocity of exhaust gases, and the design of the nozzle). He sighed when he thought about the more advanced models – Scud C and especially Scud D – which were beyond the reach of ISIS. Just one Scud D would solve his problem with its 450 mile range, payload of almost one ton, and an accuracy of 165 feet. Praying to Allah could also help but he would need something more tangible to accomplish his mission.

He made sure that everything he needed would be transported to Al-Raqqah where he would be working in the relative safety of the main stronghold of ISIS. In fact, he placed his workshop in an underground shelter that was located under a vegetable patch in an enclosed park surrounded by stone wall not far from the center of Al-Raqqah.

The Farm near Stavern, June

The laboratory staff held their weekly meeting in the living room of the farmhouse. If Frau Brandt would have seen the farmhouse and yard from the outside, she wouldn't have noticed many differences but had she been allowed inside she wouldn't have recognized the place.

The interior walls were rebuilt with prefabricated boards and the structure was strengthened with support columns. Most of the old furniture was chopped down to pieces suitable for heating in winter, but the beautifully crafted dining table and chairs that Kasim had appreciated were spared. The small bedrooms were furnished with new beds, mattresses, fresh sheets, and quilts, which were laundered every week. The odors of neglect, stale air, and moldy walls were now replaced by the smell of fresh air, pine trees, and fresh paint.

The wooden door leading to the basement was repainted and the metal door at the bottom of the stairs was opened with a large key hidden at the bottom of the dark staircase.

Kasim and Afrin were surprised to see that the basement was as large as the farmhouse above it but was completely bare of furniture or even shelves. They couldn't figure out what it was used for and why it was built in the first place. But after assessing the thickness of the concrete walls and floor, and especially the ceiling, Kasim announced this would be the ideal place to house the metallurgical laboratory where the final stages of production of the device will be carried out.

He explained to Afrin that the metallurgical laboratory in which the plutonium would be shaped needs to be shielded to minimize radiation exposure. She thought about this and said the basement had another advantage as it would be easy to control access to the most sensitive part of the project – the part where the final product; the plutonium sphere – can be seen for what it really is. Kasim agreed and they decided to lock the door always and permit only two or three people, that would be responsible for the final construction of the device, to enter the basement.

The laboratory staff occupied all four bedrooms. The plan was for Kasim and Afrin to take over the largest bedroom after disposing of Frau Brandt's old bed and mattress. The two leading scientists (a physicist and chemist) resided in the second bedroom. The third bedroom was to be occupied by the three engineers in charge of the three work shifts. The three technicians, each assigned to an engineer, shared the last bedroom. Thus, the entire staff of 10 professionals were to be quite comfortably lodged in the renovated farmhouse and able to run all the operations in the laboratory.

However, like all good plans, reality demanded that some changes and adaptations be made. First, they had to find a place for the French housekeeper, the one that Colonel Husseini jokingly said looked the part of Kasim's wife, and they managed to clear a small space for her in the pantry adjacent to the kitchen. Next, they wondered what they could do if the Colonel or the Major wanted to stay overnight and the only solution was to move the three technicians to the barn – something they would not welcome, of course.

***

The professional staff members were quite a multinational lot. They were recruited in a fashion that reminded Kasim of the movie, *The Dirty Dozen* – one or two at a time, each with their uniquely sad story.

Farres Shuweika, whose real name was Abdallah Nabil, the

Palestinian whom Afrin and Kasim interviewed, was the first to join the laboratory staff. Farres received his degree in chemistry at a technical university in Berlin after leaving his small village in the West Bank near Nablus where he had excelled in mathematics and science. He would have preferred to remain with his family in the village where his ancestors had lived for centuries and study at An-Najah National University in Nablus but got mixed up with the wrong crowd. He had to hastily escape from the territories of the Palestinian Authority after he was implicated in providing a homemade improvised explosive device used in a terrorist suicide bombing.

The bombing took place on one of the very few buses that were used by Arab laborers and Jewish settlers because the confused youth who carried the bomb got on the wrong bus and the explosion indiscriminately killed and maimed Arabs and Jews. Thus, Farres was wanted by the Palestinian police and by the Israeli Security Agency and only by the grace of Allah, and considerable help from the local Hamas cell, did he manage to cross into Jordan. From there he immigrated to Germany where he assumed his new identity as Farres Shuweika.

While still a student at the technical university in Berlin, he met a German woman a few years older than him and after marrying her received German citizenship, which gained him access to his job at the Emsland nuclear power plant. When the minor leak of radioactive material occurred, he was the scapegoat and held responsible and duly fired from his job. For his wife, this was the straw that broke the camel's back, she used this exact phrase to remind Farres where he had come from. She kicked him out of their house and divorced him.

After losing his job at the power plant, Farres delivered groceries for a living and couldn't find gainful employment in his profession despite going on several job interviews. He was, therefore, excited and enthusiastic when Kasim offered him a job in his laboratory, only hinting at the real objective of the project.

***

Mustafa Darii was originally a Turkish engineer who sought a better life for himself and his family in Germany. He worked as an electrical engineer on the automation of manufacturing systems in one of the most advanced plants of a prestigious car maker. All was well for ten years until he suffered a terrible blow of fate. His beloved wife and three-year-old twin daughters were involved in what started as a minor traffic accident when she failed to come to a complete stop in time at a traffic light. Her car swerved and its fender scratched the side of a shiny, new 700 series BMW that waited for the red light to change.

The driver of the BMW got out of his car to check the damage and was enraged by the sight of the ugly scratch. When Mustafa's wife lowered her window, the driver saw that the driver of the offending car was obviously a Muslim woman and without pausing for a minute took a tire iron from the trunk of his car and pounded the poor woman with its sharp edge. He then poured some flammable liquid from a container he had in the trunk through the open window and threw in a match. Before the flames could be extinguished the two young girls also perished.

When Mustafa heard about the incident, he almost lost his mind but gathered enough strength to attend the trial. It turned out the driver of the BMW was a Neo-Nazi had a long record of racially motivated hate crimes. However, with help from a lawyer, he pleaded temporary insanity, and a lenient judge who also drove a brand-new BMW sentenced him to one year in a psychiatric ward 'for observation.'

Within no time he was back on the street and gained status as a celebrity of the Neo-Nazi movement. Mustafa decided to quit his job and joined an Islamic cultural center. This center and mosque were also attended by Farres, so that when Farres accepted Kasim's offer he proposed to bring along his friend, Mustafa, to the project.

Kasim and Afrin interviewed Mustafa and were impressed by his determination to get back at the German establishment that had failed to do him justice.

***

Abaz Nihad was a ten-year-old Bosnian youth whose family had lived for generations on the outskirts of the small town of Sibenik on the Dalmatian coast of Croatia. During the bloody civil war in former Yugoslavia, the Serbian armed forces bombarded Sibenik because they believed it served as a major base for Croatian separatists. Abaz was a Muslim and didn't really care about the conflict between the Serbian

Orthodox Serbs and Catholic Orthodox Croatians until his house was destroyed by a shell fired by one of the adversaries – he wasn't even sure which one. His mother and grandmother, who had raised him, were killed when the house collapsed. As an orphan Abaz had no option but to go live with his uncle in Banja Luka.

Life was quite good there and he attended high school and had made many friends in his new home. But then events caught up with Abaz. Together, with many other young Muslim men he was led by a Serbian militia gang to a pit dug in an abandoned stone quarry and forced to stand in line with the other men. Unlike almost all others who were murdered at the quarry, Abaz miraculously survived.

When the shooting started, he fainted and fell into the pit just before being shot. He was covered by the blood of the men standing beside him and the murderers didn't notice he was still alive. When he came to, he understood what had happened, and after he was sure there was no one alive around him, he waited until dark and crawled out of the pit. He made his way back to Banja Luka, where he lived for years as a street kid.

After the war ended, he was accepted to join a training program set up by the United Nations and became an accomplished technician. He got a job in an Austrian firm that specialized in radiation monitoring and the handling of radioactive materials. This was mainly due to a scientist who worked for the International Atomic Energy Agency, the IAEA, in Vienna, who had taken a fancy to young Abaz.

When the scientist started making sexual advances, Abaz

was at a loss. He appreciated the help and friendship of the scientist but had no gay tendencies. Eventually the scientist became more and more aggressive and one night, when he was completely drunk in his third-floor apartment, he physically attacked Abaz. The young man tried to get away by running to the veranda where he planned to escape. The intoxicated scientist chased him blindly and stumbled over the railing and fell to his death. Abaz left the apartment in a hurry before the police got there and crossed the border to Germany.

He joined the same Islamic center as Farres and Mustafa and on their recommendation, was also invited to join the project. He, too, had an axe to grind to avenge the death of his mother and grandmother by the Christians, his own near-death experience in Banja Luka, and the coercion by the scientist.

***

Amal Al Rabia was the only woman, except Afrin, who was a member of the laboratory team. She was a self-minded woman who had escaped from Syria when the civil war there reached the town of Aleppo where she lived. Intense fighting between President Assad's loyalist army and unruly groups of rebels broke out and both sides tried to gain control over the city center. Door to door fighting and mutual shelling led to the destruction of most of the center of the town. Amal's apartment was on the top floor of one of the buildings that were near the center of the city and was strategically located, especially after most of the surrounding buildings were turned into rubble.

A small group of five soldiers from the Syrian army took over the apartment and established an observation post there. At first, they treated Amal with respect and only asked her to cook for them using the food rations provided to them by the army. Amal was happy to do this as she could remain in her apartment and got food supplies that were very scarce and not available to the city's residents.

After two of the soldiers were killed by rebel snipers, the remaining soldiers started to behave like stray dogs that bit anything in sight. They became violent and turned Amal into their sex slave, taking turns raping her and beating her. She seized a moment when two of the soldiers were asleep and the third one on guard duty went to the bathroom. She grabbed a gun from one of the sleeping soldiers and proceeded to shoot him and his sleeping friend. When the third guy burst out of the bathroom, she shot him through the head.

She ran down the stairs, out of the building, and continued to run until she reached the line held by the ISIS fighters besieging the city. She was taken to their commander and after telling him her story he commended her for her heroic act and sent her to ISIS headquarters in Al-Raqqah. She was one of the many refugees that reached the town that had been the stronghold of ISIS since 2014.

The story about her brave act preceded her and she was taken directly to Ibn Chaled, the commander in charge of intelligence for ISIS. He slowly looked her up and down and said, "Amal, we have all heard about your bravery and were impressed by it. Killing three enemy dogs is a good start but I am sure you can contribute more to the cause of Islam. Are you willing to do so?"

Amal didn't hesitate. "I am willing to become a *Shahid*, a martyr, a suicide bomber and sacrifice my life. In any case, no true Muslim man will take me after having been ravished by these vile mongrels who call themselves Muslims and soldiers."

Ibn Chaled was pleased with her answer. "You know our real enemies are not the animals that serve the snake, Assad. These we can easily deal with as we have been doing up to now. The Messianic Crusaders are the pigs that worship the wooden statue of their so-called son-of-God, they are responsible for the poor state of Islam and the Arabs in particular. We seek revenge on an unprecedented scale – killing millions in one stroke – with Allah's blessing. I was told that before the war started you were trained as a computer analyst and software engineer."

Amal shyly acknowledged this, and Ibn Chaled continued, "You would be of a great help to our most ambitious project by providing help professionally. Would you be willing to go to Germany and live there?"

Amal responded, "I have nothing left here and no reason to stay here."

Ibn Chaled replied, "You will be sent to Turkey and there you'll join a group of skilled refugees that were legally given permits to live and work in the European Community. Once there, you will contact our man in Germany who will safely transport you to the scientist in charge of the project I was speaking about. For the time being – the less you know about the project the better it is."

Amal Al Rabia reached the farmhouse three weeks later. Her journey could be considered as 'first class' because she was legally permitted to live and work in Germany. She didn't have to risk her life in a flimsy boat, then live in a camp set-up for refugees, and then walk for miles to illegally cross one border after the next until she reached Germany – the Promised Land in the minds of the homeless refugees.

Afrin greeted her warmly, glad she was no more the only woman at the farm, except the housekeeper. She told Amal she would have her own bedroom in the farmhouse, even if it meant the male members of the team had to squeeze themselves into the two remaining bedrooms or move to the barn. Eventually, Amal and the French housekeeper moved into the room vacated by the technicians sent to live in the barn with the security guards.

CHAPTER 5

Mossad Headquarters, Tel-Aviv, June

The weekly meeting of the section heads in the office of the Chief of Mossad, Haim Shimony, proceeded according to the list of routine items on the itinerary.

Shimony was about to conclude the meeting. "Well, gentlemen…" Then he saw the female section head in charge of operations and adhered his greeting. "And lady. It looks as if the external threats to the well-being of Israel are at an all-time low. Egypt is busy with its internal problems with the fanatic religious Muslim Brotherhood party and their terrorist friends; the King of Jordan has his own worries with the million or so refugees from Syria and the badgering of the large Palestinian population in his country; Syria is in total turmoil and its army is in a complete mess and busy fighting its own population with intervention from near and far neighbors; Iraq is no longer a real country but is effectively a Shiite province of Iran in the south, a Sunni unruly entity in the center and a Kurd enclave in the north; Lebanon is, as it has been for half a century, a battleground between Shiites, Sunnis, Druze, and Christians with shifting alliances. Iran is, as always, at the top of the list of our enemies and the greatest potential threat but appears to be busy restoring its economy and providing food for the growing population and jobs for the graduates from its universities. So far, they haven't been found to be in violation of the nuclear deal they signed but their support of terror organizations and their involvement in the Syrian conflict has not abated. Our relations with our European and American allies have seen better days but so far they have refrained from taking any practical steps to show their concern about the policies of our government and the behavior of our leading politicians."

Shimony looked around him and saw that his closest people were nodding in agreement. He hesitated before adding, "Our mandate prohibits us from operating inside Israel, but I do wonder where we are going. Are we rushing into another round of conflict with our neighbors with open eyes or are we being led there blindly? I fear that an unexpected event, especially if it is a large scale one, would find us unprepared. A reflexive, instinctive response by the government may place the whole country in a terrible predicament. You all remember how we found ourselves in an undeclared war with Hezbollah in 2006, that cost over 160 lives of our soldiers and citizens after an Israeli patrol was attacked and two bodies of our soldiers were snatched across the border. Those of you that are older," he saw he was the oldest person in the room, "or have studied their history, know that even the Six Day War in 1967, resulted from a series of miscalculations. True, our war plans were excellent and they were brilliantly executed, and in three hours we destroyed all opposing air forces, and in six days we captured, some say liberated, territories that were three times larger than the area of Israel before the war."

This time there were no nods of approval. No one liked to be reminded that the great victory of 1967, was something of a mishap. Shimony realized he was tramping over a sensitive issue. Almost half of the attendees of the meeting lived beyond the recognized international border of 1967, and several of them were Orthodox Jews who belonged to the so-called national Zionist movement. They viewed the Six Day War as a Godsend and the beginning of redemption and were still anticipating the footsteps of the Messiah.

Finally, Shimony said, "Is there anything else on the agenda? Or does anyone wish to raise another issue?"

David Avivi, who was now a Deputy Chief, raised his hand and said, "My biggest concern is that after the notorious terrorist acts in Europe and the US by ISIS supporters and sympathizers, the organization has kept a low profile. I fear that the setbacks they have recently had on the battlefields in Syria, Iraq, and even Libya, will drive them to more extreme acts against Western civilization and Israel. I think we should especially focus our intelligence gathering on potential operations that involve weapons of mass destruction. WMDs could provoke the world into a response that could be the beginning of the Third World War and instigate the clash of civilizations between Islam and the Western world they are so keen to initiate."

Shimony asked, "David, is there any specific threat that you know about?"

David thought about this for a moment before replying,

"No specific information, but I suggest we alert our agents in Western Europe to increase surveillance on supporters of ISIS that have access to technical information that may be related to WMDs. I am not very worried about chemical or biological weapons because there is hardly any activity nowadays in those fields and their use in the civil war in Syria has proven to be of limited value. I think the attempts by Islamic extremists to obtain a nuclear device or even a dirty bomb are still as persistent as they were." David was referring to the incidents that were described in detail in *The Dreadful Alchemist, The Dreadful Renegade,* and *The Dreadful Patriot.* Three plots in which his personal involvement was crucial.

The Chief of Mossad summarized the meeting. "As the final action item, I am issuing a directive to all Mossad offices to keep a close eye on any activities by Muslim scientists and engineers who work in the nuclear industry or have done so in the past."

As the section heads were leaving the office, David hung back for a moment and quietly said to Shimony, "Haim, you have to be very careful with your assertions about the Six Day War. Some of the section heads do not like to hear your theory about the events leading to the war. They tend to see these events as being due to divine guidance and God's intervention. Some of them may relay your words to the politicians, especially the Prime Minister, who would seize the opportunity to replace you with someone more to their liking."

Shimony knew he was barely tolerated by the PM and managed to keep his job only because of his publicly recognized achievements in thwarting threats to the survival of Israel.

The PM wouldn't risk his political career and high public rating just to get rid of a very popular Mossad Chief. One of the PM's cronies, possibly even the PM himself, was quoted as saying that when someone was appointed to head the Israeli Security Agency or Mossad, they suddenly became moderate leftists. His opponents claimed that reality and responsibility changed one's point of view. The PM didn't like this claim, to say the least, but time and again his appointees followed this pattern.

CHAPTER 6

The Farm near Stavern, July

Colonel Husseini and Major Aswadi visited the clandestine laboratory and after being given a tour of the facility they met with Kasim and Afrin.

Kasim concluded the tour by saying, "I can state that everything is in place and ready for receiving the shipment of spent nuclear fuel and reprocessing the plutonium that is contained in the fuel elements."

Afrin gave Kasim a steely look and he hastened to add, "This would not have been possible without the help of Afrin."

The Colonel said, "I am impressed with what you have done. Although I don't really understand the scientific problems and technical challenges, I do appreciate you have constructed all the necessary facilities needed for the project."

Major Aswadi cleared his throat and said, "We have also made all the preparations for hijacking the next shipment of spent fuel. I have three teams in place ready to intercept the convoy that will carry the cask with the irradiated fuel. It is best that you don't know all the details but make sure that the barn is ready."

On the way to the farmhouse Colonel Husseini ordered

Major Aswadi to personally supervise security at the farm once the shipment of spent fuel arrived at the farm. The Major listened closely to Kasim's presentation on the state of readiness of the laboratory. He asked a lot of technical questions and was particularly interested in the aspects of radiation hazards and safety measures. Kasim tried to answer all his questions but suggested that for a more detailed account, his experts on handling radioactive material should be consulted.

He summoned Abaz who was a trained technician with a lot of practical experience, and he explained to the Major that if you knew what you were doing and took the necessary precautions you would be safe. The Major, like most of the world's population, feared things he couldn't grasp with his five senses, and radiation was very high on his list, so Abaz's reassurances were welcome but not convincing. He decided he would try to keep his distance from radioactive materials.

***

The logistics for the hijacking of the shipment of spent nuclear fuel were very complicated but the planning was in its final stages. The discussion between Colonel Husseini and Major Aswadi tried to address the three main problems: overpowering the security force that guarded the shipment and taking control of the truck carrying the cask; preventing an alarm that would alert the authorities a shipment had gone missing; and getting the hijacked truck to the barn at the farmhouse without incident.

While the first task was simple, if that term could be used, and required enough brute force and some inside cooperation, the second task was formidable, and the third task depended on the success of preventing, or delaying, the alarm. They had pondered this problem for several months and the Major now spoke, "We have enlisted the driver of the truck carrying the cask. Johann Auslander, as Yusuf now calls himself, is a trusted employee of the company responsible for transporting the spent fuel elements. He immigrated to Holland from Egypt 20 years ago and married a Dutch woman. She persuaded him to abandon his old religion and assimilate in Holland but after he caught her in bed with her Dutch boss, he divorced her and reverted to Islam. He became a secret supporter of ISIS and made sure that none of his workmates knew about his new allegiance. He is more than willing to help us."

The Colonel didn't like ideological volunteers because they were unreliable. He preferred to use lucrative incentives and intimidation. "Did you offer him money?"

The Major nodded. "He realized that after this job he would not find employment anywhere in Europe, so I promised him 200,000 Euro so he could live like a prince in areas controlled by us in Iraq. He gladly accepted." He looked at the Colonel and added, "Of course, we can make him disappear after he delivers the cask. I am sure you and I can find better use for the money he was promised."

The Major proceeded to present the plan in more detail. "The truck with the cask will be escorted by four armed guards in a van that will be just behind the truck. This vehicle is protected by armor just like the vans used to transport cash to and from banks. Two police officers on motorbikes usually lead the convoy and clear traffic out of the way. In addition, there will be police officers at the main intersections to stop traffic from crossing the convoy's path. The truck will be equipped with an active GPS device that continually transmits its position to police headquarters."

All of this was supposed to be insurmountable obstacles. Colonel Husseini knew this, of course, and raised his eyebrow in an unspoken question.

Major Aswadi continued, "The crude approach is to have the convoy ambushed. The police officers on the motorbikes can be shot by snipers positioned on rooftops and the escort van can be neutralized by a rocket propelled grenade, an RPG. We don't have to do anything about the police officers at the intersections because they are lightly armed, if at all, and cannot give chase to our heavily armed fighters."

The Colonel didn't like this because such a public attack would alert the whole country. "Major, this is a really stupid plan. You have been watching too many TV movies."

Major Aswadi smiled. "I said this was the crude approach, not our plan. Now comes the more sophisticated part. We will use no brute force, only subterfuge. The driver, Yusuf, our man will pretend to have a problem and signal to the escort he needs to pull over to a side street to take care of the problem. He will announce there appears to be a leak of radioactive material and send his second driver to examine the problem. The man will don protective clothing and get out of the cabin and go to the rear of the truck with a hand-held radiation detector. He will report a high reading on his radiation detector and warn the escorting officers to stay away at a safe distance while he checks the cause of the radiation. Then he will return to the truck's cabin and Yusuf will say he needs to drive the truck into a parking garage to deal with the problem. An identical truck, with a fake cask will be waiting there. Yusuf will remove the GPS device and place it in the other truck, get in the cabin, and drive it out as if everything was back to normal. The convoy will continue its way and deliver the fake cask. Meanwhile, our people waiting in the garage will throw a cover over the cask and disguise the truck to look like thousands of other trucks crisscrossing the highways of Holland and Germany. They'll make their way to the farmhouse and deliver the cask with the spent fuel to the barn. Colonel, what do you think of this plan?"

Colonel Husseini's initial reaction was to have the Major committed to a lunatic asylum, however, after giving the plan some more thought he said, "I am now convinced that you've seen too many TV programs as well as movies, but I must say this may work. You must have heard the favorite phrase used by many elite Special Forces units: 'Who dares, wins' to come up with such an audacious plan. Can our Yusuf be trusted to pull this off?"

The Major expected this question. "We must send an assistant, the second-driver, who will sit in the truck's cabin with Yusuf. He will be one of our bravest fighters." He smiled and added, "I'll do it myself. I'll pretend to panic when a high level of radiation is detected and make sure the escort keeps its distance. My presence will ascertain that Yusuf complies with the plan and doesn't lose his nerve."

The Colonel became more enthusiastic by the moment and

said, "I am impressed. We need to think about every small detail and run a simulation and a couple of exercises before I approve the plan. Major, I really appreciate your willingness and personal bravery."

***

Major Aswadi had already enlisted six men and one woman for the security detail of the laboratory. All vowed they were ready to sacrifice themselves for the chance to become martyrs. He had told them the job will involve a vital part of the most ambitious project ever attempted by ISIS. He explained that during the first phase of the project they will live on a farm in Germany and will serve as the security detail while training for the real mission. Then they will carry out the assignment and continue to provide security to a team of scientists and engineers. He promised he would personally lead them through the whole project.

For the last three months, these eight people – the Major, the six men, and one woman – had guarded the laboratory personnel, had transported the laboratory equipment that was purchased, and had helped install it under the supervision of Kasim and Afrin. Only the Major and one of the other men were ever allowed to enter the basement and this was because their muscle power was needed to move some of the heavier stuff down the stairs and through the metal door.

The Major had worked for hours on end to perfect the plan for hijacking the truck with the cask. A truck exactly like the one used to transport the cask with the radioactive material was stolen from the depot of the contractor that worked for the company that oversaw this delicate task. The contractor assumed no one would be interested in a truck of this kind and it was usually left at a parking lot unattended after work hours and during weekends.

One late Saturday night, Yusuf and the Major walked into the parking lot and with the set of keys Yusuf had copied a few days earlier, simply got in the cabin and drove the stolen truck to the farm and parked it in the barn. It was out of sight and no stranger had any idea it was there. Yusuf had another mission that turned out to be much more difficult than stealing the truck – teaching one of the six men to drive it.

Progress in these driving lessons was slow and the truck did receive quite a few dents when the student-driver tried to drive through narrow streets – simulated by two rows of poles – and especially when he practiced how to reverse the truck. The Major was worried this relatively minor detail would delay the whole project, so he kept badgering the Colonel to find him a professional truck driver. Finally, it was Yusuf who solved the problem by persuading one of his colleagues.

Christian was in debt to a local loan-shark threatening Christian's family. Yusuf invited him to join the project, without saying anything about the plan to hijack the truck. Christian was told he would receive 100,000 Euro for a six-hour job. All he had to do was wait in the garage with the fake truck and when Yusuf and the Major arrived with the truck that carried the spent fuel cask, he was to take that truck and drive it to the farm. Christian was so excited about the chance to clear his gambling debt he didn't ask any questions.

The next problem was easily addressed by the Major. With the help of the woman volunteer, Aziza, who had been an art student in Marseille until she was attracted to ISIS because she wanted a life of excitement and adventure. She and the Major soon became an inseparable couple, especially after he told her he had divorced his wife in Iraq. Aziza designed a fake cask made of cardboard and painted it like the original cask with signs warning of radioactivity. This was placed on the substitute truck and looked exactly like the original item and was used for the practice runs.

Getting a van that looks like the armored van that escorted the shipment was a simple matter. Apparently old and used vans were up for sale on e-Bay and all that was needed was to paint it to look superficially like the real armored escort. The two motorbikes were also readily purchased legally. The six security guards the Major had enlisted will provide the fake escort – four in the van and two on the motorbikes – that will lead the truck with the real cask of spent fuel to the farm. After all, the fake convoy with the truck carrying the real cask would not be closely scrutinized by spectators as it made its way to the farm.

The main challenge remained to convince the original escorting officers that the truck with the fake cask was legitimate, because if an alarm was sounded that a cask with radioactive material was snatched then the whole country would go mad seeking it. The plan was for Yusuf and Major Aswadi to present themselves clearly before the switch of the trucks and after the operation so the officers in the escort would not suspect anything was amiss.

***

The Colonel heard the overview of the plan and looked troubled by something. "This is a fine proposal but has a fatal flaw. As soon as the crane operator will hook up the fake cask to lift it from the truck and transfer it to the ship, surely, he will notice the weight of the cask is not right. He'll immediately raise an alarm and that will be long before the real casket is safely hidden in the farm."

The Major replied, "We have thought about this problem and have come up with two possible solutions. One is manufacturing a fake cask that is as heavy as the real thing, or better yet get a hold of a discarded cask and install it on the truck. The other option is to delay the loading of the fake cask on the ship. Each approach has its draw backs."

Colonel Husseini considered these ideas for a moment before saying, "I think that further delaying the loading of the cask is bound to raise a lot of suspicion. I insist on having a fake cask that looks and weighs like the original cask. I think inserting some truly radioactive material in it would make it more convincing."

Kasim had been quiet while the operational aspects of the hijacking were being debated but spoke up. "We do not have access to radioactive material now. Of course, we'll have quite a lot after we reprocess the spent fuel elements, but until then it is not feasible."

The Colonel said, "Dear Dr. Walid, obviously you have not heard about the plan that was described in *The Dreadful Alchemist*. You may not be aware of the abundance of 'orphan sources' – radioactive sources used mainly for medical treatment that go missing every year. These are either discarded when the intensity of the radiation decreases below the threshold needed for radiotherapy, others may be misplaced, or stolen by thieves that are not aware of the radiation hazard."

Kasim said, "In that case, getting hold of one of those and extracting the radioactive material is a relatively simple task. We can even make sure that some radioactive contamination on the external shell of the cask will be convincing that there is more radioactive material inside even if we don't use any. Thus, even a small amount of radioactive material will keep away any curious observers. I like this idea, but we still need a heavy fake cask."

The Colonel turned to Major Aswadi. "Major, this is top priority. I suggest you ask Yusuf what the company does with the casks that are disqualified and discarded and then make sure you get one."

Major Aswadi's dark skin turned pale. "I should have thought of this myself before stealing the truck. Getting hold of a discarded cask would be much more difficult now because we would need to transport it separately to the barn." He was glad the proposal to contaminate the fake cask with radioactive materials was ignored now.

Kasim said, "On the contrary, now we have the means to transport it – the stolen truck. We will need to get Yusuf or the other driver we enlisted to take the truck from the farm and load a discarded cask that we will buy legally."

The Colonel summed up the meeting. "We have encountered a minor setback but once we overcome this our plan

Major and Colonel. His intuition told him that while there was quite a detailed account of their activities before they pledged allegiance to ISIS about a year earlier, there was a scarcity of information on their present activities. He read about their distinguished military careers in Saddam's Iraqi army and understood they had joined Al Qaeda for practical, rather than for ideological reasons, after the Iraqi army was disbanded and they couldn't get jobs in the new Shiite administration.

What he didn't understand was why they had joined ISIS and that bothered him. He wondered if the Americans or Brits had more information about these two gentlemen and considered calling his Dutch colleagues from the Domestic Security Service (simply BVD for short as it is quite a mouthful in Dutch Binnenlandse Veiligheidsdienst to be pronounced aloud only by those readers that have good dental services). Then he remembered that this organization had changed its name and was now called the General Intelligence and Security Service (Algemene Inlichtingen – en Veiligheidsdienstor AIVD for short).

First, David called his good old friend Dr. Eugene Powers, who was still working for the US NNSA (National Nuclear Security Administration) and asked him if he had heard anything about a grand plot by ISIS involving weapons of mass destruction. Eugene was glad to hear from his friend and promised to check if there was any relevant information. When David mentioned the names of the two gentlemen he was particularly interested in, Eugene said that the names sounded familiar and he would get back to him.

Colin Thomas, who was now back at MI6 as a deputy director and in charge of counterterrorism was also pleased to hear David's voice. He acknowledged that the Colonel and the Major had been on the list of prime suspects for quite a while and said he would try to find the latest intelligence reports on their recent whereabouts.

David tried to recall who he had been in touch with at the Dutch AIVD. Suddenly an image of the striking face of the section head in charge of monitoring specific left-wing extremists, Islamic groups, and right-wing extremists came to mind. He looked through his notes from the last multi-national informal meeting that dealt with the threat of terror cells among the refugees from Syria and Afghanistan and remembered the name of the cool woman, introduced as Anika Anraat, who represented the AIVD.

When he tried to contact her, he was told by her administrative assistant that she was out of the office and he could leave a message. A few hours later he received a phone call from Anika and asked for her cooperation. He was surprised by her response – she said she could not discuss this on the phone and urged him to come to Amsterdam as soon as possible because there was sensitive information she needed his help in assessing.

***

David called Shimony and gave him an update. The Chief of Mossad was intrigued by this unusual response from the Dutch AIVD and told him to prioritize the matter and investigate it.

The flight to Amsterdam was full and it was only with great difficulty that David managed to get a seat on it. He was squeezed between a sweaty, heavy-set woman sitting in the aisle seat and a thin man in the window seat. It turned out the man had an overactive bladder and whenever David tried to take a nap the man politely excused himself and said he had to go to the toilet. Each time, the woman placed one hand on the seat in front of her and pulling while pushing herself up by leaning on David's seat with her other hand. The passenger seated in front of her was also trying to nap when this irresistible force pulled him back and almost tore the entire row of seats out of its mooring.

Some sharp words were exchanged, and the flight attendant had to be called to pacify the passengers before words turned into blows. David, the innocent bystander suggested that the woman and the man change places, and both turned on him and shouted at him to mind his own business.

When the man finally made his way to the toilet, the flight attendant whispered in David's ear that the thin man was the heavy-set woman's husband. Now David began to understand what the soldiers of the United Nations peace keeping force must feel like when posted between two dire enemies. The flight attendant saw his distress and took pity on him. She offered to move him to business class but when the woman heard this, she started shouting it was discrimination against obese people and she would write to the airline's manager.

David once again made a proposal that was unwelcome – move the lady to business class, he said, and bring peace to the world. Now the flight attendant, and the thin man who had returned from the toilet, both turned on David, but the woman took her bag and walked up to the business class section like a royal yacht sailing into the harbor.

David was glad when the plane landed at Amsterdam airport and walked out of the airport as quickly as he could without appearing to be running. He called Anika and she asked him where he would be staying and when he told her she arranged to meet him there for a coffee an hour later. David took a taxi to the 4-star hotel that had been reserved for him by his office and after a refreshing shower and a change of clothes was ready to go down to the hotel's modest restaurant.

He entered the restaurant and made his way to a table farthest from the kitchen door and sat down facing the entrance. He was nursing his second cappuccino when Anika majestically entered the restaurant. There were not many customers at the time but every single one of them ogled the blonde beauty with their eyes and searched for the lucky man she would be joining. David didn't like the unwelcome attention but there was nothing he could do about it. As she approached his table, he rose to greet her but failed to beat the waiter who followed her closely and pulled a chair back to accommodate her. David formally shook hands with Anika and noticed that the other customers went back to their conversations.

As she took her seat Anika gave him one of her rare smiles and his heartbeat fluttered for a moment. He kept wondering how such a striking and unforgettable woman could be a senior officer in an organization that conducted covert operations. He didn't consider that this act was essentially a kind of double-bluff that allowed her to get away with almost, literally, murder because for the same kind of reasoning no one would suspect her of any underhanded behavior.

"I am glad you called me and really grateful that you arrived here so promptly. Before you called me, I had been thinking of contacting your organization because of some information that my people have discovered." David discerned that she didn't use the words Mossad or AIVD as she continued, "I didn't want to meet in my office as people would start wondering and gossiping about me meeting with someone from your country. As you probably know, your country's popularity in Holland is at an all-time low. People blame your country for causing the refugee problem, blame the occupation and settlements in the Palestinian territories, and anti-Semitism is still rife among the extreme right-wing supporters that are now gaining considerable political power. True, they hate the Muslim immigrants more but your people are next on the list of 'undesirables.'"

He barely waited for her to finish speaking before he spoke his mind. "First of all, the influx of refugees from Syria and Iraq has nothing to do with my country. The Muslims are doing the killing and ethnic cleansing to one another, with considerable help by other Muslims and some Christians. Second, the settlements and Palestinian problem have been around for decades, even half a century, and although they don't publicly acknowledge it, those Arabs living in the territories controlled by Israel have better lives than their brethren anywhere else in the Arab world. Finally, the right-wing parties all over Europe are using the refugee problem to incite the people against all foreigners and tend to forget that the Jews have been here for centuries and have made great contributions to the economy and culture of this country. But I understand why our meeting could get tongues wagging and undermine the cooperation we both need. Could you please be more specific about the information you want to share?"

Anika blushed when she heard David's righteous eruption and for a moment hesitated with second thoughts about divulging the information. She took a sip of her coffee. "I am very concerned that Colonel Husseini and Major Aswadi are planning an operation on Dutch soil. We have noticed that the Major has been here for several months and has been seen associating with suspected ISIS supporters in Islamic cultural centers here in Amsterdam and elsewhere. The Colonel has been in and out of the country several times for short visits. He travels very light and all he brings with him is a small suitcase. We have had our customs people open it or secretly X-ray it and have never found any contraband materials. But every visit here includes a trip to the Hamas unofficial embassy where he picks up a stuffed backpack."

David knew all about the unofficial Hamas representatives. They were treated with kid gloves by the Dutch government and considered to have the equivalent of diplomatic immunity. Police officers that tried to harass them received an anonymous warning to lay off and strange 'accidents' happened to members of the families of those that persisted. Hamas used contractors to do the dirty work so were never caught red-handed. David asked, "Did you ever apprehend Colonel Husseini and search the backpack?"

Anika nodded. "We did do it once and found the backpack was stuffed with old newspapers. Apparently, he had been tipped off and had a good laugh at our expense. The Dutch police force is rife with Muslims and supporters of Islam and there is nothing we can do because if we try anything there will be a public outcry about discrimination and illegal profiling. That is one of the reasons I wanted to meet with you because we know that your organization has the ISIS supporters under constant surveillance–"

David interrupted "We would never do such a thing on the territory of a friendly country like Holland."

Anika was not impressed. "Well, this has happened before, hasn't it? Your people were caught carrying out illegal operations in Norway, in the US, in Switzerland, in Cyprus, not to mention Dubai?" She was referring to some of the widely publicized cases in which Israeli intelligence agents were caught breaking the local law.

It was David's turn to blush, and he kept silent while Anika continued. "I can give you the location and time of the next visit by Colonel Husseini. Do what you think you should with this information. There are only two caveats: don't get caught and don't tell me anything about your plans."

David nodded and when Anika rose to leave, he noticed that she passed him a small note when he shook her hand. He looked around the restaurant and saw that most of the men were looking at him with a smirk of satisfaction arising from the envy inbred in every male. *If I can't have this lovely woman, I am glad that none of you can either.* He shrugged and left a nice tip on the table before walking out of the restaurant.

CHAPTER 8

Amsterdam, August

All the vital pieces were in place for the daring hijacking of a shipment of spent nuclear fuel. Yusuf and Major Aswadi were in the cabin of the truck and on their way to load the cask with the irradiated nuclear fuel. The fuel elements had been placed in the cooling ponds, or pools, for several months after they were removed from the core of the nuclear power plant.

The level of radiation was still so high that a person standing near the exposed fuel element would suffer extreme radiation sickness in seconds and would die within minutes. Obeying the laws of physics, the level of radiation decreased with the square of the distance from the fuel elements. Thus, a person standing thirty feet away from the source would receive only one percent of the radiation of a person just five feet from the source. The heavy cask reduced the amount of external radiation because its thick walls absorbed most of the radiation and considerably attenuated the more energetic electromagnetic rays.

In fact, the amount of radiation emitted from the cask was in compliance with the transportation regulations. The risks of radiation exposure to the driver of the truck and his assistant were acceptable and conformed with international commission radiation protection (ICRP) guidelines.

The cask weighed twenty-five tons, including the four fuel elements that were removed from the pressurized water reactor. Its dimensions were not very impressive with a length of twenty feet and an external diameter of less than seven feet, but the cask was a sophisticated piece of engineering. Inside, was a basket that contained the spent fuel elements, surrounded by an inner steel shell and then by a layer of lead that served for gamma radiation shielding. All this was encased in an outer casing made of steel and a neutron shielding shell. At both edges, there were impact limiters to provide extra protection in case of an accident during transport.

Yusuf had done this many times before and was whistling quietly as the truck approached the loading crane. The Major, on the other hand, was perspiring profusely. He was afraid of things he couldn't see, hear, taste, touch, or smell. The radiation emitted from the cask was a source of concern and fear.

Yusuf saw this and jokingly said, "Major, don't worry, when your hair starts to fall out, blisters appear on your skin, cataracts develop in both eyes, then you'll know you have been exposed and will soon die."

The Major gave him a nasty look that conveyed, 'drop dead.' Yusuf was amused by the thought that the Major would be the one who must get out of the cabin and convince the officers in the escort van there was a leak of radioactivity. He was sure the Major would put on a very convincing show without having to act at all.

No more words were spoken until the cask was placed on

the back of the truck and secured with steel cables that ran from the bed of the truck through special hook eyes on the cask.

Aswadi looked at the radiation detector that Yusuf took out of the truck's glove compartment and switched it on. Its monotonous clicking was slow, and the reading was in the safe green zone. He got out of the cabin and climbed on to the truck's bed, keeping his distance from the cask. He appeared to be satisfied with the reading of the detector and with a forced smile returned to the truck's cabin. From the corner of his eye he saw that the people in the escort van were closely observing his every move. However, they were too far away to notice he had spilled a small amount of some liquid from a vial concealed in his other hand. He made sure the spill was confined to a small area near the back of the truck's platform.

Yusuf gave the 'all clear' signal on the radio's communication channel and it was acknowledged by the officer in charge of the escort. He motioned to the lead motorbikes to start moving. The bikes slowly pulled out of the loading area followed by the truck and then the van that kept a safe distance behind the truck. The main gate of the power plant was open, and the security guards halted all cross traffic to allow the small convoy to exit without interruption. The convoy moved through the streets of the industrial area and approached the garage in which the substitute truck with the fake cask was waiting.

Yusuf turned on the radio and in a tone that was supposed to convey controlled panic said, "Escort, I have a problem. The reading on my radiation detector has increased. I am stopping to check." He stopped in the middle of the road and Major Aswadi got out of the cabin and donned protective clothing and a full-face protective mask. Once again, he made his way to the back of the truck with the radiation detector in his hand. He held the detector far away from his body pointing it at the cask and took a reading.

In a fluid motion, he jumped off the truck's bed and started to frantically wave his hand and shout something to Yusuf. Yusuf announced on the radio that there appeared to be a leak of radiation and invited the officer in charge of the escort to see for himself. The officer got out of the van and cautiously approached the truck. Aswadi told him to stay a few feet from the truck and pointed the radiation detector at the spot where he had spilled the vial's contents a few moments earlier. The fierce clicking sound of the detector was audible even at a distance and the officer abruptly turned about and quickly returned to the van.

Yusuf said on the radio, "I need to pull into a garage to check the leak. I suggest you wait here and make sure nobody approaches. This could be a minor problem like some external contamination or a more serious leak. I need to check this." Without waiting for an answer, he drove the truck into the garage while the van and motorbikes kept their distance and remained outside.

Yusuf and the Major quickly jumped into the waiting truck with the fake cask and started to drive it out of the garage. At the last moment, the Major remembered the GPS tracker, told Yusuf to wait a minute and quickly removed the tracker from the original truck and positioned it on the truck with the fake cask.

Yusuf announced on the radio. "Escort officer, this was only some external contamination. We are fine and ready to move on."

The sigh of relief that escaped the officer's lips could be heard on the radio. "Okay, let's continue as scheduled."

The convoy once again made its way to the port and stopped next to the ship that was ready to transport the cask to the reprocessing facility across the channel. The fake cask was loaded without a hitch. Major Aswadi used his walky-talky to inform Colonel Husseini that everything went as smoothly as planned.

Yusuf and the Major invited all members the escort team to have a drink, but they declined wanting nothing to do with the people who may have been contaminated by radioactive material. The Major patted Yusuf on the shoulder and said, "Why don't we get the drink we so justly earned."

***

Meanwhile in the garage, the driver of the other truck, Christian, jumped into the cabin of the truck with the original cask and waited for the signal to drive out. The man sitting next to him, one of the Major's henchmen was holding the walky-talky and speaking to Colonel Husseini, who was in control of the entire hijacking operation. The Colonel was seated in the fake escort van dressed in the uniform of the security firm that oversaw the safe transport of the spent fuel.

When he heard from the Major that the fake cask was

loaded on the ship, he gave the 'go ahead' signal to Christian in the other truck. The two motorbikes led the way out of the garage with the fake security guards driving behind them. No GPS signals were emitted from either vehicle.

The convoy made its way from Amsterdam across Holland without any interference from Dutch highway patrols. A police officer in a patrol car parked near the highway was a bit surprised to see the small convoy and was about to offer assistance but his colleague said that she needed to get to the restroom urgently and got out the car. He muttered something to himself about females in general and policewomen in particular but joined her to get a cup of coffee.

There was no real border control on the well-travelled highway that led from Holland into Germany and within minutes after crossing the border the convoy left the highway and travelled on rural roads to the farmhouse.

One of the lead bikers opened the gate to the farm's driveway and waved the truck through. The narrow driveway was just barely wide enough for the large truck, but Christian was an experienced driver and safely negotiated the curves along the dirt road that led to the barn. The barn doors were open, and Dr. Walid directed the truck to its parking spot. The escort van also entered the barn and parked at the other end while the two motorbikes took positions on both sides of the large doors.

The silence that pervaded the barn when all the engines were switched off was broken by the cheers of the laboratory crew and the security guards.

The Colonel stepped out of the escort and approached the

scientist with a big smile. "Now, Dr. Walid everything is up to you."

Kasim also smiled. "You can rest assured we are well prepared to carry out the work of Allah."

***

David Avivi was back in Tel Aviv when he received a call from Mossad's station head in Amsterdam, Albert Gadol. Gadol was a veteran field agent who had taken part in some of the most daring operations that Mossad conducted in Europe. To his credit, was the fact he had never been caught by a foreign government, although he had been responsible for the elimination of some of his country's dire enemies.

In some of these operations the victim's body was found with the obvious signs of a professional hit job, but in most cases the person had simply disappeared from the face of the earth, literally so in many of the successful operations.

"David, the note you passed me a few weeks ago was very helpful. We managed to track Hans." The codename they had given Colonel Husseini. "We followed him around Amsterdam. He met with several people, who we recognized as ISIS supporters. But after a couple days, he vanished into thin air, and I mean this figuratively not literally. Unfortunately, we lost track of him."

David tried to get a better understanding of Husseini's reason for visiting Holland, but Albert had no further information and suggested that David try to glean some data from his contact in the Dutch AIVD. Albert didn't know who the contact was, and David preferred it to remain that way. So, he called Anika again and was surprised by her warm response and invitation to meet again.

Once again David boarded the flight from Tel-Aviv to Amsterdam and made his way to the hotel reserved for him by his office. This time it was a 5-star-plus hotel that boasted it had one of the best bars in Amsterdam, so he silently thanked whoever it was in Mossad's administration that oversaw booking the hotel. He didn't usually care where he stayed as long as there was a roof over his head, a comfortable bed, and clean shower, but he had a feeling that this time he would need more than the most rudimentary facilities.

Amsterdam, September

Anika was waiting in the most secluded booth of the bar, nursing some kind of a red cocktail when David approached her table. She gestured to him to take a seat and said she would like another one of these cocktails and recommended he should try it. David detested any drink that looked as if it contained artificial flavoring and ordered a single malt whiskey for himself and another red cocktail for Anika. He noticed this wasn't her second cocktail and probably not her third one either and wondered if that meant she would be more forthcoming than at their previous meeting.

David picked up his drink. "Anika, I am really glad to see you." For a moment, couldn't help thinking about the beginning of the quote attributed to Mae West (and many others) – 'is that a banana in your pocket, or are you just happy to see me?' forgetting that she was supposed to lead with this line. To cover his embarrassment, he added, "Thanks for the tip you gave me last time, it was helpful although we did lose sight of the target."

Anika giggled and David, whose mind was for some reason fixed on famous quotes by movie stars, thought of Marilyn Monroe and wondered if there was any truth in her saying, 'If you can make a woman laugh, you can make her do anything.'

Finally, Anika managed to sober up a little and say, slightly slurring her words, "It appears that your infamous friend is back in Holland and up to no good. We know that he met with his sidekick, Major Aswadi, and they were photographed several times in deep conversation with a man we later identified as Johann. It turns out that this Johann is a truck driver and works for a company that is one of the contractors that specializes in hauling toxic chemical and radioactive materials for disposal."

David heard the word "radioactive" and his mind refocused on the job, forgetting all about famous quotes, movie stars, and the lovely woman sitting opposite him in the bar.

Instinctively, he said, "Do you know what they were talking about?" When Anika shook her head, he added, "Do you know where I can find this Johann?"

Anika smiled and said this piece of information will cost him another cocktail. David signaled to the bartender for two refills and considered the best approach. The drinks arrived and they toasted each other once more. Anika was already having trouble sitting up straight and she motioned to David to come and sit beside her in the booth.

David hesitated when another of Marilyn Monroe's quote came up, 'If you're gonna be two-faced at least make one of them pretty,' so he put on his best smile and moved across the booth.

Anika mumbled something about being passed over for promotion by her boss, who was also her lover. This offended her deeply. First, as a woman because he refused to leave his wife, and second, as a brilliant intelligence officer whose work was not properly appreciated.

David tried to ignore the implied invitation but when she leaned toward him and placed her head on his shoulder and her hand on his knee, the last shreds of his resistance broke down. In a hoarse voice, he said, "I think we should continue this conversation somewhere else."

Anika nodded and said, "I agree. I need to take a shower and sober up before we do anything stupid. My apartment is at the other end of the town. Can we go up to your room so I can use your shower?"

David wasn't sure what she meant by this as the sobering up part confused him, so he nodded, thinking he would never understand women. He signed the check and left a nice tip for the bartender, who thanked him profusely. He helped Anika make her way out of the bar to the bank of elevators.

The bartender and everyone in the bar, men and women alike, followed their exit with their eyes and a knowing look.

***

Anika walked out of the shower wearing the white

bathrobe the hotel provided its guests and obviously nothing underneath, with a smile she said, "It is time we revealed all, don't you think?"

David's mind was spinning, the two whiskeys were affecting him, and another of Marilyn's quotes flashed across his mind, 'It's not true that I had nothing on. I had the radio on.'

David smiled as the cord holding her robe slipped open and said, "Indeed, I have a revelation." His mind was playing tricks on him and another Marilyn quote that he thought to be appropriate in the present state of affairs escaped his lips. "Dear Anika, I'm selfish, impatient, and a little insecure. I make mistakes, I am out of control, and at times hard to handle. But if you can't handle me at my worst, then you sure as hell don't deserve me at my best."

Anika recognized the quote and burst out laughing. "I think you have our roles reversed. I am supposed to say this, not you. But it's fine with me because I am selfish and at the moment quite insecure and sure that I have already made a few mistakes tonight. So, shut up and come here."

Sheepishly, David approached her and revealed all, as requested, including his pretty face. She looked him over and chuckled. "You certainly don't wear your heart on your sleeve, but there are other telltale signs of what's on your mind."

Afterwards they lay in the bed with her head on his chest. Following the fun part, they were ready for serious business. Anika said, "My office has examined Johann's history and has come up with some very interesting and disturbing information. It turns out that his real name was Yusuf Osman when he originally came to Holland from Egypt. He married a Dutch

woman and changed his name to Johann Auslander, meaning foreigner in German. Until his meeting with Colonel
Husseini, we had no indication he was involved with radical
Islam, although we knew that after his divorce, he regularly
attended the Islamic Cultural Center. When we found his
divorcee and questioned her about him she refused to say
anything, claiming she had put that part of her life behind
her. After a little digging, we discovered she cheated on him
with her boss and when he found out he became violent and
beat her up. The divorce was ugly, and he was lucky to escape
charges for his violence and perhaps a prison sentence. Our
courts do not regard unfaithfulness in a marriage as grounds
for violence, especially when a foreigner beats up one of our
own."

David had come across several cases in which a traumatic
experience had sent people back to their original religious
faith and made them more extreme and radical than they
had ever been. He had seen that happen to survivors of wars,
terrorist attacks, and even traffic accidents. He asked, "Have
you kept tabs on the Colonel?"

Anika replied, "You know we are understaffed and were
instructed not to profile people because of their religious
beliefs. Our American allies don't like this and keep preach-
ing that all people should be treated equally, regardless of
their political and religious persuasion. That is why we
randomly select babies and 90-year-old women in wheel-
chairs for screening at airports and let single young men
of Middle Eastern appearance and haunted looks pass
through unchecked. I prefer the methods you Israelis use

so successfully but Holland is trying to play according to Political Correctness rules."

David replied, "I hope this doesn't come and bite you in the ass. Like many other Western governments, you have put Political Correctness before survival. Democracies have to defend themselves against those who want to abuse the system to destroy it." After venting some of his pent-up frustration he continued, "Do you know where any of the characters – the Colonel, Yusuf, and Major Aswadi – are at the moment?"

Anika nodded and replied, "The three of them were last seen together a few days ago. We know that Johann, sorry Yusuf, had informed his firm he would be taking a vacation after completing his last job yesterday."

David enquired, "Do you know what this final job was?"

Anika replied, "It was another routine delivery of a cask with spent fuel. He collected it from the storage pond, or cooling pool, at the nuclear power plant and transported it to the ship waiting to take it for reprocessing across the channel."

David sat up so abruptly that Anika's head was tossed away from his chest. "I don't like this. Could he have disappeared with the spent fuel?"

Anika shook her head in the negative quickly and replied, "Impossible, every shipment of spent fuel is accompanied by an escort that consists of a pair of motorbikes in front and an armored van with four officers in the back. The truck with the cask has a GPS tracker that tells the control center where it is at all times. There have been no reports of a missing shipment or, God forbid, an attack on the convoy and hijacking the cask. An incident like this would have made the world headline news. No, it's impossible."

David who knew of some of Mossad's operations that were no less daring, did not share her confident statement that nothing could have happened to the shipment. He said, "Anika, I don't like this. It stinks like bad herring which your countrymen are so fond of."

Anika pulled him back down and said, "Enough talk. Let's get some sleep afterwards."

CHAPTER 9

The Farm near Stavern, September

Work at the farm proceeded at a frantic pace. Safety issues were ignored because the deadline for the delivery of the plutonium core had been advanced. Instead of having six months to reprocess the irradiated fuel elements and extract the plutonium, Dr. Kasim Walid was informed he only had six weeks. 'Informed' is really a mild way of saying he was directed to do so 'or else…'

The Colonel didn't need to elaborate what 'or else…' meant because Major Aswadi had given a clear demonstration of the ruthlessness and total disregard to human life by garroting one of the security guards he caught napping while supposedly on patrol duty. The guard's body was buried in the courtyard and was marked by a pole painted red that served as a reminder to the others.

After the cask arrived at the farm and was placed in the barn, the most frightening maneuver had to be performed – opening the cask and removing the spent fuel elements.

Kasim had looked for two volunteers to carry out this task and when no one volunteered he quietly pulled the Major aside and said he would only need one volunteer as he himself would be willing to do the job. The Major looked at him as if he were out of his mind and told him not to worry – he would make sure to bring the necessary manpower either from the outside or have two of the security guards "volunteer." The Major added that the project could not afford to lose Kasim.

Within less than 24 hours two young men arrived at the farm, escorted personally by the Major. They were introduced as new recruits of ISIS that were among the stream of refugees from war-torn Syria. They were brought to Stavern from Frankfurt where they had been staying in one of the houses a local church charity organization had set up for refugees.

The two men, Arref and Makram, didn't ask what they were needed for but declared they were willing to give their lives to the Islamic Caliphate represented by ISIS. It turned out that Arref had some experience in operating a crane at a construction site in Al Salamiyah before that village was practically destroyed and he barely escaped with his dear life into the waiting arms of ISIS. Makram had been a dental technician in the same village and joined Arref when he escaped.

Kasim saw that the two men were tired and hungry after their journey and told the Major they should eat and rest before starting their work. He explained that tired and hungry people made mistakes and an accidental lapse of concentration could be devastating for the whole project. The Major was impatient but had to accept the scientist's words. Kasim was pleased when he learned they had some relevant experience with delicate mechanical operations.

The next morning Kasim described the work that had to be done. Arref and Makram were eager students and within a few minutes understood two things: the work involved a considerable risk to their health and this risk could be minimized if they meticulously followed Kasim's instructions. First, they had a 'dry run' mimicking the steps of removing the lid of the cask, pulling out a fuel element, unloading it into a waiting lead-covered container, and transporting it to the dissolution tank on the other side of the barn. From that point on the laboratory personnel would take over and continue with the chemical processes needed to extract the plutonium from the irradiated fuel element.

They repeated the practice of the 'dry run' three more times until Kasim was satisfied they were in control of the operation. He then had everybody clear the barn and stood near the large doors to supervise the movements of Arref and Makram from a safe distance, or at least from a spot from which he could slip away if they accidentally dropped the fuel element before placing it safely in the lead container.

To everyone's great relief the two young men performed faultlessly, and the first fuel element was transferred from the cask to the lead container and from there to the stainless-steel reactor.

Concentration nitric acid was slowly poured into the reactor and the cladding surrounding the fuel element started to dissolve. During this operation, a copious amount of gas was released. Some of these were radioactive gases entrapped inside the irradiated fuel element and others were merely toxic gases arising from the dissolution reaction by the nitric acid. All the gases were vented through a chimney and carried away with the help of strong air stream that diluted the gases before releasing them into the atmosphere.

Had a radiation detector been placed downwind it would have gone off-scale, but none were positioned there. A curious neighbor may have visibly seen the puff of yellowish-brown nitrogen oxides, but nobody seemed to notice as it was already dark outside. According to Kasim's calculations, the size and configuration of the reactor and amount of fissionable materials, plutonium and uranium, would not be enough to cause an accidental chain reaction. Such an event would have ended the project and probably also the lives of the people close to the reactor.

In order to expedite the dissolution of the fuel the acid inside the reactor was gently heated. With the help of remotely controlled manipulators the solution was transferred through a stainless-steel mesh that served as a filter to the extraction reactor. An organic solvent was used to extract the plutonium and uranium from the acid leaving the highly radioactive fission products in the aqueous acid phase that was discharged into a waste holding tank.

Normally such a highly radioactive solution would be treated before disposal, but the laboratory team couldn't be bothered with such details. After all, they would be far away from the farm once their job was complete.

The organic solvent containing plutonium and uranium was mixed with dilute nitric acid and the plutonium was separated from the uranium. The solution with the uranium was sent to a second waste holding tank and the plutonium was transferred to the next reactor, where it was precipitated from the solution. The solid precipitate was treated by a few more chemical operations until metallic plutonium was obtained. This product is highly toxic if inhaled or swallowed (who in the world would want to swallow plutonium?) but emits little electromagnetic radiation.

The plutonium metal was now transferred to the basement under the farmhouse, where it would eventually be further purified and cast into the shape needed to produce the core of the atomic bomb.

In the following week, this operation was repeated twice more without any incident. Kasim had arranged the process so work on the second fuel element could begin as soon as the dissolution and extraction of the first fuel element was completed. So, the three fuel elements were processed, and the plutonium purified and converted to metallic form.

Kasim called the Colonel and using code words informed him the total amount of plutonium was enough for construction of one nuclear device and asked what to do with the remaining spent fuel element. He was ordered to leave it in the cask, because every additional handling of the radioactive material increased the risk of an accident. Kasim was not pleased with this directive and decided to ignore it and reprocess the fourth fuel element. Wisely, he didn't say anything to the Colonel.

Amsterdam, October

The Colonel had returned to Syria after the cask was delivered to the farm but was now in Amsterdam again. He arrived late at night and didn't feel like taking the two-hour drive to the farm, so decided to take a taxi from the airport to his hotel and pick up his rental car in the morning.

He was pleased with Kasim's progress reports and wanted to be present during the final stages of casting of the plutonium core. He was worried the other part of the project – the preparation of the improved rocket will be behind the updated schedule. It was fair to say that the 'Rocket Man' protested vociferously when he was ordered to expedite the job and have the improved rocket ready almost four months ahead of the original timetable.

Raymond claimed that this would not leave him enough time to test the new rocket but Colonel Husseini cut him short and said the severe losses of personnel and territory that ISIS had suffered on the battleground meant their deathblow to the heart of their enemies cannot be postponed much longer.

The Colonel knew time was crucial because the flow of fresh volunteers was no longer making up for the losses of ISIS fighters. It was even much worse than the official, and unofficial, estimates had been because those were based mainly on body counts and didn't consider the ever-growing number of deserters.

Many of the foreign volunteers realized they didn't have a real prospect of coming out of the battle alive. Much to their remorse they understood they would probably die in an air raid on one of their convoys or hiding like cowards in a hole in the ground and not get a chance to die fighting. The mass desertion of the European volunteers also had an up-side – they would be able to carry out heroic acts for the grandeur of Allah in their home countries, as some already have done.

Many of these acts were not part of a coordinated campaign but rather carried out by individuals and were based on local initiatives. ISIS was usually quick to claim responsibility, which in an indirect way was genius because they provided the ideology if not the actual weapons or explosives.

In one infamous case, an ISIS supporter with a long criminal record rented a heavy truck and drove it through the throngs of people celebrating the French National Day on the 14th of July in the town of Nice on the French Riviera.

In other cases, individuals that had a grudge against society or were simply mentally unstable took an axe, a sharp knife, or a pistol and ran berserk killing and maiming as many people as they could before being stopped. Once again, ISIS was there to take credit although its leaders in Syria or Iraq had no idea or direct involvement in the actual attacks, referred to as 'hate crimes' by the Western media.

The Colonel could not share these thoughts with anyone but his trusted friend, Major Aswadi, and was looking forward to seeing him at the farm. He was so occupied with his thoughts about the fate of ISIS and the rising doubts about the success of the project that he didn't notice Albert Gadol.

The Mossad station chief was sitting in his car and could see Husseini walking from his hotel to the car rental office nearby. David had received a tip from Anika about the Colonel's arrival at Schiphol and immediately alerted Albert, who easily discovered which hotel Colonel Husseini would be staying at and posted two agents, Eyal and Natalie, to keep him in sight.

David's impression that Albert was an experienced and

resourceful field operator was now proven correct. Natalie, a tall, dark-skinned young woman, was stationed in the car rental agency closest to Husseini's hotel and Albert watched with great joy as the Colonel entered the very same rental office.

Eyal appeared to be waiting for the car he had reserved and was busy pulling his wallet with the Maryland driver's license and credit card. The Colonel went directly to the woman serving the Priority Customers and demanded to get his car immediately.

Natalie overheard the discussion and figured the Colonel will take the black Mercedes already parked next to the door. She realized that time for action was short so pretended to have forgotten something and rushed outside. She stooped to pick up her sunglasses that had fallen out of her handbag right near the Mercedes and with one fluid motion stuck the tracking device under the back fender as she rose. Any man who happened to see her bend down would naturally focus on the curves of her trim figure rather than on her hands, so no one noticed the little trick she did with the tracking device.

By the time she returned to the desk, Husseini was already getting into the Mercedes and adjusting the driver's seat and side mirrors. He also switched on the built-in GPS guidance system and entered the address of the farm near Stavern.

Eyal unsuccessfully tried to see the address he keyed in but didn't worry because the tracking device would enable Albert to follow the Mercedes at a safe distance.

Colonel Husseini pulled out of the parking lot in a hurry and almost collided with a bicycle. He stuck his head out the window and shouted a series of derogatory curses in fluent Arabic at the old man riding the bicycle and at his whole chain of ancestry from the apes downward. A few pedestrians shook their head in disgust, probably thinking about the swarms of rich Arabs that were taking over their country and not suspecting that this particular individual was the harbinger of a much deadlier type of foreigners – mass murderers.

Eyal and Natalie got in Albert's car. Albert saw that the signal from the tracking device was very strong and coolly followed it. The Mercedes was exceeding the speed limit and Albert was surprised because a professional would try to avoid drawing the attention of the police in such a blatant manner. He said to his colleagues, "Husseini must be in a real hurry to drive like this."

Eyal and Natalie nodded and said nothing. The Mercedes was heading to the A10 ring and the Israeli agents were not sure which exit the Colonel would take and in which direction he was heading until he turned south-east on the A1/E231. After a few minutes, he switched to the A28/E232 toward Zwolle with the Mossad agents following at a couple miles behind.

Albert wondered where Husseini was going because the direction now was north-east. When he passed Zwolle, and headed due east, Albert started suspecting they were heading into Germany. The Mercedes slowed down and pulled into a gas station. The Colonel did not stop at one of the pumps and after parking the car headed straight for the rest room.

The Israelis pulled into the parking lot and waited in the car. Natalie said she also needed to use the rest room, but

Albert said it was too risky because Husseini would surely have noticed her in the car rental office.

A few minutes later the Colonel walked out with a cup of coffee in one hand and entered his Mercedes. He placed the coffee in the holder and took out his cell phone to make a call. From his animated gestures, Albert figured he was getting worked up about something. Finally, the Colonel hung up and took another sip of coffee before continuing eastwards on the A37 and crossing into Germany on to the B402.

The Colonel seemed to be more relaxed now and was driving at a much slower pace on the rural roads. Albert had to shorten the distance between the two cars but made sure he would stay out of sight from the Mercedes. After several twists and turns the Mercedes came to a stop. Albert also stopped but a moment later he saw the Mercedes moved a few feet and stopped again. A few seconds later it was on the move once more but going very slowly.

Natalie was the first to understand. "He must have turned off into a gated driveway. He stopped to open the gate, drove through it, and stopped once more to close it before continuing."

Albert looked at her with new respect and said, "Eyal, you'd better get off here and try to see where the Mercedes is now. Be very careful and stay out of sight. I'll drive past the gate and wait for you about two miles down the road. If there is a problem, call me."

Eyal got out of the car and made his way through the trees that surrounded the farmhouse while Albert continued on the narrow road and drove past the gate. A couple miles further, he pulled over and stopped the car on the shoulder of the road. He told Natalie to wait in the car while he also tried to get a look at the farm from the other side.

Natalie responded, "Wait a minute. Let's first try to see the area on Google Earth and then decide how to approach the farm." Albert felt quite stupid because he didn't think of this obvious step. He quickly called Eyal and told him to wait before getting any closer to the farm, so the agent found a nice quiet spot in the copse of trees where he was hidden from the road on the one side and from the farmhouse on the other side.

The low-resolution image of the area did show there were several farms within a radius of ten miles. Most were surrounded by open, cultivated fields and obviously not suitable for hiding any clandestine activities. However, Albert noticed that one farm stood at a distance from the road and was isolated by trees. Even from the fuzzy image it looked as if the farmhouse was in disrepair and it was unclear if there were any functioning additional buildings besides the house and barn.

After carefully checking their position Albert was sure the gate they had driven past, and the dirt road led to this farm. He called Eyal and told him to get a good view of the farm and photograph it but make sure he is not seen by anyone.

Albert told Natalie to move to the driver's seat and turn the car around so it would be facing the direction from which they had come in case they needed to pick up Eyal in a hurry. He said he would try to get a look at the farm from the other side.

Eyal noticed there were no footpaths through the copse of trees and figured that people didn't hike or picnic in that area. He made his way slowly through the wooded area avoiding the edge of the tree line. The flat ground on which the road was built became hilly and a little steep as he got closer to the farm. This provided him with some extra cover as he climbed up the hill. As he approached the ridge he lay on the ground and crawled forward until he could observe the farm buildings.

He lay still for a few moments enjoying the peaceful surroundings. At one point he thought he heard voices of people speaking in Arabic but the noise from some kind of engine, probably a generator he thought, interfered and the words were not very clear. He saw the black Mercedes parked in front of a rundown farmhouse and next to it he could see three other cars. The large barn was in no better shape than the farmhouse and he wondered what all these cars were doing there.

He saw a couple men leaving the farmhouse and walking toward the barn and recognized one of them as Colonel Husseini. The other man appeared to be older, probably in his early sixties, and by the way he was moving his hands, Eyal guessed he was trying to get some point across to the Colonel.

A small door on the side of the barn opened and he got a glimpse of a man with a gun slung on his shoulder and smoking a cigarette. As soon as the guard saw the Colonel, he threw his cigarette to the ground and gave a clumsy salute. The Colonel ignored him and strode into the barn. Eyal couldn't see what was inside the barn. He took a few photos with his cell phone and then called Albert and in a low voice, a whisper, told him what he had seen. Albert instructed him to carefully return to the road and wait.

After Albert left Natalie in the car, he approached the farm from the opposite side, but the hilly terrain blocked his view. He decided he might expose himself if he got too close, so he remained hidden in the trees and all he saw was the back of the old farmhouse and the barn. He couldn't make out much detail of what was going on there, so he retreated to the car.

Natalie drove back and after passing the gate saw Eyal stepping out from behind a large tree. After picking him up Albert told Natalie to drive to the closest village, that happened to be Stavern. They found a small café and ordered coffee and sandwiches. They avoided speaking Hebrew and kept their voices down and quietly spoke in English about the countryside, the weather, and about tourist sites.

Once they were back in the car, they discussed their next steps. Albert said he had to call David and tell him about the farm and their suspicions that it was the focus of ISIS activities in Europe and perhaps the site where they are planning their big project.

CHAPTER 10

Mossad Headquarters, Tel-Aviv

David received Albert's report with mixed feelings. On the one hand, he was relieved the search for the site of ISIS's main effort in Europe has come to an end.

There was little doubt in David's mind that whatever was going on in the farm near Stavern was at the hub of activity and Colonel Husseini's presence there was proof enough.

On the other hand, the involvement of Yusuf, the driver who's last accounted for job was to drive a truck with a cask of irradiated fuel, was a serious concern. The fact that Yusuf had disappeared afterwards was troublesome as was his involvement with Colonel Husseini and Major Aswadi.

The news that one of the casks of spent nuclear fuel that arrived at Dounreay for reprocessing did not contain the fuel elements the manifest listed was very disturbing. It was quite easy to put two and two together and reach the conclusion that the missing shipment was somehow diverted and was now in the hands of the Colonel and his buddies from ISIS.

The fact that this diversion was discovered weeks later, only after the cask had been opened at the reprocessing facility, indicated a sophisticated hijacking operation was involved.

This wasn't a crude armed robbery and attack on the convoy transporting the irradiated fuel elements that would have been discovered instantly and alerted the whole country.

This was a well-planned and flawlessly executed operation by a clever and devious adversary who managed to get away with one of the most closely guarded items on the world's watch-list. Evidently there was inside cooperation in getting the information about the shipment and then planning the switch.

In addition, the proven organizational skills pointed to a strong group with vast resources not afraid of taunting the authorities in, at least, two of the most technically advanced countries in Europe – Holland and Germany. The involvement of people with known Islamic backgrounds like Yusuf, Husseini, and Aswadi could only mean one thing – ISIS was up to something on a grand scale.

David had made his career in Mossad by chasing the 'bad guys,' who were determined to produce a nuclear device and detonate it in Israel, so he was worried this would be another such attempt. He knew, better than anyone else, that such a successful operation could precipitate a global war with nuclear weapons, or at the very least, an all-out regional war the outcome of which would change the Middle East. So, he would enlist all Mossad resources, and perhaps the help of other intelligence agencies, to nip this new hazard in the bud.

He met with Mossad Chief Haim Shimony and explained the situation. "Haim, this time we are facing a very dangerous plot. ISIS is desperate to produce a major coup because it is losing ground on the battlefield. As far as we know they have initiated a project that involves radioactive materials and we strongly suspect they have managed to hijack a shipment of spent nuclear fuel without anyone noticing until it was too late."

Shimony intervened, "Perhaps they are after a 'dirty bomb' – something that can cause mass disruption but hardly mass destruction. Of course, it would be terrible if they detonated such a device in Tel Aviv, but Israel can overcome such an event." Shimony was not an expert in nuclear physics and believed, as did many other people, that spent nuclear fuel contained low-grade plutonium that could not be used in an atomic weapon. He correctly assumed that the high radioactivity from the fission products and the large amount of other radioactive contaminants would make it ideal for a 'dirty bomb.'

David was not inclined to speculations based on wishful thinking. "Haim, I believe they wouldn't go to this effort for anything less than a real nuclear device. So far, they have tried to smuggle such a device in a container through our Haifa port, a suitcase bomb across the border from Jordan in a tourist bus, and a booby-trapped plane from Iran. I must get to the bottom of this and find out if this is their grand-coup against us."

He then gave Shimony a short review on the plutonium content in spent nuclear fuel. "The most important isotope in weapon grade plutonium is plutonium-239. There are other isotopes of plutonium that are produced when the uranium fuel is irradiated, and they complicate the functioning of an atomic bomb because they may cause a premature detonation that would result in a low yield called a 'fizz out' or 'fizzle.' But with a sophisticated design, and we have always suspected that ISIS has obtained the necessary blueprints from its secret supporters in the Sunni Islam world, a considerable atomic explosion may result."

Haim was obviously still skeptical, so David added, "Dr. Theodore Taylor, a former US weapons scientist testified before the congress in 1975. He explained that a small, simple, inexpensive facility for extraction of plutonium would require only a few months and a crew of less than a dozen skilled people using published information and commercially available equipment. Furthermore, in 1997, the US Department of Energy warned that reactor grade plutonium could fuel a nuclear weapon despite the difficulties and hurdles."

"How do you intend to find out what they are planning and what they have done?" asked Shimony, who was now much less skeptical.

David replied, "By politely questioning Colonel Husseini or Major Aswadi. They are the brain and brawn behind this scheme."

The Mossad Chief sniggered. "You'll have to be very polite with these two gentlemen. Do you think you could use some leverage like you did with Alan Ross? I doubt that the two gentlemen have ever seen a dentist."

Shimony was referring to an event that took place and was described in *The Dreadful Patriot.*

David laughed. "Every man has his vulnerabilities. I do need some information on the personal histories of the two gentlemen. For example, it is well known that many Iraqis have favism." David saw the questioning look on Shimony's face and added, "That is a deficiency of glucose-6-phosphate dehydrogenase."

Shimony's expression of impatience prompted David to get on with it. "This is susceptibility to certain foods like broad beans that can be life-threatening as it affects the red blood cells."

Shimony was now really dismayed. "David, this is nonsense. There are many types of drugs and substances in our arsenal that can induce similar or worse effects regardless of a person's susceptibility to fava beans. Why look for some rare and exotic genetic problem?"

David was taken aback by Shimony's atypical outburst and responded, "This is a very sensitive issue among Iraqi macho men. It is fine if they die in battle or an accident or even from a fatal disease but dying from something stupid like fava beans is an offense to their pride and manhood."

He recalled the joke about the man who was about to die of diarrhea and requested that on his tombstone it would say he died of syphilis so people would think he died like a man rather than like a wimp. Wisely, he refrained from mentioning this anecdote and continued, "The nice thing about this idea is that we don't have to really induce favism, it is enough if we threaten the distinguished gentlemen that we'll spread the word they died because they ate a handful of fava beans."

At last Shimony got the point. "So, if you get your hands on one of these gentlemen, you'll tell them they must cooperate if they want to die like martyrs or else, they will be remembered as weaklings that ate a plate of fava beans? Now I am beginning to understand the idea, although I still don't like it. There is only one small flaw – how can you capture them?"

David smiled. "You taught me that there are three main strategies to enlist collaborators: money, women, and perverted sex. Obviously, money cannot work in this case and I am not sure if any of these two men is inclined to perverted sex, so the good old 'honey trap' with the right woman seems to be the best way to entice one of them."

Shimony responded, "I'll get our analysts to dig deep and find out what they favor in that department. Go to Amsterdam and do your magic. Good luck."

CHAPTER 11

Amsterdam, October

Albert Gadol was at the Schiphol airport when David's flight landed and approached him as soon as he exited from the custom's 'green lane' portal.

On the way to David's hotel – again the fancy one with the best bar in Amsterdam – Albert gave David an update on the trip to Stavern in the tracks of Colonel Husseini and the information he managed to gather on the farm and activities within it.

David thanked him for the information but had some trouble answering Albert's question. "Why don't we go to the German intelligence service and police and tell them about the farm? After all, it is within their jurisdiction and they can raid it and arrest everyone on site for illegal handling of radioactive materials as well as half a dozen other offenses against the law in Holland and Germany. They can confiscate the nuclear materials and neutralize the threat."

David had known that such a raid could easily curtail the operation, so he decided to share his line of reasoning with Albert. "True, this will stop them and remove any immediate risk to our country, if indeed Israel is the target. But there are two reasons why I prefer to keep the authorities out. First, I want Mossad to lay its hands on Colonel Husseini and Major Aswadi because they must have information on all the plots that ISIS are hatching against Israel and the West. We can make them sing like canaries while the Germans with their 'human rights' approach will respect their 'right to remain silent' and so on. Second, the Germans will rush to release all the perpetrators as soon as some hostage situation develops, as it surely would when ISIS captures some German citizens and threatens to behead them publicly. Mossad needs to maintain its well-earned reputation as an intelligence service that will stop at nothing when the fate and security of Israel are involved. We need a televised confession by the Colonel that will be screened globally and show the world that ISIS is willing to murder tens of thousands of innocent people. There are still people that regard ISIS as some kind of national liberation movement that wishes only to establish equal rights for the Muslims and erase the heritage of Colonialism."

Albert thought about David's words and conceded that he had a few fine points. He asked, "So, how do we proceed? If we want the Colonel alive, we need to separate him from his entourage and get him somewhere we can snatch him. Do you have a plan?"

David smiled and said, "He is a man, isn't he? We can get a beautiful woman, someone so classy he could only dream about, and she would make him an offer he cannot refuse. This basic ploy has worked throughout history almost without failure. I am waiting for feedback from our analysts about the Colonel's secret, or not so secret, preferences."

Albert wondered if the Colonel would be so gullible. He expected Colonel Husseini to be extremely careful, especially as the stakes were so high just before the project is ready for launching. He said, "Should we keep following him? There is a risk that he'll spot the surveillance team. I suggest we keep him in sight but at a safe distance until our little 'honey trap' has the queen bee in place."

***

David received an electronic file from the analysts that had been investigating the Colonel's history since the days he served in Saddam Hussein's army. Apparently, Mossad had a very thick file on Colonel Husseini although information of his activities since he joined ISIS was not as detailed as David had wished.

It turned out that the Colonel had been happily married to Zina who was Saddam's niece, after all he was also a member of the leader's clan. She was killed in one of the bombing raids that American stealth fighters launched at Saddam's palace where she had taken refuge. At that time the Colonel was in the south of Iraq trying to fend off the American troops that invaded Iraq from the Saudi border. He was torn with grief when he heard about Zina's demise and swore to avenge her death.

This was one of the reasons he had joined Al Qaeda and later became one of the military leaders of ISIS. The attached photos showed a petite slim, dark woman with large black eyes and a shy smile. David immediately recalled the beautiful

Mossad agent whose real name was Miriam, but everyone called Mata due to her physical resemblance to Mata Hari and her manipulative skills. Mata had easily lured Alan Ross as described in *The Dreadful Patriot* to his fate and David had an immense respect for her.

David turned to Albert and pointed to the photo of Zina. "This is the Colonel's weakness and I know how to exploit this." He noticed Albert's expression and added, "We have what he will think is the salve for his open wound – a beautiful woman that we will turn into a mirror image of his dead wife. I'll ask Shimony to send Mata here and we'll engineer a meeting with Husseini."

Albert, who was the veteran of many daring Mossad operations, smiled and said, "I'll make sure that the Colonel does not slip away this time."

Al-Raqqah, October

Colonel Husseini had returned to Amsterdam after his last visit to the farm, unaware he had been followed by the Mossad team. In the same afternoon, he boarded a commercial flight to Istanbul arriving in the evening. From there he had no trouble slipping into Al-Raqqah, which still was the headquarters of ISIS in Syria to pay a visit to Dr. Raymond Mashal and read him the riot act.

In a steely voice, he talked to Raymond and explained that there were two options: either deliver the rocket on time or face the consequences. This last part of the sentence was accompanied by drawing his open hand across his throat, a gesture needing no interpretation.

After the Rocket Man recovered his wits, he invited Husseini to see the large underground workshop where one of the old Scud B rockets was being modified.

Raymond proudly showed the Colonel the modified nozzle and explained, "The performance of the rocket engine has improved by over 25% as our preliminary tests show. Our calculations show that the superior thrust of the engine should lead to an increase of the rocket's range that would now be close to 400 km."

The Colonel didn't have much faith in scientists in general and even less in theoretical calculations. His sour expression made this very clear to Raymond, who was discerning his reaction with great concern. Raymond pointed to the tip of the rocket, where the payload would be placed, and said with some tremor in his voice, "With this new configuration, the rocket could house a larger warhead."

The Colonel was still skeptical and wanted more details. "Dr. Mashal, can you provide the exact dimensions of the new warhead?"

The scientist replied, "It conforms to the dimensions on the blueprint I was given." He was too afraid to say anything about his worry that the weight of the warhead would deleteriously affect the range. He then pointed at the fins and said, "The navigation system has also been modified. These fins are controlled by a modern GPS system, so the CEP is smaller."

He saw that the Colonel was about to ask a question, so the scientist clarified this by adding, "The circular error probable is the term we use to describe the accuracy of the rocket. The old Scud B could easily hit a city; the newer model could be aimed to hit a suburb and now I can aim the rocket to hit a street block from a launching site several hundred kilometers away."

He saw that the Colonel was impressed by this, so he continued his explanation and pointed at the rocket. "You can see where the fuel tank and oxidizer tank are. They take up most of the rocket's size and weight. We have increased their size by 10% and that also adds to the range."

The Colonel asked, "If that adds 10% to the range why didn't you increase the size of the tanks by 20% or even more?"

The scientist explained, "Increasing the amount of the fuel and oxidizer also adds to the weight of the rocket and beyond a certain point this is counterproductive. Furthermore, the whole structure may fall apart and disintegrate during lift-off or flight if the weight is too large. This has happened to some of the modified rockets that our army used in the Iran-Iraq war and in the Gulf War. There is a fine line between improved performance and total failure."

He wanted to say, 'Do you understand my problems now?' but rightfully thought that offending the Colonel's feelings by showing off his superior intelligence would not serve him well, so he just said, "I really need more time for testing the overall effect of all the modifications. The best way to do so is to carry out a full-scale field test."

Colonel Husseini grunted. "Dr. Mashal, with all due respect, understand that we don't have more time. The whole project is at a risk and every day increases the chances of it being discovered and stopped. Launching a rocket for your desired field test is suicidal. There are satellites focused on the territories we control, and they will surely detect such a launch within seconds and before we know it we'll be under aerial attack. No, you need to cool down a little. I am pleased with your progress although I can perceive that you have some doubts."

Dr. Raymond Mashal, the Rocket Man, didn't comment and tried not to react to this last observation, so he said, "Inshallah, we shall reign with the help of Allah."

The farm near Stavern, Early November

Colonel Husseini returned to Amsterdam and rented a car at the airport – a black Mercedes, of course. He drove straight to the farm near Stavern. He arrived there in the evening and was met by Major Aswadi, Dr. Kasim Walid, and Afrin.

They led him to the basement under the farmhouse and proudly showed him the metal sphere they had produced. The Colonel found it hard to believe that such a small, innocent looking object could destroy a whole city in an instant.

Dr. Walid noticed the expression of disbelief and said, "I know that it is hard to grasp the destructive power of an atom bomb by looking at this thing that is only slightly larger than a tennis ball. This is all because of an infidel, a filthy Jewish dog, hypothesized that converting mass into energy would yield so much power. In fact, a few pounds of the right stuff could either supply electrical power to millions of people for a year or destroy the lives of hundreds of thousands of people in seconds."

The Colonel knew all about Einstein and other Jewish scientists and the role they played in developing atomic bombs for the hated Americans and the godless Russians. So, he just said, "Convince me that this little sphere will do the job to bring death and destruction to many Jews that are now conveniently concentrated in one small country."

Kasim tried to avoid the complicated issue of explaining the difference between the weapon grade plutonium produced in dedicated nuclear reactors and the isotopic composition of plutonium extracted from spent fuel of commercial nuclear reactors. He said, "Colonel Husseini, the plutonium we have here is second or third rate compared with plutonium the nuclear powers produce for atomic weapons. It may be more prone to incomplete nuclear detonation..."

The Colonel jumped up and shouted, "You knew this all along and said nothing? If this thing doesn't work, you will wish that you were dead. Do I need to be more explicit or can you use your imagination Dr. Walid?" The way he drew out the word doctor left no doubt in Kasim's mind that it was a lowly derogatory title in the list of insults.

Kasim turned so pale he could be mistaken for a Scandinavian living north of the Arctic Circle. He stuttered, "Colonel Husseini, I assure you I am doing my best to make sure the device works as advertised. I have used a large excess of plutonium and added the material extracted from the fourth fuel element although my calculations showed that it was not necessary, and I did this despite your instructions not to do so. I am glad to say this also went without a hitch and we now have a better chance of complete success. I know what's at stake and am aware of the consequences of failure to perform fully."

Afrin opened her mouth to say something but one warning look from the Colonel was enough and she held her silence. Major Aswadi didn't like the direction this conversation was heading as he knew he would be almost as accountable as the scientist. After all, he had spent the last few months with the people at the farm and was up to his neck in this part of the project.

Despite the pleasant diversion provided by Aziza, the art student from Marseille, Major Aswadi regarded the project as the most important and significant in his life and had worked day and night for its success. He felt responsible not only for the physical security of the personnel but also for the administrative leadership of the laboratory team and the security detail. He saw himself as a kind of General Groves working side by side with Dr. Walid, whom he thought of as the Dr. J. Robert Oppenheimer of the project.

After a long moment of silence, he said, "Colonel, these are the best people risking their lives working with dangerous materials for the cause of ISIS and the New Caliphate. Each and everyone know what is at stake and they are all willing to die, if this can help the project. Kasim here had provided excellent scientific leadership and shouldn't be intimidated or threatened."

The Colonel was simmering. "Major, I think you have grown soft living here with your mistress. You are no less responsible for whatever happens than Dr. Walid. If it works you will be given medals and will be mentioned in the prayers of every true believer, but failure will not spare you your fate." After a long pause, he continued in a softer tone, "I guess that we must trust Allah that the task you have carried out in His name and for His cause will be successful. Please gather the whole team – the laboratory personnel and security detail – so I can thank them all in person."

Within five minutes they all gathered around Colonel Husseini who smiled and said, "On behalf of Allah and Muḥammad ibn ʿAbdullāh ibn Abdul-Muttalib ibn Hashim his envoy, and the New Caliphate I wish to thank you all for your work. You will be fully rewarded in heaven but here on earth you have earned the gratitude of the Muslim people. They will never know your names and what part each and every one of you had in this grand project, but they will thank you five times a day. In the New Caliphate, you will earn a seat of honor at Muhammad's feet."

A round of applause and broad smiles cut him short, so he waited a moment before continuing, "Today, your product will be sent on its way to its destination. For your own protection, you have not been told where it will go or when or how it will be used. This also allows you all to leave here safely." He waited a moment to allow the implications to be understood. After all, they had all known that in some cases all participants in projects of this kind were summarily executed to keep the secret, and some had worried they would suffer a similar fate.

The Colonel concluded, "Each of you will receive a handsome sum of money that will enable you to start a new life, far away from this farm. I plead that you behave discreetly and not draw unwanted attention by the authorities. I can arrange to take those of you who want to continue to contribute to the cause to the actual battlefields, but I believe that you have already done more than your share to further the advance our New Caliphate. Go, and Allah be with you and watch over you."

He departed after giving Major Aswadi and Aziza the task of taking the plutonium sphere from the farm and arranging for its shipment to Al Raqqah where it will serve its purpose.

He got into his rented Mercedes and accelerated so fast that pebbles were splattered at the jubilant group that came to see him off. Once the cloud of dust left by the car settled down, Kasim said he needed a stiff drink and invited Afrin, the Major, and Aziza to join him in the living room of the farmhouse.

Within a couple of hours, the farm was as deserted as it had been before it was purchased by Kasim and Afrin.

CHAPTER 12

Evening, Amsterdam, Early November

The Colonel almost rammed the gate at the end of the driveway as he left the farmhouse. He kept cursing all scientists and engineers and relaxed a little only after reaching the outskirts of Amsterdam. He was lucky not to get stopped by the German or Dutch highway patrol for reckless driving and speeding, but he didn't think about that as he was too busy planning how to let off some steam and unwind in Amsterdam.

He arrived at the hotel he had reserved and left the car for the valet to park. He checked in and made sure his single bag was sent up to his room. He thought of going to one of the "coffee shops" and get some legal marijuana but couldn't be bothered so he entered the hotel's bar to indulge in some good alcohol. This was strictly forbidden by his religion, but he thought none of the patrons of the bar would care. However, just to be on the safe side, for the sake of appearances, he asked the waiter that came to take his order to serve him a double Scotch whiskey in a teacup.

The waiter had heard this before and told the barman, "We have another of these pious Muslims who thinks they can deceive the world by having whiskey in a teacup."

The barman looked at the customer and told the waiter, "I would like to assign the new waitress to serve this gentleman." He pointed at the diminutive dark girl who was standing at the far side of the bar "Her name is Asma. Please call her."

The waiter was not very pleased but said, "You're the boss. Pour him a lavish portion of your best whiskey and I'm sure he'll give her a generous tip, which we should split three ways."

The barman groaned softly. "Why do people have to pretend to be something that they are not?" He did as requested. He summoned Asma and told her the customer she had waited for had arrived and handed over the teacup filled almost to the brim with whiskey.

The waitress made sure that a generous expanse of her cleavage showed when she bent down at the Colonel's table and gave him his cup of 'tea.' She smiled and said suggestively, "Would you like anything else with your tea? Or perhaps something special after that?"

Colonel Husseini looked up and noticed the lovely waitress for the first time. He froze. She reminded him of his beloved wife, Zina. He took out his wallet and paid for his drink with 100 Euro bank note, telling her to keep the change. Mata, in her new role as Asma the waitress, thanked him profusely and said she would check with him in a few minutes if he wanted another drink or perhaps something to eat.

The Colonel gulped down half of his whiskey and felt the liquid sliding smoothly down his throat and warming his stomach. His eyes followed every movement of the waitress and saw that she seemed to flirt with every male customer.

Nevertheless, he couldn't take his eyes off her as he slowly sipped the remainder of his drink and considered her words.

David and Albert were seated at the bar and speaking quietly. The bartender came up to them and asked if they wanted a refill and when their wine glasses were filled with red wine Albert slipped him another 500 Euros, as promised when he agreed to hire Mata.

The bartender whispered that she was the best waitress who ever worked in his bar and he could easily hire her on a permanent basis as the tips she split with him that evening were more than he normally made in a week. David hadn't found out the number of the Colonel's room but knew that Mata would soon have it and hand it to him.

***

The Colonel's gaze didn't leave Mata for one second. As promised, she returned to his table and in a low husky voice said, "My name is Asma." She bent even lower to show him the tag with her name and giving him a glimpse of her breasts. "I just came to check on you, as promised. Would you like *anything...* else?" The last few words were delivered in a tone that implied anything.

Colonel Husseini now looked very closely at this woman, with the help of the alcohol clouding his brain, she looked more and more like his lost Zina. He slid his hand slowly into hers and said softly, "Asma. A beautiful name that goes well with your beautiful face. You remind me of someone I used to love. Tell me about yourself."

Mata knew he half expected her to brush him off. This pick-up line was so much of a cliché that no one used it anymore so in the absurd circular way these things happen it had started to gain acceptance again. No one in his right mind would use it on a strange woman but she took his statement at face value and responded with a modest smile. "I am so plain looking that many men tell me I look like someone they know. I hear this all the time, but you seem to mean it."

The Colonel was encouraged by her reaction – he had half anticipated she would ignore his advance. He said, "Would you mind bringing me another glass of my special tea and sit with me for a few moments."

Mata put on her best smile. "I'll gladly bring you more of your tea, but I am working at the moment. I wouldn't mind sitting and talking with you after my shift ends." When she saw the look of expectation and excitement on his face, she added, "In about an hour. Enjoy your drink but it would be wise to get something to eat. We have an excellent menu." She suggested some of the dishes from the menu she had memorized earlier.

The Colonel didn't normally like to get advice from women, but this was an exception, so he ordered filet mignon. When she asked him how he liked it cooked, he replied, "Very rare. I feel today that the sight of blood dripping on my plate is appropriate."

Mata was taken aback by the last statement and started to wonder if she was not putting herself in harm's way.

***

Once her shift ended Mata walked over to the Colonel's table. She had served him his drinks and food and the busboy had cleared the plates from his table. He had paid his check and once again tipped her generously, if you consider a 200% tip generous.

The Colonel motioned for her to sit down and order a drink, but she said she had seen enough of this bar during her shift and preferred to go somewhere else for coffee. Colonel Husseini gathered all his courage – he was brave and ruthless on the battlefield but dealing with independently minded women was not his forte – and blushingly suggested room service in his hotel room.

She appeared to consider this proposal and declined it gently saying they should first go to a public place for coffee and hinted that she might reconsider his offer later.

The Colonel didn't expect anything else. He would have been suspicious, and a little disappointed in her, if she had agreed to come up to his room immediately. He said he was a visitor to the city and would follow her suggestion of a café. She had been ready for this – the whole evening had gone strictly according to the playbook she and David had prepared – and told him she needed a moment to refresh herself. He rose politely and she made her way to the restroom in the lobby. On her way, she gave Albert who had been waiting just outside the bar the 'all clear' signal with her thumb and index finger.

By the time she got back to the bar Colonel Husseini was standing and as soon as she appeared, he took her by the arm and asked her to lead the way. Mata successfully tried not to shrink at his touch and let the back of his right hand "acciden-tally" brush against her left breast.

***

The café was quite crowded, but Mata led the Colonel to a table that had just been vacated by a young couple who hap-pened to be Albert's agents, Natalie and Eyal. The table was positioned near the window overlooking the street and the young couple crossed the street and stood on the other side partially hidden from view by a tree and some bushes, where they could observe Mata and the Colonel.

The Colonel looked around him and said, "Asma, this is a nice place and the people here seem to be enjoying them-selves as if they have no worry in the world." A waitress came over to take their order and they both said they only wanted strong coffee and chocolate cake.

After the waitress left, Mata laughed. "This is why I like it. I must confess that for a while I was intimidated by the looks you gave me in the bar. I felt you were watching me like a hawk watches a rabbit and it was not a pleasant feeling. After you told me I reminded you of someone you used to love and realized you were being sincere, not just spinning me some yarn, I could feel your sadness. I too have lost the man I loved, Maxim, and I know the feeling of *deja vu* whenever I see someone who reminds me of him."

The Colonel, who was not normally very sentimental, looked at the beautiful woman sitting across the table and said, "Do I remind you of your Maxim? I am sure that he must have been much younger than me."

Mata put on a self-conscious expression. "It's not the way you look, it's your mannerism, your shyness mixed with self-confidence, and your attitude. Maxim was very much like that." She placed her hand on the table in a gesture of friendship. He hastened to pat her outstretched hand.

Mata shyly and slowly pulled her hand away from his and said, "I know I shouldn't pry, but are you a tourist enjoying Amsterdam or are you here on business?"

The Colonel didn't want the conversation to become too personal, so he said, "A little of both." He saw she was looking at him expectantly and added, "I'm a businessman from Iraq and here to arrange a deal with a Dutch firm to sell crude oil. I have been here several times so am not compelled to visit the tourist sights and museums, just enjoy the food, the free atmosphere, and the beautiful people." He smiled at her, then said, "I don't want to sound too trite, but tell me what is a beautiful woman like you doing in a hotel bar?"

Mata gave the well-rehearsed answer. "I am trying to earn enough money to cover my rent and save some money to send to my family back in Sri Lanka. You must have noticed that my Dutch is not very fluent and that is why I work in a bar where most of the clientele consists of tourists and foreigners that speak English."

He looked at her inquisitively and she added, "Maxim was my fiancé and we had plans to get married here in Amsterdam when he lost his life in a terrible accident. He was run over by a drunk driver returning from a party for the players of Ajax football club. Apparently, the financial backers of the team were rich Jews who celebrated the fact they had made a fortune by investing in the team. One of them was driving along the icy street and didn't even see Maxim trying to cross the road." She couldn't hold her tears back when she told this story.

Colonel Husseini patted her hand and offered her a napkin. He said, "I am not surprised that the Jews have no regard for human life. They deserve whatever happens to them."

Mata picked up her coffee mug and seemed to be surprised that it was empty. The Colonel noted this and said, "Would you like to continue the evening in my room? We seem to have a lot in common and are both looking for some consolation for our losses."

Mata didn't expect such a direct invitation as she thought he would have more finesse. She replied, "Okay, but I can only come up for a short nightcap."

They both got up to leave and then she said, "I cannot be seen walking through the lobby with you. You go first and I'll join you in 10 minutes."

He nodded. "I understand. The hotel staff know you work in the bar. I am in room 1007. Knock quietly three times and I'll open the door. Meanwhile, I'll check the minibar and see that it is well stocked." He summoned the waitress, paid the bill, then marched out of the café with a smile.

When the Colonel was out of sight, Mata took out her cell phone and sent a text message with the room number to Albert and quickly deleted it from her phone. She then checked her bracelet to verify the small vial hidden in one of the metal links was intact.

She had full confidence in Mossad's technical division and smiled as she thought what Q from the James Bond books and movies would have done under similar circumstances. She took her time getting to the hotel, assuming correctly that building up Husseini's anticipation would make her job so much easier.

***

The Colonel was pacing nervously from the window to the bathroom in his room when he heard the gentle tapping on the door. Instead of the three quiet knocks he had expected there was a long series of noises that sounded like a cat scratching the door. He made sure the security chain was engaged before opening the door slightly and was gratified to see Mata standing there with a rueful smile on her face. She said, "I forgot what we had arranged and was afraid to raise too much noise so I just scratched the door hoping you would open it."

The Colonel peered around her to make sure she was alone and then closed the door to disengage the security chain before opening it widely. Mata moved into his open arms but before things got out of control, she gently but firmly disengaged herself from the embrace. He was a bit disappointed but assumed she was simply playing hard to get so he became a perfect gentleman and said, "Asma, I am so glad you came. What would you like to drink?"

Mata knew that the liquid content of the hidden vial would be impossible to detect by sight, taste, or smell in an amber colored drink so she said, "I would like some cognac if you have it. It puts me in the right mood."

The Colonel was a bit surprised by her choice but went to the well-stocked minibar and saw a couple miniature bottles of Hennessey's very special cognac. He picked one up and showed the bottle to Mata, who nodded her approval. He found a couple snifters in the little cabinet the minibar was placed and poured the contents of one mini bottle of cognac into a snifter, then another. He passed a glass to Mata then raised his own and in a slightly hoarse voice said, "Here's a toast to the beautiful woman that reminds me of my one true love." Then he added, "I have another reason to raise a glass of fine cognac, but alas I cannot share it with you, beautiful Asma. I can only say that today a milestone in the history of the world has been crossed."

Mata was a bit embarrassed but raised her own snifter, saying, "Here's to a man who reminds me of the real brave men in my country." She then moved over to sit close to the Colonel. Her mind was spinning with the implication of his last sentence – did it mean that they had completed the task at the farm?

She urgently had to convey this information to David. She couldn't help feeling that her meeting with the Colonel was being conducted simultaneously on two separate levels – a lonely man trying to seduce a woman and a secret agent trying to extract information from an archenemy.

At that moment, the phone rang, and the Colonel got up to answer it. The prearranged diversion gave Mata the opportunity to quickly slip the contents of the vial into her own drink. A moment later the Colonel returned and mumbled something about the ineptness of the hotel's telephone operator misdirecting calls to his room instead of room 2007. Then his suspicious mind began to work overtime and he looked at Mata and said, "Asma, why don't we swap our drinks?"

Mata pretended not to understand what he was talking about and appeared to take a sip of cognac from her snifter. She said, "What? Is this some kind of ritual or silly game that you play?"

The Colonel's suspicion grew stronger, but he put on an innocent face. "This is a tradition we have. When you have your first drink with a beautiful woman you exchange your drinks – this is symbolic for other exchanges that should follow."

Mata now looked flabbergasted, trying to ignore the crude insinuation of his last words, she replied, "Fine, I won't stand in the way of tradition. Here's my glass of cognac." She gave him her snifter and took his. She lifted it up before taking a mouthful of the amber liquid and saying, "May all our days be as pleasant as this one will turn out to be."

The Colonel smiled broadly. "This is the most original toast I have ever heard." He gulped down the cognac from the snifter that had been hers and contained the drug.

Mata snuggled up to him and held his head in her hands. His eyes became unfocused and the deadweight of his head seemed to weigh a ton as he slid down the sofa and onto the carpet. She took out her cellphone and texted a short message: *Come.*

CHAPTER 13

Amsterdam, The Mossad safe House

Five minutes later she heard some quiet commotion in the corridor and opened the door. David, Albert, and Eyal were there with a large trunk on wheels. Eyal took a nasty looking syringe out of his pocket and injected its content none too gently into Colonel Husseini's exposed vein. The Colonel groaned quietly and fell into a deep, drug-induced stupor. The three men lifted the limpid man, gagged him, folded him into the trunk, and locked it.

David said, "Mata, you did a great job and your timing was perfect. Are you okay?"

Mata smiled, picked up her snifter, took another sip, and then told David about the Colonel's second reason for a toast and her fear of its meaning. She didn't need to say another word. He then asked, "What would you have done if he didn't suggest you switch your drinks?"

Mata smiled, "In that case I would have made the proposition and say that it was our traditional ceremony." David nodded and made a mental note that men were so gullible when the blood supply to the brain was diverted to other parts of their anatomy.

David then addressed Albert. "Wait for us to roll the trunk to the elevator and take it down to the parking garage before you restore the surveillance cameras, we neutralized on the way up. Then join us in the van. We'll have to go to the farm and check it as soon as we get Husseini to the safe house."

Albert nodded and they all left the room with David and Eyal rolling the trunk. Albert put on his cap making sure it covered most of his face and waited until the two men with the trunk entered the service elevator while Mata took the guest elevator down to the lobby and walked out of the hotel. He then removed the opaque lens cap from the camera in the tenth-floor corridor and made his way to the service elevator. There he repeated the act and did the same with the camera in the parking garage before taking the stairs up to the street exit. He quickly removed his cap and reversed the jacket he was wearing. In any case, he was also wearing a wig with smooth blond hair to cover his naturally curly brown hair.

David and Eyal pushed the heavy trunk into the side door of the van and drove out of the hotel's parking garage. David had smeared some mud over the stolen license plate of the van knowing that even after the forensic experts of the Dutch police managed to decipher the license number of the van from the photos taken by the cameras at the entrance and exit of the garage they would be barking up the wrong tree looking for a nonexistent van.

***

The van with the three Mossad agents, David, Eyal, and

Albert who joined them in the van a couple of blocks from the hotel, made its way to the safe house in one of Amsterdam's busiest quarters. The house looked exactly like its neighbors on both sides – it had a narrow street front and stretched quite a large distance away from the street.

According to the common legend, this was due to the heavy taxes imposed on the basis of the width of the house on the street front or the canal front. A large hook extending from the front of the upper floor served in the old days as a means of carrying heavy and large pieces of furniture to the higher floors because the staircases were very narrow. With modern mobile cranes it was no longer put to use and was more of a decorative reminder of the old days.

The basement in the back of the house, the part most distant from the street, was soundproof and that is where the trunk was brought. Natalie was waiting for them in the living room, where they all retired after making sure the trunk was locked and secured in the basement with Husseini still folded in a fetal position inside.

David had discussed the interrogation strategy with Albert, while Natalie and Eyal were in the kitchen making good, strong coffee. Albert who had a lot of experience from his days as a field agent suggested the 'good cop – bad cop' approach but David said the Colonel wouldn't fall for such a simple ploy and then came up with a risky ploy. "Albert, Husseini doesn't know what really happened to him. He is not aware of the fact that Mata drugged his cognac purposefully. If we bring Mata to the basement and treat her as a prisoner, he might think all the cognac had been spiked and she too was an innocent victim of Mossad."

Albert was shocked by the proposal. Getting a comely agent to spike a drink while pretending to be willing to go to bed with him was standard operating procedure – a 'honey trap' – but locking an agent in a basement with a known cruel and ruthless terrorist was something else altogether. "David, this is a crazy idea. What if he suspects her and attacks her? He could kill her with his bare hands before we can intervene. He has nothing to lose and is apt to be violent under the circumstances. I don't see what we can gain by this approach. I only see that we are putting Mata in harm's way."

David had thought about this and said, "Of course, we'll only do this if Mata fully agrees. I am sure she understands the risks involved. If we can create a situation in which Husseini believes she can escape or will be released, while he is doomed, he may trust her to deliver a message to his collaborators. This will allow us to capture them long before we can break the Colonel."

Albert said, "I don't like this, but I am pretty sure Mata would agree to play along with this crazy plan. So, we need to keep Husseini sedated until we set the stage."

***

David called Mata and asked her to join them in the safe house. The petite, dark-skinned girl arrived and was greeted with quiet cheers by her three male colleagues and Natalie who looked up to her with undisguised admiration. Her dream was to join the elite Mossad exclusive unit that carried out the most dangerous assignments for Israel.

After having coffee and relaxing a little, David outlined the devious plan he had concocted. Eyal and Natalie listened open mouthed, while Albert's body language couldn't hide his reluctance, and they all watched Mata's reaction to the proposed plan.

She said she needed some time to consider it but David told her they needed her consent to set the stage and time was short because it would be risky to keep Husseini sedated for too long. Mata wanted to know how quickly they would be able to react in case she was in physical danger.

Albert looked at David and said, "One of us will be posted by the basement door and we have installed a surveillance camera that covers the entire room." They all knew that even with these measures the response time would be too long.

David added, "We'll make sure there can be no physical contact between the two of you. The Colonel will be chained to hooks in the wall and his movements will be restricted to a small area where a bucket will serve as his toilet. His food will be placed by one of us at the edge of the range of his movement. You will be tied with plastic cable ties on your hands but will not be chained. You'll have to keep your distance from him."

Albert interjected, "Maybe tie his hand behind his back and Mata will be responsible for feeding him."

Mata strongly objected. "And I'll take him to the toilet and hold his 'thing' while he urinates!? This is out of the question. And I'll have to feed him and bring him water? There is no way I'll do it like this."

David understood there were some lines she would not cross and said, "Okay. So, we'll stick with the original plan."

***

The three men wore masks that covered their faces when they entered the basement and moved Colonel Husseini's inert body from the trunk and chained him to the hooks on the solid basement wall. They left the basement, so Mata and the Colonel were there alone.

He regained consciousness slowly, shook his head to clear it a little and blinked a few times to wet his dried eyes. The first thing he realized was that his whole body ached and then he discovered the movement of his arms and feet were constrained by chains attached to the wall. He was humiliated to see he had soiled himself and looked around the room to see if anyone had noticed this embarrassing situation.

When he saw Mata lying on a Styrofoam mattress placed close to the opposite wall, his embarrassment grew. Her eyes were closed, and a bright red welt stretched from her forehead to her mouth. She appeared to have trouble breathing through her nose and her lips were parted. For a moment he thought of his late wife, Zina, but then grasped the circumstances of his predicament and noticed Mata didn't look as if she'd fared much better than him. He coughed to clear his parched throat and noticed that Mata shivered slightly when she heard his dry cough.

She opened her eyes and looked at him. He said, hoarsely, "Asma, where are we? What happened?"

Mata had obviously been crying and in a choked voice she answered, "I have no idea where we are. The last thing I remember before waking up in this room is that we were in your hotel room and sipping cognac on the sofa. You put your head on my shoulder and the next thing I know was waking up from a deep sleep here in the basement with my hands tied. You were out for longer, but I had no strength to come over to you."

Colonel Husseini considered her statement and wondered if she was an innocent victim or a participant in his kidnapping. He had no doubt that Mossad was behind his abduction and knew they often employed female agents or hired prostitutes for entrapment of men and women alike. He tried to get a closer look at Mata but the dim lighting in the basement and the distance between them made it difficult to read her expression.

Mata was aware of the scrutiny and his qualms and was very careful not to overact and overplay her hand. She said, "They must have removed my watch and jewelry, so I don't know how long we have been here because I have been sleeping and waking on and off. I used the bucket in the corner and had quite a lot of urine so I guess it must be several hours."

Husseini asked, "Did you hear the kidnappers speaking? Did they interrogate you?"

She shook her head slightly. "No one has spoken to me, but I overheard them speaking among themselves when they thought I was still unconscious. I didn't understand any words, but I am quite sure they were speaking some strange language, perhaps Arabic or Hebrew."

Husseini nodded as if that confirmed his suspicions. He said, "Did you try calling the captors?" Mata shook her head and he added. "I think we were taken by Mossad, but I don't understand why they took you. They should have left you in the hotel room – dead or alive. Why would they bring you here?"

Mata had expected this and had her answer ready but paused as if to consider his question before saying, "I don't know. Who are you really? Why would the Israelis be interested in a merchant that deals with oil contracts?"

Colonel Husseini tried to maintain his cover story. "It must be a case of mistaken identity. This will not be the first-time Mossad hit teams got the wrong man. You may remember the heinous murder of an innocent waiter in the Lillehammer affair in 1973, whom they thought was a master terrorist. More recently two dozen of their agents were compromised when they were caught on camera in a hotel in Dubai and charged, *in absentia* I must add, for the assassination of Mahmoud Al-Mabhouh. They claim to be the best intelligence organization in the world, but they make mistakes and our kidnapping is just another of those blunders."

He looked at Mata to see how she received his speech and was pleased to note that she swallowed every word. After a long pause, he said, "They are very careful to prevent us from seeing their faces. They wear masks all the time. This is a good sign."

When he saw her bewildered expression, he added, "They can release you without worrying that you'll be able to identify them to the police."

She said, with undisguised hope in her voice, "So, they should soon discover their slip-up and release us."

Husseini almost laughed at her gullibility but kept a straight face. "I'm sure you'll be able to convince them of your innocence, but they will probably give me a hard time."

The basement door opened and a slim man wearing a mask over his face entered. He grabbed Mata by her arms and pulled her up, making sure to give her a resounding slap on the face as he did so. He then took a knife out of his pocket and slashed the plastic tie cable that held her ankles together.

She managed to kick him in the shin and swore at him loudly, but he tightened his grip on her arm and force marched her out the basement making sure to lock the door behind him.

When they climbed the stairs to the ground level, he removed his mask and stated, "Mata, you didn't have to kick me so hard."

Her answer was a long curse and then, "David, you didn't have to slap me so hard." She continued to tell him about the conversation she had with Husseini, emphasizing her interpretation of his body language.

David had every word recorded and videotaped, but he needed her personal impression and mainly if she was gaining his confidence. Mata said, "Husseini immediately knew he was in Mossad's hands and reacted as if he was certain his death was near. He was obviously suspicious of me because I was also kidnapped and not murdered in the hotel room. So, I am not sure he will be convinced that he can trust me. I think you need to first live up to his expectation and interrogate him, perhaps even torture him, to get all the information out of him. When this fails, and I am sure it will because he is willing to die for the cause he believes in, he may become desperate to get word out and give the order for the plot to continue and then may see that I am his only chance to do so."

David thought about this and agreed with her. He said, "Mata, you understand that we should appear to interrogate you to ascertain your innocence. It must look realistic and will be unpleasant."

Mata's reply didn't surprise him, "I knew what I was getting into from the moment the plan was conceived. Please don't leave any permanent marks I need my pretty little face."

David told Albert to start the bogus interrogation session and left the room. He tried to close his ears with his hands when he heard Mata screaming – it was much too realistic and convincing.

***

Mata was taken back to the basement by Albert and Eyal who kept their masks on and thrown none too gently on the mattress and the nylon cuffs were placed on her hands and feet. The top of her dress was torn and what was left of it barely covered her breasts. The raw scars on her shoulders and body were telltale signs that Albert had enthusiastically played his part in the charade, but he had heeded Mata's request to leave her beautiful face unscathed.

Mata didn't have any difficulty displaying her pain and rage – they were genuine. When Colonel Husseini looked at her and saw her scarred body and broken spirit, he was finally persuaded she was not one of his captors.

He didn't have much time to ponder on this point as a third man, also wearing a mask, brought a metal chair into the basement and attached it to the floor with four large metal bolts. Eyal left the basement and returned a minute later wheeling in a cart with two car batteries and a set of cables and wires with nasty looking clips on both ends.

The Colonel had seen these devices before and knew exactly what they were used for – and it was not to start car engines.

Albert addressed the Colonel in fluent but slightly accented Arabic. This was due to the fact that his parents had come to Israel from the Kurdish part of Turkey, a fact he hastened to convey to the Colonel. In a quiet but menacing voice, he said, "Colonel Husseini, we know what you are doing at the farm near Stavern and we can easily guess what your target is."

He watched the Colonel's attempt to hide his surprise and added, "We have been on to you and your operation for a long time. We could have easily informed the German police and BND or the Dutch authorities, but we know, as you do, that all your men would have been given light prison sentences, if at all. Worse than that, your colleagues at ISIS would then take some unfortunate European or American journalists or humanitarian aid volunteers as hostages and demand your release and that of your team in return for the hostages. No, this time we decided to cut off the snake's head – yours – and do so in such a manner that will send a message to ISIS supporters worldwide."

Colonel Husseini tried to put on a show of bravado and laughed. "I am not afraid of you Zionist dogs. Allah will take me to sit by his Muhammad's side while the 72 virgins serve us sweet tea."

Albert cut him short. "You have made sure there would not be enough virgins left by raping and killing every woman you lay your filthy hands on. In any case, once we finish with you here you won't be able to do anything to any woman, virgin or not, and Muhammad would be forced to watch your agony when you see the missing parts."

He motioned to Eyal to undress the Colonel and tie him to the metal chair and pour a bucket of water over his body. He then added, "Do you see these car batteries? They are joined in parallel so you will get double the current and then we will see how high pitched your voice becomes and how high you can jump in your chair."

Eyal made sure the cable was connected to Husseini's genitals and threw the switch. The smell of singed meat permeated the basement and the Colonel's soprano almost shattered the light bulb before he passed out.

A fresh bucket of water and a few slaps across his face brought the Colonel back. He bared his teeth in what could be loosely interpreted as a smile. "Do you know how many times I have used this method to get traitors to speak? I can give you a lesson or two about the effects of direct current on choice human anatomical parts."

Albert groaned inwardly but kept a straight face. "Yes, but have you ever allowed a beautiful young thing," he said pointing at Mata "to watch how your balls play ping pong with each other."

The Colonel's head swerved to see if Mata was watching and he was relieved to see she was facing the wall and trying to cover her ears with her hands. Albert followed his gaze and motioned to David, who was standing by the door, to turn Mata's head toward the metal chair and to remove her hands from her ears.

He noticed the Colonel's smile fade away and a look of rage caused by insult to his manliness replace it. David motioned for Eyal to throw the switch again.

The Colonel's scream reached a new high and he fainted once again. David motioned to Albert to take a break and join him outside the basement and told Eyal to keep an eye on Husseini in case he tried to harm himself in some way.

Once they left the room, he said to Albert, "You are doing a great job. I know it is an unpleasant thing to do, even to a monster that has killed many innocent people and plans to murder many more. I suggest we let him stew for a little while. Meanwhile, we'll take Mata to another fake interrogation session and after that tell her she'll be released after dark as we were convinced she is not involved in the Colonel's plot."

Albert was still a bit skeptical if their plan would work but realized they could always resort to more physical torture if the Colonel didn't fall for it. Now came time for the end game.

***

Mata was dragged back into the basement and thrown on the stinking mattress by Eyal. Her hands and feet were not tied by the plastic cuffs.

Albert walked in carrying a plastic bag. He did his best to look intimidating, not an easy job when one's face is hidden behind a mask, and rasped, "Missy, we'll let you go after it gets dark. We'll drive you to a place near your apartment in a roundabout way so don't think you'll be able to find us. If you ever see us again it would be most unfortunate for you and your family. Here are some clothes – put them on and be ready to leave in one hour."

He tossed the plastic bag on to the mattress, just barely missing her face and shouted, "What are you waiting for? Put the clothes on now."

Eyal and Albert stood leering at her and Albert added, "Do it while we watch to make sure you don't try anything."

Mata glared at them and it wasn't all a show. She said, "At least try to behave in a civilized way and turn your heads." To no avail.

She shrugged and said to the Colonel, "Look at these representatives of the civilized world. Taking advantage of a poor girl."

She turned her back to the men ogling her and put on the clothes that were a couple sizes too large for her elfin figure. Eyal stepped forward and cuffed her hands again warning her not to do anything until they returned to release her, and the two captors left the basement.

The Colonel had followed all this from his secured seat on the metal chair. The stench in the closed basement was terrible as he had not been released from the chair since his interrogation had begun several hours earlier. He had no option but to soil himself several times and none of his captors bothered to clean him or the chair.

This was not pleasant for Mata to watch and smell but was part of the ploy. She got up from the mattress, not an easy task with her cuffed hands, and hobbled up to him with a look of concern and pity on her face.

The Colonel tried to avoid her glance but finally looked up to her and whispered, "Asma, I am sorry to have put you in this situation. You should never have been taken here. They should have left you in the hotel room."

Mata looked sympathetic and whispered in his ear, "I know they have the basement covered by video – they showed me how we were brought here. I am now with my back to the camera so they cannot read my lips or hear me. I'll go to the police and get their help and save you."

The Colonel knew that if the Dutch police got anywhere near the place, which he strongly doubted, he would be killed on the spot. He assumed his people were anxiously looking for him and waited for his final directive to execute the plan. He had warned them to wait for it because the correct timing of the attack was crucial and had given up any hope of being able to deliver the final order.

He wondered if he could trust Mata but other options were non-existent, so he whispered, "Come closer."

She brought her ear close to his mouth he said, "Dial 964-66-737200 and ask for Akram. When he answers just say one word 'kazabeen' and hang up. Can you remember this?"

Mata put her mouth against his ear and repeated the number and code word and then gave his ear a small kiss.

The Colonel smiled and said out loud, "We could have had a great time together. I'll die with a smile on my lips thinking of you."

She returned to her mattress and lay down waiting for the hour to pass.

***

The door opened and Mata was pulled up and half carried out of the basement before the plastic cuffs were removed. Eyal and Albert took a good look at the Colonel and noticed he had a small smile on his lips. They wondered if it was because he had read through their ploy and duped them or because he thought he had managed to deliver the death warrant to countless innocent people.

David hugged Mata and tried to comfort her. She gave him the phone number and he recognized the 964 prefix as Iraq's country code and checked to see that 66 was the prefix for Erbil city code. He was surprised to see that 'kazabeen' meant 'lies' or 'liars' in Arabic and was worried they were conned by the Colonel.

He passed the information to Mossad headquarters and they promised to get back to him with the identity of the registered owner of the telephone number and its exact location.

David summoned the team that included Albert, Eyal, and Natalie from Mossad's Amsterdam station and Mata was sent from headquarters to carry out the most dangerous and difficult part of the mission. He said, "Thanks to Mata's exceptional performance we have what might be the breakthrough we were seeking. There is still a chance Colonel Husseini had duped us by giving false information. But my gut feeling is he was persuaded that his only chance of issuing the order to proceed with the plan was by giving Mata the contact and code word."

Albert, always the skeptic, said, "I am surprised that an experienced operator like Husseini fell for our simple ploy. I think we have to apply more intense physical pressure that will surely break him."

David answered, "What do we do if he repeats the same contact information under torture. If he duped us once he would gladly do that again and pretend to have been broken physically. If he says something else while being tortured, we won't know if he just made this up to stop the torture. So, I don't think afflicting physical pain would gain anything, except of course, revenge for all the innocent people he had killed and plans to kill."

Albert protested, "I think that physical pain and suffering applied wisely will clarify the situation. I am bothered by the choice of the code word. In Arabic, a language I am familiar with, and in Turkish culture, the word 'kazabeen' has a strong connotation. It is much more than simply 'a lie' or 'liars' as we understand it. It implies that someone is fundamentally untrustworthy, that the person is a habitual deceiver or that he is not to be believed. Someone you wouldn't rely on to tell you the time of day."

David knew a thing or two about the cultural differences between Western gentlemen who felt bad about telling even small lies and used to think that opening someone else's private letters was dishonorable, while Arab culture adopted the motto if you believed something was true then it was not a lie.

This last part was taken almost directly from the Seinfeld episode in which George Costanza prepared Jerry for a polygraph test "Jerry, just remember. It's not a lie... if you believe it."

On the other hand, David was wary of the falsehood behind another cliché that stated, 'gentlemen wearing suits and ties don't lie' and knew that some of the biggest liars in history appeared to be well-mannered and dressed in tailored suits and wore silk ties.

David shook his head to chase these distractions aside and said, "Okay, Albert, we'll torture Husseini and see what he has to say, but I want to keep him alive so be careful. I have another notion - if we don't torture him at all he'll think we are softhearted. So, we'll go through the motions. If he doesn't break and confess all then we'll tell him we know everything because Mata was our agent and we are just being spiteful to inflict physical pain as punishment. I believe this will be the final straw – when we show him how gullible he had been."

Albert nodded. "A little waterboarding can do wonders to strengthen someone's memory, and our friend in the basement has earned it." He motioned to Eyal to accompany him.

***

David and Natalie drove to the farm near Stavern, leaving the task of interrogating the Colonel to Albert and Eyal. The two-hour drive seemed to stretch forever as David's mind was still milling with the Colonel's statement about a 'milestone in the history of the world.' As he understood the situation, it could only mean they had succeeded in their mission, which he suspected was to produce a nuclear device.

There was almost no other traffic on the road near the farm. Just to be on the safe side, he drove past the gate and was surprised to see that it was open.

Natalie also noticed this and said, "It looks as if they have all left."

David was acting cautiously and replied while pointing at the trees, "Let's turn around and then drop me off where I can approach the farm through the copse of trees over there."

He got out of the car and climbed the small hill to the point from which he could survey the farm. No cars were parked near the farmhouse and he couldn't hear the generator. He assumed it was now deserted. He returned to the car and they drove through the open gate and up the dirt road.

No one came out of the farmhouse to greet them or inquire why they were there and who they were. Natalie parked the car and the two of them got out and walked up the stairs to the front door.

There was no response when they cried out, 'Anybody home?'

They tried the door and it was unlocked. They entered the farmhouse repeating the call. David noticed there was some food left on the dining table and the refrigerator was silent. He opened it and was greeted by the smell of spoiled food. He figured that once the generator was shut down, or ran out of gas, there was no electric power.

They walked out of the farmhouse and entered the barn. The first thing they saw was the fake convoy – the escort van, the two motorbikes, and the special truck used to transport the real cask. David noted a large stainless-steel vessel and recognized it as a reactor for dissolving irradiated fuel elements. He also saw the other pieces of the equipment used for the extraction and purification of the plutonium.

He grabbed Natalie's hand and said, "Let's get out of here. I am sure the level of radiation here is high."

Once they were out of the barn he said, "There must be another laboratory for handling the metallic plutonium and casting the sphere that will serve as the core of their atomic weapon."

Natalie was the first to notice the small door on the side of the farmhouse and pointed to it. They cautiously descended the stairs. They had to use some force to open the heavy metal door, but one look was enough for David to identify the metallurgical laboratory. A large metal object caught his attention and he could read the German label that said it was a special high temperature inductive furnace.

David knew that this type of equipment could be used to melt metal before casting. On the floor of the basement he saw two crucibles that had concave spherical shapes slightly larger in diameter than a tennis ball. He approached the glovebox in which a lathe was installed and understood it had been used to shape the plutonium into an almost perfect spherical configuration. He found a small metal shaving in the glovebox. It looked so innocent, but he suspected it could be deadly if somehow it entered a human body.

He had read somewhere that a few micrograms of plutonium could cause an agonizing and painful death. He found a pair of gloves and tweezers and carefully placed the shaving in a plastic bag and then placed that bag in a small box.

He said to Natalie, "Let's get away from here now, before we receive a dangerous dose of radiation or get exposed to highly toxic and radioactive substances."

They didn't speak at all during the drive back to Amsterdam. Each was absorbed in their own thoughts and concerns, not only about the potential effects on their health from being in the laboratory without any protection, but also about the significance of what they had seen.

David knew that the amount of plutonium in the spent fuel elements would be enough to construct at least one atomic device. In the wrong hands, this could be a 'game changer,' whether used just for blackmailing or if, indeed, detonated.

**

David asked Natalie to drop him off at the Israeli embassy and exited the car with the container and precious sample he had collected in the basement of the farmhouse. He went straight to the ambassador, who fortunately was a professional diplomat and not one of the political appointees whose only qualification was that they were members of the ruling party and cronies of the foreign minister and explained the situation.

He told the ambassador that the Mossad station chief and

his people were occupied with an urgent operation and he produced the container, delivered directly to Mossad head-quarters without being opened. The ambassador was cooper-ative and said it would be sent in the diplomatic pouch with a special courier on the next flight to Tel-Aviv.

David thanked the diplomat and called Shimony. He updated him on the findings at the farm and explained the urgent need to analyze the sample. Shimony said he would alert the expert laboratories and make sure the sample receives top priority.

David was satisfied and after hanging up returned to the safe house where the Colonel was being interrogated by Albert.

***

Strangely, Colonel Husseini felt a sense of relief the beauti-ful woman who so reminded him of his beloved wife was no longer present to see him so humiliated. He was embarrassed that she saw his nakedness and how he had soiled himself and how badly he smelled and now that she was gone, he was no longer bothered by that. He still nursed an elusive feeling of distrust she may have been planted by the devious Mossad agents or even that she had been coerced to tell them what he had whispered in her ear before she was released, if indeed she was.

He wondered what would have happened if he gave her false or partly incorrect information. For example, the right phone number and wrong code word would probably confirm to his colleagues he was taken prisoner and they wouldn't know whether to proceed with the grand plan or abandon it. Giving her the wrong phone number would achieve nothing, obviously.

Then he considered the best-case and worst-case scenarios. The best case would be she would place the phone call, give the correct password, and the plan would be fully executed. He smiled when he thought about that.

The worst case would be that Mossad got the information and managed to trace the phone to Erbil in Iraq. Then what? He wondered what they could do with this knowledge and concluded that no grave harm could become the grand plan because the Israelis couldn't operate in the parts of Iraq that were controlled by ISIS.

Finally, he thought that it would be a telltale sign she was cooperating with his captors if they didn't come to interrogate him any further. In that case, a fleeting smile crossed his lips, he would at least not suffer before meeting his certain death. These thoughts were interrupted when the basement door was opened and two of his captors wheeled in a large metal table on which a bucket of water and some linen cloths were placed.

He knew what these simple, everyday household items meant and started shivering. He had seen the most stubborn and strong men break down and sing like canaries after a few sessions of waterboarding. There were only two routes of escape – death or being released by outside help. He regarded death as the more likely route and considered it to be just another form of external, perhaps even divine, intervention.

Albert noticed how the Colonel recoiled when he saw the items brought into the basement and understood he was fully aware of their meaning. He said, "Colonel Husseini, I am glad to see you don't need the 101 class on waterboarding."

Eyal looked at Albert and by the tone of his voice realized he was smiling although his face was hidden by the mask he was wearing. Eyal couldn't speak Arabic fluently but he grasped the word 'waterboarding' that was said in English and figured out the rest of the sentence.

Albert motioned for him to release the Colonel's chains that tied him to the metal chair and move him to the metal table. As the chains binding him to the chair were unshackled Husseini's body went limp. When Eyal tried to lift him up and move him to the table the Colonel jumped up and tried to run to the basement's door. Albert had anticipated this and had locked the door and now took out a Taser and fired the pair of small darts into the Colonel's naked back.

The effect on Husseini's weakened body was immediate – he started convulsing and lost all control of his sphincter muscles. The smell was terrible as it was an unwholesome combination of feces, urine, fear, and desperation.

Eyal wanted to take out a gun and finish the job but Albert shook his head and said, "We continue with the interrogation until he tells us what we want to know." He winked under his mask, although Eyal couldn't see the gesture, he was sure that Eyal understood that this was said for the benefit of the Colonel.

Albert and Eyal lifted the motionless body of Colonel Hussein and carried it to the metal table. In fact, it was easier to handle him in this position than to struggle with a kicking and writhing conscious man who knew exactly what to expect. A bucket of cold water was sufficient to raise Husseini from the comfortable and cozy realm of being unconscious to the cruel reality of torture, pain, and suffering brought about by waterboarding.

The Colonel knew from his experience of being on the delivering end of the maneuver rather than on the receiving end that resistance was futile, yet he tried to withstand the feeling of drowning and choking for as long as possible. He did his best to hold his breath and pass out or die even before the wet linen towel was placed on his face. His captors anticipated that and whenever he tried to stop breathing, they whipped his feet with a thin electric cable making him gasp with pain and involuntarily also take a deep breath.

This version of the game of cat and mouse, if that is the proper term for what was going on in the basement, went on for a couple hours before Albert motioned to Eyal to take a break. Once outside Eyal said, "I cannot take this anymore. We don't need his confession. Let's consult with David."

Albert knew that the young Mossad agent had a point, so granted his request and they climbed the stairs up to the living room where David and Mata were drinking coffee and reading the information they had received from Mossad's analysts regarding the message the Colonel had whispered in Mata's ear.

The phone number and address in Erbil had been located and a special Mossad operations team was being organized to go there and discover what was going on.

Albert and Eyal left the basement, entered the living room and with a sigh of relief, and removed the masks from their faces.

David took one look at Eyal's face and guessed what was on his mind. He said, "It looks as if intense physical pressure will not break someone as experienced and dedicated as the Colonel, so now it's time to apply psychological leverage. I'll go down to the basement with Mata and tell him that he was duped. That he was a real sucker, a loser, who lost his rational thinking when he saw a lovely face. We'll tell him that he fell for the oldest trick in the book and literally add insult to his injury. Mata can then tell him how he gullible he was to think that someone like her would fall for a man like him. She'll say that seducing him was one of the easiest but most disgusting jobs she had ever done. She'll insult his manhood."

At first Albert thought that more brute strength would achieve better results. But on second thought his knowledge and understanding of the Arab mind, if one could really attribute character trends to an entire population, took over. He said, "Well, if this fails, we can always go back to the good old methods."

***

Colonel Husseini welcomed the break his tormentors had given him when they left the basement. He knew they would be back and braced himself to continue with his strategy of passing out when the pain became intolerable. Part of his conscious mind understood that continuous oxygen-depravation would eventually cause irreversible damage to his brain. He didn't care about that outcome but worried that in some intermediate stage, before his brain was totally ruined, he might start blabbering and disclose everything he knew about the grand plan. He was satisfied with the knowledge the plutonium core was on its way to Syria in the hands of Major Aswadi and Aziza.

He was also aware the entire work force that produced the core had dispersed before he was captured, and they were probably trying to get as far away from the farm as possible. Of the team that worked in the farm, there were only three other people who knew the details of the grand plan, Aswadi, Kasim, and Afrin, and as soon as they became aware he had been taken by Mossad they would try to disappear to a safe place.

So, he only needed to hold out for a few more days, or even just a few more hours, to give them a better chance of escaping the claws of the Mossad.

Husseini heard the basement door opening and tried to turn his head toward it as far as the restricting iron frame that held his head in place allowed him. At the very edge of his peripheral vision he saw the masked figure of the slim man who was obviously the head of the Mossad team that had abducted him. He stiffened when the petite figure of the beautiful woman he knew as Asma came into view and his mouth fell open in recognition of what had caused his downfall.

David saw the expression changing on the Colonel's face and could effortlessly imagine what was going through his mind. He said, "Colonel Husseini please meet, Mata, the Mossad agent that so easily duped you. She told me that alluring you to her honey trap was one of the simplest and most disgusting jobs she had ever done. Did you really think she would convey your message to your contact person? In fact, as we speak a special unit is on its way to Erbil."

Mata looked scornfully at the naked figure on the metal table and said, "I played you for a fool, imitating some of the mannerisms of your beloved Zina. You fell for it without even considering you are old enough to be my father and ugly enough to be my pug-nosed dog. What made you think you were in my class? That I would have a real interest in you? That I would come up to your room because I instantly fell in love with you? That I would whisper in your unwashed ear because I cared for you? You were merely a target, a gullible, easy unchallenging sucker."

Husseini seemed to shiver and shake with rage with each additional word and muttered a series of curses that would have made the hardiest soldiers of ISIS blush with embarrassment.

David assessed the situation and said, "As much as I would like to allow my boys to continue enjoying themselves playing with you, I think that I can offer you a deal. We don't need much more information from you about your scheduled operation – we have most of it and the rest we'll get in Erbil. But if you come clean and tell us where we can find the people behind your plan then we'll set you free with a new identity and send you to a country of your choice. If not, we'll play with you a little longer until your mind is so demented that you no longer know who you are. Then we'll make a nice video and put it on public display and tell the whole world exactly how you fell into the honey trap we set for you. You will be ridiculed in the marketplaces all over Iraq and Syria, your colleagues in ISIS will be shamed, and your entire movement will be the laughingstock of the Arab world. People in the West will toast Mossad in the bars with a good alcoholic drink in their hands like the 'tea' you had at the hotel bar and raise a glass to the weakness of the primitive Arabs. Yes, Colonel, you will be remembered by history as the most stupid man who lost his good judgment when he saw a pretty face."

The Colonel, as any person who had grown up and lived in the Middle East, recognized this speech was an overture for negotiations. His position was very weak, he knew, but there was probably something in his possession that Mossad wanted. He tried not to show that, but a glimmer of hope engulfed his mind. He responded, "Cut the bullshit, no more nonsense. We are not babies born yesterday. Let's negotiate my release. What do you want in return?"

David appreciated the fighting spirit of his opponent. Apparently, the speech he had just made achieved the opposite result. He had hoped to break Husseini's resistance and get him to confess all to save himself from further humiliation, but the Colonel was tough. He had already reconciled with the fact he would die in this basement, and suffer excruciating pain, so there were not many things that could really scare him. David said, "I can let you die like a man rather than like a stupid fool that was duped by an exquisite face."

The Colonel's reply was not quite expected. "Dead men don't feel anything. No shame, no humiliation, and no pain. Why should I care? Do you think that my honor or my name in history can be affected by something that is beyond my control? I never ran away from a battle, I didn't freeze when fired upon, I didn't cower in a shelter when my soldiers were bombed and strafed. I didn't hesitate to shoot my enemies, my hand didn't waver when I cut the head off an infidel journalist who was a CIA spy, my voice didn't quiver when I issued an order to burn down a village or bomb a Shiite mosque and set it on fire when it was full of worshippers. No, no matter what you do to me I'll always be considered as a hero by the only people I care about – my warriors. Allah will take me to heaven and seat me beside Muhammad, as I have been promised." He waited a minute before continuing, "If you want my cooperation, you'll have to guarantee my freedom."

Mata looked at David, obviously impressed by the demonstrative outburst. David recovered quickly and said, "We can discuss this tomorrow." He left the basement with Mata on his heels.

CHAPTER 14

The outskirts of Erbil, Iraq

The two unmarked Hercules turboprop planes were making their way in tight formation along the flight path used by commercial aviation flying from Damascus in Syria to the city of Tabriz in Iran. This flight was supposedly full of Iranian army officers who were assisting the poorly trained forces of Bashar al Assad in his fight against what he called 'the rebels' who were now due to some leave and relief in their home country.

These flights were not a daily occurrence because some of the planes returned to Iran with coffins rather than live officers. Anyhow, this particular flight transported 22 elite troops of Sayeret Matkal that was the special operations spearhead of the Israeli Defense Forces. The seasoned soldiers were accompanied by two civilians, who were in fact senior operatives of Mossad.

The man in charge of the operation, Dan Maggen, was seated in the cockpit of the lead plane and receiving on his laptop live feeds from the camera and infrared sensors that were installed in the unmanned drone circling over the target. The photos showed an isolated house in the Mamizawa area, a few kilometers south of Erbil airport and city center.

The phone number that Mata had gotten from Colonel Husseini was registered as being in that house. The house stood aside from its neighbors and was patrolled around the clock by ISIS troops. The two sentries and a three-man patrol could be clearly seen on the thermal imaging camera.

Maggen noted a sudden bright flare when one on the sentries lit a cigarette, probably in an effort not to fall asleep while on the most boring routine duty that had never been interrupted by anything even remotely exciting.

The pilot of the lead plane lifted his right hand showing five raised fingers, signaling the number of minutes until the drop. Maggen shut down the computer and stepped into the hold of the plane. Twelve soldiers in each plane were already standing up checking each other's equipment and making sure everything was in order.

In each plane, there were two of the latest model Hummer all-terrain vehicles also ready for the drop. The plan was for six soldiers to jump out of the open cargo door before the two Hummers were dropped and six more after the vehicles.

This was not the conventional way of doing things but then this was not your regular unit of paratroopers. The noise from the open cargo doors was deafening but the earphones not only allowed communications but also reduced the external noise level.

The red light started flashing and within seconds each plane hurled 12 human figures dressed in black overalls and two Hummers. The planes continued their assigned route until they almost reached the Iranian border and then dropped down to the deck and turned north-west penetrating the Turkish airspace in a blatant violation of international law.

Before the Turkish aerial defense system could react – it was still trying to recover from the arrest of the officers and soldiers that participated in the unsuccessful attempt to overthrow the government – the two planes were back at their base in Israel.

***

The soldiers gathered next to the Hummers and except for a sprained ankle and a painful shoulder there were no other injuries. They mounted the vehicles and drove the short distance to the Makhmur highway that led to Mamizawa, then veered off the highway and approached their target. One of the Hummers drove with their headlights on as if they owned the place while the other vehicle travelled around the back without any lights.

One of the men, Sergeant Kogan, silently alighted and snuck up to the sentry whose attention was drawn to the commotion at the front gate. Within seconds the sentry was garroted and dead before he was gently set on the ground. The other men joined the sergeant and they all headed toward the small building that housed the soundly sleeping ISIS fighters, while the Hummer and the driver remained just outside.

Meanwhile, at the front gate the lone sentry and the three-man patrol looked uncomprehendingly at the vehicle that suddenly appeared in the middle of the night. The ISIS officer in charge of the patrol approached the vehicle to enquire what they wanted.

The window on the driver's side opened and the ISIS officer was shot in the face by a silenced pistol wielded by the driver, while black clad soldiers in the back of the Hummer shot the three other ISIS men. One of the Israeli soldiers opened the gate and the vehicle glided in to the complex. The troops spread out per plan and silently seized control of all the buildings.

The Israeli soldiers subdued the dozen ISIS fighters sleeping in the barracks before they were even fully awake and locked them all in the largest room that happened to be the officers' dining room.

The Israelis were surprised to see that their prisoners were mostly older men, probably in their late fifties and older, or teenagers who had yet to grow any facial hair.

Three soldiers stood guard while the base commander, if the bedraggled old man who said he was in charge could be viewed as the leader of the motley crew of frightened ISIS fighters, was taken to the headquarters. Maggen looked at the commander and immediately realized the man was terrified and didn't know how in the world a group of Israelis took over his base that was hundreds of miles away. Maggen said, "What is your name?"

The base commander hesitated and was rewarded by an open hand slap on his left cheek. He stuttered, "I am Ismail and I am in charge of the ISIS fighters."

One of the Israeli soldiers emptied the commander's pockets and presented Maggen with a Syrian ID card. Maggen was a bit surprised as Erbil is in Iraq, but then recalled that ISIS didn't care about the old borders and all this area was part of their New Caliphate.

Maggen looked at it and said, "I see that your full name is Akram Ismail. Is this correct?" The shocked commander just nodded. Maggen continued, "Does the phone number 964-66-737200 sound familiar?" Akram shook his head.

Maggen pulled out his cellphone and dialed the number. Everyone in the room stood still and listened as the phone on the desk started ringing. Maggen smiled, but it was more like the smile of a cat playing with a mouse. "So, Akram, you know only your last name and you don't know the number of your phone. In a minute, you'll tell me that you were not told that you will receive a phone call from Amsterdam."

Akram started trembling and tried to utter something. He was cut short by Maggen who raised his voice and said, "What were your instructions?" Emphasizing his words by slapping Akram on both cheeks.

Akram started weeping, more from humiliation than pain, and said, "If the correct code word is given, I am supposed to call someone at Al Raqqah and repeat it. If any other message is given, I was ordered to call my immediate commander who is at Erbil airport and inform him."

Maggen believed the man and asked, "What's the correct code?" He saw that Akram hesitated, so he gave him another taste of the medicine that seemed to work so well and slapped him across the face twice more.

Akram sniveled. "Kazabeen was the word."

Maggen knew he had intimidated Akram and gained his unwilling cooperation, so he said, "Who is your contact at Al Raqqah?"

Akram replied in a whisper, "It is my nephew, my brother's eldest son, who is one of the senior commanders of our forces. He got me this job here and put me in charge of this base."

Maggen was pleased that they were getting somewhere. "What is his name?"

Akram mumbled, "Salah Ismail, but most people call him 'the Slitter' because he made his reputation by slitting the throats of the enemies of the Caliphate."

Maggen realized they have already gathered all the relevant information, which was pitiful and disappointing. He assembled his men and told them to make sure all the captives were securely tied and locked in the dining room. The Israelis made sure to cut all land lines of communication but were not sure that a cellphone or two escaped their search so they planted a powerful scrambler that had been carried in one of the Hummers and left it just outside the door of the dining room.

Maggen knew that by leaving the captives alive he was taking a huge risk but didn't want to execute these old men and teenager youths.

***

The two Hummers made their way to the exfiltration point where four large helicopters were waiting to take the troops and Hummers back to their secret base set up on the eastern edge of Jordan.

They were coming to the end of their 750 mile journey across the vast expanses of largely unpopulated areas in Iraq, making sure to avoid army and air force bases. Their flight path had been monitored by American satellites that were forewarned of the operation, but no enemy forces had spotted them.

Each Hummer was loaded on a helicopter, the troops in the other two helicopters, and the invading force left Iraqi airspace as quietly as it had entered it. A flight of eight F-15I fighter jets of the Israeli Air Force were on stand-by to come to the aid of Maggen's troops should they require aerial support and defense. Fortunately, the whole operation was executed perfectly and without incident.

***

Haim Shimony, the Mossad Chief was furious. He had risked the lives of 24 of his country's elite warriors and the flight crews of four helicopters only to learn that Salah Ismail, 'the Slitter,' was the contact person in Al Raqqah. He was frustrated also because he knew that Salah was beyond the reach of Mossad. He called David, who was still in Amsterdam, and updated him on the outcome of the daring raid deep into ISIS held territory in Iraq.

David responded, "I'll use this information in my interrogation of Colonel Husseini without telling him about the futility of the operation. We need to know what ISIS intends to do with the plutonium core that was manufactured at the farm. Once we know that we can try to intercept it or at least eliminate their plan to use it against Israel. I'll give Albert a free hand."

CHAPTER 15

Istanbul, Early November

Major Aswadi and Aziza were entrusted with the most valuable and most important object that ISIS had – the plutonium core that had been manufactured by Dr. Kasim Walid's team in the farmhouse near Stavern.

It didn't look like much – a gray sphere, slightly larger than a tennis ball. However, it had three unique features – it was a lot heavier than it looked, it was hot, and it was deadly.

Kasim had made sure that the radioactive core was wrapped in several layers of aluminum foil and the whole thing was placed in a box with two steel petanque boules.

Kasim had never seen petanque boules in his life but Afrin had played the game with some of her French and North African friends in Amsterdam. She came up with the brilliant idea of placing the plutonium core in the box that was used to carry the petanque boules, although it weighed as much as 20 standard boules that weigh only about two pounds.

These too were wrapped in aluminum foil supposedly to protect them from being scratched in transport. For good measure, the box also contained the small jack ball (called chochonnet by the aficionados of the game) that served as the target ball. The box itself was reinforced to safely hold the extra weight but to the naked eye it appeared to be completely mundane looking.

The Major carried the heavy box onto the commercial flight from Hamburg to Istanbul and although the box was X-rayed by airport security the three boules looked practically identical, even though one of them produced a kind of fuzzy image. The machine operator thought nothing of it and waved the box through.

The Major pretended that it was just another petanque box although the extra weight was a bit difficult to handle. The problem was solved by placing it on the larger trolley suitcase. Afrin and Aziza were on hand to distract overanxious security guards and Kasim was also ready to create a diversion if needed.

Upon landing in Istanbul, the custom's people were too busy trying to catch people smuggling tax-free liquor and cigarettes and paid no attention to the middle-aged guy with the wooden box. Radiation monitors were not operational in Hamburg or in Istanbul, so getting the plutonium core to the van sent to meet them at Istanbul airport was a piece of cake.

***

Kasim and Afrin said they wanted to spend a few days in Istanbul as their role in the grand plan had been successfully completed. Major Aswadi wanted to know what Colonel Husseini's thought of this unexpected request but the Colonel didn't answer his cellphone.

The last they saw of him was when he stormed off the farm in his Mercedes after thanking the laboratory team and security people for their successful endeavor. What was even more disturbing was the fact he hadn't even heard from the Colonel. This was not typical behavior as Husseini was something of a control freak who didn't like delegating responsibilities to his underlings.

Although Aswadi had been the Colonel's closest friend and partner for a couple decades and had learned to anticipate his reactions he had noticed that the Colonel was under immense pressure. Moving up the deadline for the grand plan had taken its toll and the Colonel was short-tempered, as noted from his comments about Aziza.

Major Aswadi assumed the Colonel was jealous he had found happiness in his relationship with Aziza and envious that Kasim and Afrin seemed to be inseparable while he had nothing except one-night-stands with prostitutes.

Major Aswadi considered Kasim's request for another long moment and finally said, "Dr. Walid, you have performed a great service to the grandeur of Allah. Spend a week here in Istanbul but after that come to Al Raqqah to observe up close what is done with your product."

Kasim replied, "Thank you. We'll take a taxi to the center of Istanbul and stay there for a week. I'll text you the details once we settle in. We'll make our own way to Al Raqqah next week. Allah will protect us all."

***

Major Aswadi instructed the driver of the van to take the most direct route to Al Raqqah, almost 1300 miles, and around a twenty-hour drive on the highways. He knew that he could have taken an internal flight to some town in Turkey that was closer to his destination but was worried that his precious plutonium core would be discovered.

The driver who only knew there was an important piece of cargo but not what it was, said, "Major, let's buy food supplies and water before we leave the city. I have heard that there is a food shortage in the countryside and perhaps it will be difficult to buy supplies along the way, especially if we need to use dirt roads to avoid roadblocks."

The Major considered this and agreed, so they stopped near one of the stores and the Major remained with the van and its prized cargo while Aziza and the driver did the shopping.

The Major tried to call Colonel Husseini on his cellphone but there was no reply, so he called the hotel in Amsterdam. The receptionist refused to give him any information about the guests so after insisting that it was important, he was transferred to the manager on duty. The manager was only willing to say that the Colonel had not been seen in the hotel recently.

Major Aswadi persisted but the manager said that Colonel Husseini was a grown-up adult and the hotel's policy was not to enquire what the guests did. After the Major promised him a sizable sum of money to 'refresh his memory' the manager volunteered some useful information. He stated that a tall young woman had paid the Colonel's bill and collected his belongings from his room before checking out. She said that the Colonel had moved in with her and left a name and address.

For double the original sum, the manager agreed to send the Major the information as soon as the money was deposited in his personal account. Meanwhile, the driver and Aziza had returned to the van with the supplies. Aswadi said there was a change of plan and ordered the driver to take him to the nearest branch of Ziraat Bankasi, the oldest bank (founded in 1863) in Turkey and had the largest number of branches.

The Major entered the bank and walked straight to the manager's office. He presented his credentials and told the manager what he wanted. The manager guessed that this was one man he didn't want to mess with and carried out the requested money transfer.

The Major added that he also needed some cash in Euro currency, and this too was instantly granted. The Major left a nice tip for the manager and walked back to the van.

He called the hotel manager in Amsterdam and was put on 'hold' while the manager checked his bank account. A moment later the manager was back on the line and gave him the name and address the tall woman had left at the front desk. The manager added that he was informed she had paid the bill in cash, and as an afterthought said he was surprised to see the bill included a large sum due to use of the most expensive alcoholic beverages in the room's minibar.

The Major thanked him for this additional piece of information and was now sure that the Colonel had entertained someone with a lavish taste for alcohol in his room. He shook his head as realization that something bad befell the Colonel due to his irresponsible and unprofessional behavior. He knew that he was now in charge of completion of the grand plan and his determination to succeed had grown stronger.

Al Raqqah, Early November

The road trip to Al Raqqah turned out to be closer to 24 hours. The main difficulty was they had to circumvent all roadblocks. Some were manned by ISIS fighters or supporters that would have let them through without delay, but others were manned by opposing rebel factions, by Hezbollah or Syrian army soldiers or just by trigger-happy citizens who fired first and then sorted out the bodies.

The problem was that one couldn't tell from a distance which was which and getting close enough to find out was a gamble that Major Aswadi was not prepared to take with his precious cargo on hand.

Nevertheless, here they were in Al Raqqah driving slowly through the village partly in ruins as it had become the favorite site for target practice of the Syrian air force. The Russian pilots also liked to strafe the village streets whenever they saw movement and even the Americans delivered some of their bombs on what they considered as ISIS targets.

The village came to life after dark when the air raids were minimal and usually way off target. Major Aswadi found his way to the temporary headquarters of ISIS located 50 feet underground in a series of chambers hastily dug under some ruined houses. He was delayed a little by the sentries posted at the camouflaged entrance until they could confirm his identity but was finally allowed to enter the improvised operations center. Aziza did not accompany him, of course, and waited for him in the van.

He carefully placed the wooden box with the three boules on the floor next to his feet and greeted the two men seated at the table. One of them he recognized as Karim Sheikh Hassan, the old man that replaced the Yemenite after his demise, as the religious leader of ISIS.

The Sheikh didn't have the power and authority that the Yemenite had, and certainly lacked the charisma, so confined himself to dealing and passing sentence only on religious affairs. The young man sitting next to him had fierce eyes and a raw looking scar that stretched across his low forehead. He rose and said, "I am General Salah Ismail. Thank you for coming here safely Major Aswadi."

The Major had heard about 'the Slitter' and the rumors that he encouraged his people to fight while he himself found a safe position from which he could see the battleground and make 'strategic decisions.'

The Major, who believed that an officer should lead his people and head the fighting, did not think much about strategists that 'led from behind.' He had heard rumors that the scar that decorated Ismail's face was caused by a dagger wielded by a woman he was trying to rape and was not won in battle. Yet, he showed his respect to 'the Slitter' and said, "Sheikh Hassan and General Ismail, I bring to you this humble box in which lies a little boule that can change the history of the world and bring to us the New Caliphate."

He opened the box and lifted the plutonium core wrapped in aluminum foil and saw that while the Sheikh came closer to get a better look at the object the General recoiled in his chair and almost toppled over with it. A look of sheer terror crossed his face as if the plutonium core could jump up and land in his lap

A few moments went by in which Aswadi removed the aluminum foil and showed them the sphere of plutonium and encouraged them to feel its weight and the heat it emitted.

Ismail had no choice but to approach the object and touch it. He now looked fascinated by the globe that promised sinister mega-death and said, "Major, I expected your arrival as I have received the code word sent by Colonel Husseini, but I fear that I don't have good news." He told the Major about the raid carried out on the camp near Erbil by the Israelis and he was sure the Colonel had been compromised and possibly taken captive by Mossad.

The Major heard the detailed description of what took place at the camp and was glad they had decided to use the old man, Ismail's uncle, as a cut-off for reporting the completion of the construction of the plutonium core.

This obviously sent the Israelis on a wild goose chase that gave them nothing useful. He said, "General Ismail, we now have two more main objectives ahead of us. First, we must build the warhead using the plutonium core I have brought, and second we need to install it on the rocket."

The Slitter didn't like to hear lectures from his underlings about what should be done so he cut the Major short, "Thank you for stating the obvious. I am putting you in charge of carrying out these two tasks together with Dr. Raymond Mashal."

The Major tried to protest saying he knew nothing about nuclear physics and detonation of atomic weapons but to no avail.

Ismail said, "You can take your pick of our scientists and if you want somebody else just tell us and we'll deliver him to you, hopefully in one piece and in a cooperative mood. Go now, you have two weeks to get the job done so don't waste any time."

Sheikh Hassan suddenly spoke up. "Major Aswadi, we appreciate the effort you have put into this project and the personal risks you have taken. We have spent many hours discussing the grand plan and have decided to make a change that will magnify it and enhance the chance of successfully toppling the evil regimes of our enemies and instigating a global war."

The Major just looked at the speaker not knowing what to expect. The Sheikh continued, "We will prepare two rockets and launch one to Tel-Aviv as planned and the other one at the Shiite traitors in Tehran. Each will think that the other side is responsible for the attack and will counterattack in force."

The Major interrupted, "But we only have one nuclear device. How can we attack both sides?"

General Ismail interjected, "That's the nice part. One side will be attacked by a single rocket with a few hundred pounds of conventional high explosives, while the other side will suffer from the devastating effects of an atomic bomb."

The Major asked, "Which side will that be?"

The Sheikh and the general exchanged a glance and the general answered, "That will be decided at the last moment. Go and order the 'Rocket Man' that he is now to produce two long range rockets. I am sure he will not like it. He has already complained, and I had to clarify what will happen to him and his family if he doesn't deliver."

***

The first thing Major Aswadi did after leaving the improvised operations center was to call Dr. Kasim Walid at his hotel in Istanbul.

When the scientists answered, he said, "Kasim, I am sorry to interrupt your well-deserved vacation, but we need you and Afrin to complete the job. Take a domestic Turkish flight to Urfa and I'll send a car to meet you there and bring both of you. Check the flight schedule and let me know how soon you can get here. It is only a matter of two or three weeks and then you are free to go."

Kasim tried to protest but the Major was adamant they were needed as soon as possible and promised to send them on a long vacation after the accomplishment of the project. The distance from Urfa to Al Raqqah was about 100 miles, about one tenth of the distance from Istanbul. The Major figured the scientist and Afrin would be tired after spending a few hours in a car and believed this arrangement would be better for all involved.

CHAPTER 16

Evening, Amsterdam, Mid-November

Colonel Husseini, or rather the shell in which the once proud man now resided, was broken physically from the treatment that had been delivered by Albert and his friends.

He had received an unpleasant surprise when he realized that Mata, of whom he still thought as Asma or Zina when he was delirious, was a Mossad agent. He internally congratulated himself and the Major for devising the cut-out, so he was not too concerned the Israelis had the name and phone number of the contact near Erbil.

His daydreaming was cut short when the basement door opened, and David walked in without the mask he had always been wearing. Husseini understood the significance of this – he would surely die without seeing daylight ever again.

David said, "We have warm regards for you from Akram Ismail. You may be glad to learn that our people spared his life after he revealed everything he knew." He watched the Colonel's reaction and was disappointed that all he got was a shrug and a small smile.

Husseini mumbled, "He knew nothing and had nothing to tell you. His role was just to pass a one-word message to his nephew."

David said, "Yes, we figured that out. His nephew, 'the Slitter,' is now the most important general of the ISIS forces operating in Syria. It is no wonder your forces are receiving one defeat after the other as the general 'leads' his troops from the safety of a bunker."

He saw the Colonel's face turning red and continued, "It takes no genius to understand what you are up to and what you want to do with the plutonium your people have extracted from the stolen spent fuel elements." He paused and then added. "We also know that you have forced Raymond Mashal to work for you."

This piece of information was supplied by friendly Kurds in return for some weapons that were handed down to them. He observed Husseini's reaction to these words and was rewarded by a string of curses, so he knew he had hit a raw nerve.

The Colonel relaxed a little and said, "So, there is nothing you can do to stop what's coming to you. My life is unimportant and there are enough martyrs to fulfill their mission on earth and deliver death and destruction to the enemies of true Islam. Our Caliphate will rise from the smoke and ruins of your country."

David opened the basement door and Albert stepped in and approached the Colonel with a garrote. A couple of minutes later they placed Colonel's Husseini's body in a black plastic bag and put it inside the trunk in which he was brought to the basement a few days earlier.

They threw the belongings that Natalie had collected from his hotel room into the trunk and wheeled it out of the safe house and loaded it onto a small motorboat waiting in the canal opposite the house.

Eyal was at the helm and he headed into the Ijsselmeer shallow lake, which is the largest lake in Western Europe. The plan was to drop the trunk somewhere in the lake. They were not concerned the body would be discovered – on the contrary, they hoped that it would scare other ISIS operatives.

***

David wanted to focus on the next stage of the ISIS grand operation he assumed was to load the plutonium on a ship, a plane, or a rocket, transport it to Israel and detonate it.

From his own experience, he knew there have been such attempts before, that thanks to his own work and brilliance were thwarted. But he also knew the margin between success and failure was very small, so he was really worried. The information extracted from the Colonel was not specific about the means of delivery, target location, or schedule.

The only real clue was the Colonel's response when David mentioned Dr. Raymond Mashal, and in David's opinion this may indicate a rocket would be used to deliver the atomic bomb to its target.

At his disposal were three of the classic tools of any modern intelligence service: human intelligence or HUMINT, signal intelligence or SIGINT, and photographic evidence obtained from satellites, unmanned drones, and spy planes together known as VISINT.

HUMINT depended on the ability of Mossad and other

friendly intelligence services to get information from people in the area where the activity was taking place, from insiders in ISIS, and when all else fails then from rumors and sources that could not be validated.

The usefulness of SIGINT hinged on two factors: the existence of communications and the ability to intercept and interpret them. The area in which ISIS operated was very large but that presented no problem for the satellites that were in low earth orbit (LEO) and circled the earth every 88 minutes at an altitude of 100 miles or every 127 minutes 1,245 miles above the surface.

The problem was when a given area was not covered by any satellite, information that was classified but not impossible to obtain. Whoever wanted to carry out clandestine operations above ground could find the time when the area was not under surveillance and move people, equipment, or forces. With proper camouflage and diversions these things could be done even under the unseeing eyes of the satellite's sensors. Drones and manned planes could potentially fill in the blind spots, but it was a huge task to have everything covered all the time.

Only a superpower like the US had anything close to full coverage of the vast suspected area, so David decided to call his friend at the NNSA, Dr. Eugene Powers, and ask for cooperation. He knew that this request wouldn't be granted for free but was willing to pay the price. When his friend answered the phone.

He called his friend. "Eugene, it has been quite a while since we last talked about weapons of mass destruction that we suspected were part of the ISIS grand plan. We are willing to share the information we have but we need your help."

Eugene knew how these *quid pro quo* deals worked. "David old friend, do you mean another round of 'you show me yours and I'll show you mine?' If so, I am ready to play."

David laughed, this was the no-nonsense Eugene he knew and liked. "We know that ISIS has managed to steal a cask with a shipment of irradiated fuel from a Dutch nuclear power plant. The theft wasn't noticed at the time because the perpetrators used a sophisticated switcheroo trick."

Eugene interrupted. "How come you didn't alert the Dutch authorities and tell us about it? This is not how friends treat one another."

David became apologetic. "We wanted to know what they were up to before sounding the alarm. We have followed the trail of the nuclear material to an isolated farm in Germany, a few miles across the border from the Netherlands. We found the place deserted but enough evidence that told us they had extracted plutonium and even manufactured what appears to be the core of an atomic device, what you usually refer to as a 'pit.'"

David could perceive Eugene's astonishment over the long distance that separated them, and he continued, "We have a sample of the material. Our scientists are analyzing it as we speak, and we are willing to share the results with you."

Eugene overcame his initial surprise. "Can you send us a sample? Our analytical chemists can validate your results and perhaps even derive additional information."

This was what David had been hoping to hear, so he said,

"Sure, we can do this. Now, here's what we need."

The conversation and negotiation went on for another few minutes until the two men agreed on the details. David summarized, "The sample will be delivered to your embassy in Tel-Aviv so that your courier can take it directly to your laboratory in Los Alamos, without having to go through customs and explain why he is bringing plutonium into the US."

They both had a short laugh about this, and David added, "I am requesting you to divert one of your satellites to get high resolution photographs of Al Raqqah and the vicinity. Your drones should focus on the same area so there are no temporal gaps in the surveillance. Please send a directive to your informants and collaborators to report any unusual activities in the area. We have an agent that has limited access to ISIS headquarters, and he believes the rumors that some highly classified operation is under way but has no details. Perhaps we can join forces and find out what is really going on over there."

Eugene ended the conversation by saying, "A man's work is never done. Let's talk again in a couple days."

***

David's job in Amsterdam had almost come to an end. He knew that the body of Colonel Husseini would be discovered sooner or later and wanted to make sure the Dutch authorities did not carry out an in-depth investigation and implicate Israel. He called Anika. "It's has been a while since we last met. I miss you."

Anika knew he had been in Amsterdam for a bit and was slightly offended he hadn't contacted her sooner. In an icy tone, she said, "What do you want?"

David had expected her chilly reply, so he nonchalantly said, "I want to see you."

Anika snorted. "Business or pleasure?"

David liked her directness and attitude. "Why not have both? As my favorite movie star said, 'I am good, but not an angel. I do sin, but I am not the devil. I am just a small man in a big world trying to find someone to love.' Well, I admit I made a small gender change."

Anika couldn't restrain herself and laughed. "I see you still have a fixation on Marilyn Monroe's famous quotes, and as usual you distort them according to your needs. Yes, let's meet. Your place or mine?"

David preferred the relative anonymity of a hotel room and invited her for dinner first, followed by drinks, and then for whatever they might feel like for dessert. She laughed again and they arranged to meet at a fancy restaurant she recommended. She said she would make the reservation as it was usually required to book a week in advance.

He checked the rating the restaurant received on popular web sites and was pleased to see one review that read 'great food, slow service' and was also happy to see the restaurant offered a nine-course taster's menu. He hoped his employer would agree to pay the bill in full, even though it was about 10 times the officially approved expense for dinner. In any case, a night of immense pleasures with Anika would be worth it, not to mention the business aspect.

***

David arrived a few minutes early to survey the place and when he told the maître d' he was expecting Miss Anraat he was shown to a table set for two and in a relatively quiet corner. The background din of conversations suddenly dropped by a few decibels and David lifted his eyes from the menu he had been studying to observe what caused this.

He was gratified to see the beautiful blonde gliding from the restaurant's entrance directly to his table was Anika in a tight dress that emphasized her lithe body and left little to imagination. He was still having difficulties getting used to the way a male audience behaved whenever she walked into a room. For a moment, he worried their photo would be taken and posted on all social media web sites, but then figured to hell with it, let my friends envy me.

David rose to greet her, and they exchanged pecks on the cheeks. David said, "Thanks for agreeing to meet me."

Anika shrugged. "Let's enjoy our dinner first, then drinks, possibly dessert, as you suggested, and after that we'll talk shop. I would like one of those red cocktails you told me you detested."

Before David could raise his hand to summon a waiter there was one behind his left shoulder. In no time he returned with Anika's red cocktail and David's single malt whiskey.

They decided to have the taster's menu and simply focus on every delightful dish with its proper kind of wine. David was surprised to see that Anika kept up with him eating everything he ate and matching every glass of wine he drank. He was beginning to feel the accumulative effects of the alcohol, but she seemed to be in full control.

Two hours later, finally dinner was over, and he called for the bill. It was much less than he assumed, and he commented on it, then Anika told him it was 'per person.'

David blushed and said he had heard of such a system in a hotel but never in a restaurant. Anika started laughing and admitted she had arranged this little ploy with the maître d' and a moment later the correct bill appeared at the table handed to him by the smiling maître d' himself.

David graciously paid and added a generous tip and said to Anika, "I hope you don't have any more surprises for me tonight."

She gave him the best imitation of a Cheshire cat's smile and didn't say a word.

***

The dessert they shared in his hotel room wasn't included in the nine-course dinner but surpassed it in variety and exotic flavors. Anika turned out to be more inventive than the restaurant's chef and gave David an introductory course in molecular cuisine.

Long after, when morning broke, they took a long shower together, ordered a pot of fresh coffee and got down to business. David said, "Our mutual friend, Colonel Husseini, has developed a new hobby – feeding the fish in Ijsselmeer Lake. It is a kind of 'slow release' meal as small morsels and molecules have to find their way out of a closed trunk."

David watched her reaction and added, "He was a very tough cookie and didn't break under physical pain. We tried to mess with his brain and use psychological pressure but that didn't work either. We found out some more about ISIS plans from other sources and by using classic surveillance measures."

Anika responded, "Do you want to share the details of your findings with AIVD?" Referring to the Dutch intelligence service she worked for.

David pondered that question and answered with a question of his own. "Are you sure you want to know what we have discovered? It may force your government to take steps that are both unpopular and risky."

He knew the ramifications of the discovery that an atomic bomb had been manufactured from a stolen shipment of spent fuel that was hijacked on Dutch turf, right under the nose of the Dutch police and intelligence services could be devastating.

First, it would cause widespread panic in the civilized world. Second, it could potentially curtail the nuclear power industry. Third, it would precipitate a global clash of civilizations because a nuclear device in the hands of radical Islamic extremists, like ISIS, would necessarily bring about preemptive strikes by countries that may feel threatened.

Anika also thought of the consequences of having such perilous information. She had a good idea what David was getting at and, based on what she knew about Yusuf, the spent fuel shipment and Colonel Husseini, could make an educated guess. The responsibility was great, and she didn't want it. She said, "Only stupid people believe that 'what you don't know cannot hurt you.' In this case, I think the opposite is true. Tell me what you have, and I'll decide whether to pass it on."

David told her what he had found out about the shipment, the way its theft was not detected, the farm near Stavern, the chemical and metallurgical laboratories, and the fact that the plutonium core was missing. He also shared his suspicion that it was transported to Al Raqqah, where it would be turned into a nuclear device and then shipped by unknown means, possibly by a rocket, to its unknown target.

Anika quietly followed his narration and made no comment. After having another cup of coffee David said he had to leave Amsterdam and try to follow the fate of the plutonium core. Anika replied she was sad to see him go and she needed more time to process the information he had shared with her.

CHAPTER 17

Mossad Headquarters, Tel-Aviv, Mid November

David returned to Tel-Aviv and requested an urgent meeting with the Chief of Mossad and his senior staff.

He briefly summarized the situation. "We have located the clandestine laboratory that ISIS had set up to extract plutonium from the cask with spent fuel elements. We have also found clear evidence they had cast a spherical plutonium core. I am quite sure that by now it has been smuggled out of Germany, probably to territories held by ISIS. The interrogation of Colonel Husseini who was in charge of the project didn't yield much useful information beyond what I already told you. We tricked him, with the help of our fantastic Mata, to give us the contact details and password. As you know, our raid on the ISIS camp outside Erbil proved to be futile – it only served as a cut-off between the operation in Europe and their headquarters in Al Raqqah. I am trying to get the Americans to help us locate the plutonium core and find out what ISIS plans to do with it. There is another item that may be related – Dr. Raymond Mashal, also known as the 'Rocket Man,' has been coerced to work for ISIS. We have heard rumors that he has established a clandestine workshop in or near Al Raqqah.

So, if we put two and two together, we may have a concerted effort by ISIS to produce a nuclear device and develop the means of launching it. We have to assume that Israel is the target."

He was interrupted by Haim Shimony, "Who did you share this information with?"

David replied, "I had to share the part about the plutonium core with our American colleague, Dr. Eugene Powers, to get their help. I also shared some of it with our contact at the Dutch intelligence service, Anika Anraat, so they don't implicate Israel after the Colonel's body is found."

Shimony said, "It looks as if we were a little too late. David, this may be a bit of hindsight wisdom, but you should have involved the Dutch and German authorities as soon as you located the farm and suspected the shipment of spent fuel was taken there."

David retorted, "This would have caused an international incident, and based on past experience, the perpetrators would be released as soon as ISIS got hold of some German or Dutch hostages. ISIS would simply try again somewhere else until they succeeded. I think I made a sound judgment based on the information I had at the time."

Shimony sighed and said, "Let's not cry over spilled milk. We will now focus on finding the plutonium and the 'Rocket Man.' I'll update the Prime Minister and ask his permission to deploy our special operations units to find out what ISIS is up to. I am sure he won't like my report."

***

The conversation between the PM and Shimony was not recorded anywhere, but it is not difficult to imagine what took place in the PM's office. The bottom line was that Shimony left the office with a feeling he would be disgracefully replaced if this menace to the security of Israel is not neutralized. The PM had long sought an excuse to fire Shimony and appoint one of his cronies to the job, but Shimony's public record of successfully averting threats had prevented him from carrying out his desire.

Shimony returned to Mossad headquarters and summoned David Avivi for a private meeting. David entered the Chief's office and one look at the ashen face of his old friend and mentor was enough.

Shimony said, "David, I don't care at all about my career and personal fate, or for that matter about yours. I am deeply concerned about the consequences of a nuclear attack on Israel and the fate of the Jewish people. We must do everything to remove this threat. I am putting at your disposal all the means we have and authorize you to cooperate with any foreign service that is ready to help us."

This was something so irregular that David didn't believe his ears. Shimony saw his expression and added, "I feel that this time the risk to our country is greater than it has ever been because unlike Saddam's Iraq or the Islamic Republic of Iran that were afraid of our retaliation if a nuclear device was detonated in Israel, these ISIS fanatics actually want an all-out war to break out. They would regard this as their vengeance against the infidels."

David responded, "I'll work out a plan to intercept the

plutonium and make sure that no harm befalls our country.'"

He left Shimony's office and called for an urgent meeting of the heads of the relevant units in the Israeli intelligence community that included Mossad, the Israel Security Agency, the military intelligence corps, and the commanders of the elite commando units. He also invited senior representatives of the foreign office and the Israeli Atomic Energy Commission (IAEC), as the operation involved nuclear materials.

When they were all gathered in Mossad's most secure conference room, David opened the meeting by describing the risk to Israel and summarizing the information they had. This was met by total silence, unlike the usual wisecracks that commonly tried to relieve the tension in these meetings.

David concluded by saying, "I see from your expressions that you understand the gravity of the situation. I propose the following practical steps: Mossad will activate all its assets in and near Al Raqqah with special emphasis on collaborators that have access to ISIS headquarters; the ISA will try to find out if there are any rumors among the Palestinians about an 'act of Allah' or some unusual preparations for Jihad; military intelligence will alert its people to follow up on leading scientists that may be participants in the plot and deploy all its SIGINT resources to track any communications that may be relevant; Sayeret Matcal, the elite intelligence gathering unit will send a small team to Al Raqqah region to observe what is going on there and with permission to use any means necessary to destroy and eliminate personnel, especially the 'Rocket Man;' the foreign office will try to find out if any of our friends have picked up anything that may be related to this plot; finally, the IAEC will prepare an in-depth analysis of the magnitude of the damage that could occur from detonation of a device made of plutonium extracted from irradiated nuclear fuel. As you know, I have earned my degree in physics and know this is not the ideal fissile material for making atomic bombs, nevertheless it can be done. Please go and start working. We'll have another meeting in three days to follow up on the progress."

Al Raqqah, Syria, Late November

Major Aswadi didn't wait for Dr. Kasim Walid and Afrin to arrive from Istanbul and decided to pay a visit to Raymond's workshop. He had heard about Colonel Husseini's last visit a couple of weeks earlier but wanted to see for himself what exactly was going on there.

His arrival was unannounced, and he thought a surprise visit would give him some leverage with the 'Rocket Man.' The guards on duty at the entrance to Raymond's secret workshop recognized the Major and heeded his order not to notify their boss. The Major walked into the office and saw that Raymond was pecking at the keyboard of a computer and absorbed in some complex calculation.

The scientist raised his head when he heard the door to his office opening and said in a startled voice, "Major Aswadi, it's been quite a while since I last saw you. I heard from Colonel Husseini you have been busy with some special operation in Europe."

The Major didn't like the friendly tone, after all, he was

here to make the rocket scientist double his efforts, and if necessary, force him to do so. He gruffly said, "Colonel Husseini has disappeared, presumed kidnapped and murdered by Mossad. By order of Sheikh Hassan and General Ismail, I am now in charge of your project. Later today, or tomorrow morning, you will receive further help from Dr. Kasim Walid, whom you may have heard of."

The Rocket Man replied, "I am sorry to hear about the Colonel's demise. Yes, I have met Dr. Walid on various occasions when as young men we both worked in Saddam Hussein's grand projects. I am glad that he'll be joining me."

The Major noticed the scientist didn't comment on his role as his new boss and felt that Raymond didn't appreciate this fact. Aswadi said, "I have some other information for your ears only."

He looked around to ascertain no one was within earshot and continued, "We have managed to produce a plutonium core. With the help of Dr. Walid, we will turn it into a nuclear weapon that will be placed on top of your rocket as its atomic warhead. It will be launched at the heart of the enemy."

Raymond's jaw dropped open. He had suspected that he was ordered to extend the range and payload of the rocket for some special mission he thought would be a chemical weapon or 'dirty bomb.' He had no idea that ISIS had the means to produce an atomic bomb. He responded, "I am astonished. I had never considered we would have an atomic bomb and certainly that we would consider using it."

Major Aswadi smiled. "The days of deterrence are over. It's time for action so the world will take us seriously. The outcome of this act would ignite a global war and Islam will come triumphant in the aftermath. You have been ordered to produce a single rocket, but our revised grand plan calls for production of two long range rockets. One will carry the real atomic payload and the other one will be a decoy with conventional explosives. Each one will be aimed at a completely different target – we have more than one dire enemy that deserves death and destruction. Hopefully, they will suspect each other for the attack and start a vengeful war that would lead to their mutual destruction."

The 'Rocket Man' hid his shaking hands under the desk and stated, "As I told the Colonel, I have modified the old Al-Hussein rocket and according to the calculations I have made it should have the required range and payload capability. But I need to carry out a couple of tests to verify this. After all, you wouldn't want the rocket with its very special payload to fail. The correct way to verify this is to do full scale testing with dummy warheads." He bit his lips as soon as he said the words 'dummy warheads' because that reminded him of the cement warhead that had been launched at Israel during the First Gulf War.

The Major caught on immediately and said, "Dear Raymond, I am sure this will never happen again."

The scientist was now worried. "I barely managed to scrap enough parts and carry out the necessary improvements for one rocket. Now, suddenly you want another one on very short notice. I don't know if I can do it, especially as I cannot do any testing."

The Major turned dead serious. "Raymond, I am sure

you'll succeed and become a hero. I need not tell you that failure is not an option for someone who wants to stay alive."

***

The three men from Sayeret Matcal, the Israeli elite unit that specialized in intelligence gathering, amongst other things, were dressed in the typical garb of the foreign volunteers that had flocked to join the ISIS fighters in the days it was trendy to do so.

They couldn't pass as volunteers from any of the large Muslim countries so two of them that spoke fluent Spanish pretended to be from Spain and the third one was supposedly from Italy. Like the other fighters, they were armed to the teeth and wore a bedraggled assortment of paramilitary clothes.

The Italian, Giuseppe Bentivegna, whose real name was Yossi Ben-Tov, was presented as their commander, which happened to be true. The three men walked eastwards along the main east-west thoroughfare that dissected Al Raqqah until they reached the large market. They turned left and arrived at the stone wall that surrounded a large trapeze-shaped enclave.

According to the information that David Avivi had received from the satellite photographs, some unusual activities had been spotted there. The photos showed what appeared to be a large vegetable garden in the center of the complex and two small houses on both sides of the main gate. When Yossi peeped through the gate, he noticed a large truck that seemed completely out of place parked near the building on the right side of the gate.

A local informant had noted that the force guarding the facility had been doubled and motorized patrols regularly checked the area. A few small houses bordered on the complex from two sides and there were quite broad roads that ran along the other two sides.

The highway was patrolled by a Toyota 4-wheel drive with a mounted machine-gun. The vehicle moved slowly along the paved road and the two bored ISIS fighters in the cabin were busy arguing about something while the third fighter who manned the machine gun was trying to intervene.

None of them paid attention to the three Israelis trudging along the road as if they had important business to do elsewhere. After the vehicle passed them, Yossi released his hold on the pistol he had in the pocket of his battledress and his two colleagues loosened their grip on their AK-47 guns. The three men stepped close to the stone wall, supposedly to take a rest in its shade and have a drink of water from the bottles they carried.

When no one was looking, Yossi stretched his hand and placed a tiny video camera on the wall making sure it was facing the main gate. He peeped at the screen of his cellphone to verify the camera was working properly, when he saw a uniformed man entering the complex with two large baskets and walking straight down the vegetable garden.

Yossi lifted his head from the screen and motioned to his colleagues to take a look. When he looked again at the screen no one was there – the uniformed man had disappeared. Yossi wondered what had happened and kept staring at the small screen muttering something in melodious Italian under his breath. A moment later, the man reappeared with two empty baskets.

The three Israelis continued their leisurely stroll along the highway until they reached a house that looked deserted. In fact, the decrepit structure was more like a shack with broken windows and flimsy plywood door.

One of the men checked to see that it was indeed deserted, and he came out pinching his nose with his left hand and gesturing with his right hand that it was safe. They entered the structure and re-verified it was empty and Yossi figured that because of the terrible stench that pervaded the shack no one in his right mind would consider staying there. Yossi took the first two-hour shift of guard duty and told the other two to catch some sleep. They took turns sleeping until it was past midnight.

The three men stealthily returned to the complex and Yossi was boosted over the wall by his men. He silently made his way to the middle of the vegetable garden to the spot where the uniformed man had vanished and reappeared earlier. He could smell cigarette smoke and heard bits and pieces of a quiet conversation.

His knowledge of Arabic was good enough to gather that some engineering matter was being debated in a civilized way. He pressed a little knob on his watch and the miniature radiation detector gave him a reading that confirmed the presence of radioactive materials.

He cautiously moved back toward the wall and saw that the reading dropped to background level. He deliberated whether to go back to the spot where he had stood earlier, when he heard the main gate open and a Toyota drive through with its main headlights on.

He dropped to the ground behind a low bush and froze, holding his breath. Despite being a highly trained soldier in one of the world's best elite commando units he closed his eyes like a child does when he doesn't want to be seen. Luck was on his side, or perhaps the children knew what they were doing, and the driver of the Toyota turned back and drove through the still open main gate.

Yossi started breathing again and slowly made his way to the wall. One of his colleagues had thrown a thin nylon rope over the wall and Yossi had no trouble climbing it and dropping on the other side of the wall. He motioned for his colleagues to return to the temporary safe house until dawn.

***

The exfiltration of the three Israelis was as smooth as their infiltration. As soon as they were safe amongst a group of Kurd fighters, he conveyed the information to David and gave him the exact coordinates of the walled complex. His two colleagues were surprised to see the group of Kurds included only women and asked Yossi about this.

In a low voice, little more than a whisper, he explained that this group had the reputation of being the fiercest fighters and were greatly feared by all ISIS men. These men strongly believed that if you were killed by a woman you would not go to paradise and would not get your share of 72 virgins promised to every Muslim who died as a *Shahid*, a martyr fighting infidels. The leader of the Kurd women smiled at Yossi as she easily grasped the meaning of his explanation despite knowing only a few words in Hebrew.

The Kurd women escorted the three Israelis across the border into Turkey where they were picked up in a temporary airstrip and flown to safety in Israel.

CHAPTER 18

Mossad Headquarters, Tel-Aviv, Mid November

David hurried to the Mossad Chief's office and burst in without bothering to knock on the door. Shimony was deeply absorbed in something on his computer display and was startled by David's sudden entrance.

Haim said, "David, you look like a cat that has found a jar of milk. What is it?"

David smiled. "Not milk but sweet, whipped cream. We have located the clandestine workshop in Al Raqqah and have detected traces of radioactive materials. This must be where they are constructing the bomb. The photos that Yossi sent show the secret trapdoor and a large truck of the type that is used to transport missiles."

Shimony was not so impressed. "So, now that we know where they are, we need to discover their plan and decide what to do about it."

David was bubbling with enthusiasm. "What do you mean 'decide what to do?' We'll destroy the complex and everybody in it. We'll bomb Al Raqqah back to the stone age–"

Shimony cut him off. "Not so quickly. If you are right and the plutonium is indeed in a clandestine laboratory or workshop under this 'vegetable garden' and it is dispersed by our bombing, Israel will be blamed for using a 'dirty bomb' on an innocent civilian population. No one will believe us that the plutonium was there in the first place and we'll be held responsible for using a radioactive dispersion device, an RDD weapon."

David was not deterred. "I just received the results of the analysis of the sliver I brought from the farmhouse in Germany. Our scientists found that the plutonium consisted of 61% of the fissile isotope Pu-239 and the balance was other undesirable isotopes. Eugene Powers said these results were confirmed by the Americans. This is typical of plutonium extracted from fuel that was irradiated in a nuclear power plant and is called 'reactor grade plutonium' and considered as inferior atomic bomb material."

Shimony knew a thing or two about atomic weapons, after all he was the head of an organization in charge of securing the safety of Israel, particularly against adversaries that wanted nothing more than to produce an atom bomb and use it to destroy his country. He said, "I know that, and I know the amount of inferior grade plutonium required to make a bomb is not that much larger than the best weapon grade material. I am also aware that failure to produce a large effect is much more likely with the inferior material."

David excitedly replied, "So, what's the problem? Everyone knows we don't have a nuclear power plant and therefore no 'reactor grade' plutonium."

Shimony cynically stated, "Since when has the truth stopped propaganda? The whole Muslim world, even the most ardent enemies of ISIS, will unite against Israel if we are suspected of using an atomic bomb or even radioactive material against their fellow Muslims. No report from a myriad of analytical laboratories, even from the IAEA laboratory in Vienna, would stop them from declaring a holy war against Israel."

David was flabbergasted. "What do we do? Sit still and wait for ISIS to launch a rocket with a nuclear warhead on Tel-Aviv?"

Shimony's tone indicated he was serious, and not to be quibbled with. "We'll have to devise a plan to sabotage the plutonium without spreading it. The best place would be deep in the sea. Think of something and come up with a plan. It should be much easier now that we know where the material is and how they intend to launch it."

***

David stormed out of Shimony's office wishing he could find solace in Anika's arms but knowing he couldn't even share the information he had with her. He gathered the most brilliant minds from Mossad's operational and technological departments for a brainstorming session.

He first described the problem. "We know that ISIS managed to produce one plutonium core or 'pit' as the Americans call it, and it is now in a workshop or laboratory that lies under a vegetable garden in Al Raqqah. We have also spotted a large truck, of the type used to transport rockets parked in the same complex. We assume they want to position the 'pit' on the rocket's warhead and send it with no love to Israel. We are looking for ways to thwart their plan without, I repeat, without spreading the radioactive material. Any ideas?"

His short speech was met by total silence as the astounded audience tried to digest what they had just heard. After a few moments several hesitant hands were raised, requesting permission to speak.

David knew that within a few more moments as the participants get more involved, a more heated debate would ensue. He nodded at the oldest participant that had been involved in clandestine operations for decades. The man said, "The best thing would be to raid the place and steal the warhead. We have carried out such intrepid operations in the past and we can do that again."

There were murmurs among the audience and whispered allegations that the man was living in the past.

David intervened, "Please keep an open mind and don't shoot down any suggestion. Let's hear some other ideas."

A young physicist that had been recruited straight out of graduate school ventured an opinion. "As I see it, we have two options: intercept the rocket after it is launched by a laser beam or shoot it down with our anti-missile defensive shield."

A software engineer proposed another option. "We can interfere with the guidance system's program and divert the rocket to a place where it can cause no harm, or even send it back to its launch pad."

The research chemist that had been in attendance said, "Let's mess with the fuel system so the rocket falls down immediately after it is launched."

A nuclear engineer said, "Perhaps we can disrupt the timing of the detonators and cause a fizzle."

An experienced field operative said, "We can follow the rocket on its way to the launch pad and eliminate the launch crew. After that, we can dissemble the warhead and bring it home and present it as irrefutable evidence of ISIS plan to murder our people."

A retired jet fighter pilot who had joined Mossad after a long career in the Israeli Air Force said, "IAF had solved problems of this type before." Referring to strikes against the Iraqi and Syrian nuclear reactors. "We can simply bury the laboratory under a large amount of debris that it will be impossible to retrieve the rocket or the plutonium."

The meeting continued for another 30 minutes with all kinds of proposals raised, until David put an end to the heated discussion. "I am glad that so many ideas have been presented. We'll have to consider the merits and limitations of each and try to come up with one practical plan and one that will serve as a back-up. Please think about everything we have heard here, and we'll meet again tomorrow. I beg you to consider all the proposals and not fall into the NIH trap."

When he saw the look on the faces of the younger scientists and engineers he explained, "NIH stands for 'not invented here.' Many people tend to ignore suggestions made by someone else and blindly support their own proposals. We'll meet here at 3pm tomorrow."

CHAPTER 19

Al Raqqah, November

Major Aswadi escorted Dr. Kasim Walid and Afrin to the workshop that was under the vegetable garden in the walled complex.

Walid and Mashal appeared to be genuinely pleased to see each other and after Kasim introduced Afrin as his close personal assistant Raymond smiled broadly and said that he also needed a young talented assistant.

The Major caught on the jovial mood and said he would gladly assign one of his bearded soldiers to the job. Raymond took the new arrivals and showed them around the underground facility that was a combination of workshop and laboratory.

He turned to them and said, "You have produced the plutonium core and done a very good job, as far as I can tell. Our leaders, General Ismail and the Sheikh have provided me with blueprints for fabrication of the implosion mechanism. I told them I had no experience in this field and they assured me the blueprints were genuine and were provided by a Russian deserter. I would like you to look and confirm they are really suitable for the reactor-grade plutonium pit you have produced."

He led them to his desk and unfolded a large blueprint with markings in Russian. Kasim leaned over the blueprint and tried to understand it. What he saw was something that looked like a soccer ball that had a smaller ball, slightly larger than a tennis ball in its midst.

After pouring over the schematic for some time he looked up and asked, "Is this design operational for our lower grade plutonium core? Has it been tested or is it just an idea?"

The Major replied, "This is the best we have. The deserter had guaranteed that it would work with any kind of plutonium. Unfortunately, he met with an accident shortly after he delivered this blueprint and is no longer around to answer any questions."

Kasim and Raymond exchanged a long glance and were certainly not reassured by this last sentence. Kasim said, "The scheme is easy to follow. I believe we can arrange the explosive charges so the direction of the force will compress the plutonium core to a supercritical configuration. I assume we have the triggering mechanism to set off all the charges simultaneously." He looked at the 'Rocket Man' who just shrugged and shook his head.

The Major said, "Of course, we have already taken care of that detail. The Russian deserter sold us a couple boxes with the detonators for an exorbitant price which was one of the reasons he had this unfortunate accident."

Kasim and Raymond nodded and studied the blueprints with a little more enthusiasm than before and made a list of the items they needed. The Major waited impatiently until they were satisfied with the details. He glanced at the short list and said he would deliver all the items by the next day and left them.

The two scientists and Afrin visibly relaxed after the Major had left. Raymond said, "My dear friends, it appears we are in this together. I have given this grand plan a lot of thought, as I am sure you have done, and have done my best for it to succeed. We are working for masters we did not choose and will be held responsible for an act we would not have even considered under normal circumstance. We are expected to achieve with meager means in primitive facilities what Saddam Hussein couldn't do with a workforce of thousands of scientists and engineers and an unlimited budget."

Kasim and Afrin expressions showed that they agreed with every word. Raymond continued, "On the other hand, we have made a lot of progress. You two have produced a pluto-nium core, something that Saddam had dreamed of but never accomplished. I have improved the primitive Al-Hussein rockets and extended the range, payload capability, and accu-racy. The updated guidance system had converted the rocket from a statistical weapon to a strategic guided missile."

Kasim interrupted this overly optimistic review. "Yes, that is all true. But what we have in common is that neither system has been tested. We must believe that both systems work perfectly – that your rocket reaches the target and our atomic bomb delivers the tremendous force it is designed for. I fear that these depend more on the will of Allah than on our professional skills."

Afrin had kept her silence until this moment, and now

said, "Let's not forget we are working against an enemy that is ruthless, sophisticated, and desperate to stop us. Remember the disappearance of Colonel Husseini and the fate that probably befell him. We must watch our backs. I am also worried that Major Aswadi has given us a task that is almost impossible to carry out on such a tight schedule. He implied in no subtle way what failure would mean to us. I think that threats of this type are counterproductive. The extra pressure might cause us to make mistakes."

The two men nodded silently and Kasim put his finger on his lips as a warning sign.

***

Three days later the atmosphere in the workshop had changed. Kasim was pleased with the set of shaped charges made from conventional explosives per the blueprints. Apparently one of the engineers that Raymond had enlisted for the rocket project was an expert in this field with experience he had gained by devising advanced mines for the Iraqi army and later perfected his skills by blowing up old statues and historical monuments under the direction of ISIS.

He explained the rationale of using shaped charges to achieve the compression forces needed for the nuclear implosion device and assured the scientists that the simultaneous timing mechanism was faultless.

Raymond was also optimistic because he had enough spare parts to construct the second rocket. It, too, used all the parts that the 'Rocket Man' had modified to improve the performance of the first old Al Hussein rocket. Raymond was still worried that no actual testing could be carried out and the range of the rockets was based solely on calculations. He was also concerned the guidance system depended on the GPS controlled by the Americans and could be switched off or even fed with false positioning data. Each rocket had a back-up guidance system based on somewhat outdated optical gyroscopes that 'remembered' the coordinates that would take the rocket from the launch point to the target. This was not as reliable and accurate as the scientist had wanted but there was nothing else he could do.

The Major's visit was much more cheerful than his previous one. He heard about the progress that had been made and smiled. "So, now, gentlemen, you will take the rockets to their designated launching positions."

He addressed the 'Rocket Man' and added, "Raymond, you will oversee the rocket that will be aimed at Tel-Aviv. Ideally, we would launch it from somewhere in Syria, as far west and south as we can to shorten the range to Tel-Aviv. But given the situation with so many enemies on the ground and the frequent air raids by the Syrian and Russian air forces, not to mention the Americans and their minions, it would be difficult to travel in that direction in Syria nowadays. Furthermore, the Israelis are closely watching everything that is going on in Syria, especially close to their borders. You will have to travel toward the south and southeast of Syria, away from the fighting and then head west through Iraq. Most of the way you will be in areas that are still under our control, but there may be some dangerous parts where the enemy forces are trying to push our fighters back. In order to disguise your special cargo, after all a rocket launcher will raise suspicion from friends and foes, the rocket will be taken apart and placed in a standard shipping container. We won't use the truck that had been parked in the walled complex because it would attract too much unwanted attention. You will have two people with you: a professional truck driver and an experienced warrior who will be responsible for your security, and that of the rocket. When you reach this spot," he pointed to a spot close to the border between Iraq and Jordan, "you will reassemble the rocket, arm it, and launch it at Tel-Aviv. Then you'll get away from the launching point as fast as you can because the launch is sure to be detected and will be investigated within a short time. It is best if you abandon the container and the trailer and drive the truck back to the main highway and mingle with the regular traffic."

He saw the question forming on Raymond's lips and continued, "I know what you want to ask. No, you won't know if your rocket contained the atomic bomb or just a payload of conventional explosives. It is best you and your two escorts don't know if you have a chunk of plutonium a few meters behind your backs during the long voyage."

Raymond face lost all color as he asked, "When do we leave?"

The Major smiled. "As soon as you finish your preparation, pray to Allah for success. You have three days to reach the launch spot so don't get delayed."

As an afterthought, he turned and added, "The launch will be scheduled for one hour after dawn. This is when Tel-Aviv is most congested by the tens of thousands of people that come into work every morning. This will increase the chaos and number of casualties. You will set up everything during the night and leave the launching spot, so you'll be able to get safely away."

Kasim and Afrin followed this dialogue with great interest because they correctly assumed they would be given similar instructions. The Major surprised them and said, "My dear Afrin and Kasim, you have a much more dangerous mission. Unfortunately, the distance to Tehran from the closest point in Iraq is over 450 miles, far beyond the range of the rocket that Raymond had improved. Even with a small payload, much less than what we need for the special delivery parcel." He smiled as he said this. "So, you must travel through large areas that are populated and controlled by Kurds, both in Iraq and in Iran. When you get to the Hamedan area in Iran that is just under 200 miles from Tehran, you'll prepare your rocket for launching."

He noted the uncertain expression on their faces. "Don't worry about the Kurds. We have bribed the chieftains that are along your route. To be on the safe side, you'll have an armed escort that will travel with you. I, personally, will be in command of it and I'll be carrying enough gold to bribe our way to Tehran and back."

Kasim said. "If I correctly recall the map, we have to travel hundreds of miles through hostile territory and will be carrying a lot of gold, as you mentioned, and other precious materials. This will make us a highly attractive target for thieves, robbers, and greedy terrorists."

The Major responded, "That is true. But don't forget that our enemy's enemy is our friend. The Kurds in Iran are persecuted by the Mullahs' regime and they want their independent state that will include 30 million Kurds that are now treated as second-class citizens in Iraq, Syria, Turkey and Iran. If one of those hostile regimes is weakened by our attack, as Iran will surely be, then their chances of gaining their free state will increase."

Afrin interjected, "The Kurds are among our fiercest enemies in Syria and Iraq. Why would they turn a blind eye?"

Major Aswadi replied, "This is what makes our task so much more dangerous. We have already negotiated safe passage in return for a supply of arms. The Kurds have vowed to use these arms against the Turks and not against ISIS."

If anyone from a Western intelligence agency would have heard this conversation, he would nod his head and think that politics in the Middle East were like shifting sands. One day you were my enemy and the next day you were my friend against a common enemy.

CHAPTER 20

IDF military camp near Tel-Aviv

David looked at the ten eager young men that were members of the elite unit of the Israeli Defense Forces. Most of them had participated in the futile raid on the ISIS camp near Erbil a few days earlier and he knew they were as frustrated as he was with the meager results of that daring raid.

For many years, the unit's very name 'Sayeret Matcal' was a secret and to most Israelis it was known simply as 'The Unit.' Many former fighters from this unit had excelled in their military and political careers after leaving the unit.

None of the men looked like Rambo. They were mentally tough and physically strong and had endured rigorous training, but you wouldn't give them a second look if you happened to pass them on the street. Everyone was extremely intelligent, resourceful, and wise enough to avoid any unnecessary confrontation if there was another way to achieve their goal. They were renowned for some exceptional feats that received wide publicity, like freeing Israeli hostages being held by Palestinian and German terrorists at Entebbe airport in Uganda, thousands of miles from Israel. However, there were numerous missions carried out by 'The Unit' that were closely guarded secrets few outsiders had ever heard about.

David opened by stating, "Israel is faced with one of the most serious threats in its history – the threat of an imminent nuclear attack. Based on our intelligence, we know that ISIS managed to hijack a shipment of irradiated nuclear fuel and extracted reactor grade plutonium from it. Our most recent information brought to us by three members of your unit shows that they smuggled it to Al Raqqah, where they have a clandestine workshop and laboratory. We have also found out they have worked on improving the range of some of their old rockets and assume they intend to install their atomic bomb on one of those. We suspect their target is in Israel, most likely the Tel-Aviv area in the commercial and cultural heart of the country. The Prime Minister, a proud former member of 'The Unit' as he is keen to mention quite often, has instructed Mossad to remove this threat by whatever means needed."

He looked at his audience that were closely following his every word and added, "You have been handpicked to carry out this mission deep behind enemy lines and destroy the rockets and the plutonium core of the bomb."

One of the officers, Captain Porat, who had acquired a degree in nuclear engineering before joining 'The Unit' raised his hand and when acknowledged by David said, "How can we destroy the plutonium?"

David nodded, as it was an excellent question, and answered, "I said you are to destroy the plutonium core not the plutonium. If you splatter the core with carefully placed explosive charges, the plutonium will be dispersed over a large area and will be impossible to recover."

Porat raised his hand again and said, "This would contaminate the whole area and make it uninhabitable for thousands of years or will require a tremendous remediation effort."

David responded, "This is regrettable, but keep in mind what they wanted to do to us with this plutonium. The alternative is to get hold of the intact core and drop it somewhere in the deep ocean or in an active volcano. There are no safe ways to get rid of this deadly material."

He turned to the commander of 'The Unit' and said, "Colonel Ilani, please give the troops their tactical briefing."

Colonel Ilani who barely rose over five feet two inches of muscle and hard as a diamond, took over. "Due to the importance of this mission I'll lead it personally. Tomorrow night we'll drop with black parachutes in a desolate area 15 miles from Al Raqqah. We'll be dressed like ISIS fighters, just as our three men did a few days ago. We'll set up a roadblock and commandeer the first three jeeps that will be stopped there. Any questions so far?"

Porat raised his hand again. "What do we do with the people in the jeeps?"

Ilani replied in a chilly tone, "We'll send them to meet Mohammad and the virgins waiting for them. Let's make it clear that we cannot take prisoners on this mission."

He stared at the team, making sure he had their attention and continued, "Our colleague, Yossi Ben-Tov, will be in the first jeep and will lead us to the walled complex in Al Raqqah. He has seen the place and even ventured into the vegetable garden under which the clandestine workshop is located so he knows the territory well. ISIS has positioned a very small force to guard the place as they don't want the neighbors to start asking questions about what is going on there. Yossi and two of the men in the lead jeep will quietly eliminate the guards, open the main gate and drive into the place. I'll be in the second jeep and Captain Porat will be in the third vehicle. We'll take positions on both sides of the gate. Then I'll slip into the compound with Sergeant Kogan and together with Yossi's squad we'll force our way, quietly if possible, into the workshop. There are bound to be several people working there, but they are mostly unarmed civilians. We'll try to lock them up in one of the storerooms but if they put up any resistance they will also have to be eliminated quickly. We'll then set up a chain of explosive charges that will assure the complete destruction of the complex and of the plutonium core. The charges will be set to go off five minutes after we leave the place. The explosion will create a diversion that will allow us to travel north and join the same group of female Kurd fighters that had sheltered Yossi and his two colleagues. They will transport us across the border with Turkey. Any questions, this far?"

No one said anything. "Needless to say, if anything goes wrong there is nobody nearby who can help us on the ground." He paused for a moment before adding, "But we can always rely on our guardian from above."

He pointed at the tall man wearing coveralls and insignia of a major in the Israeli Air Force. "Major Uri Karp is the leader of a flight of four F-15I jet fighters that will come to our aid if things get bad. They cannot extract us and carry us to safety." He saw everybody smile because they knew what these planes could do and what they couldn't. "But will make sure that no enemy gets near us alive."

He looked around to see if there were any other questions or comments and then dismissed the men with a final sentence, "We leave tomorrow night so make all the preparations you need."

CHAPTER 21

From Al-Raqqah to the launch spots

Two large trucks with empty standard shipping containers made their way gingerly through the main gate of the walled complex.

The driver of the first truck, Selim, parked the truck in the middle of the vegetable garden much to the chagrin of Raymond who had cultivated it in his spare time and occasionally enjoyed the ripe tomatoes that grew there.

Major Aswadi supervised the loading of one rocket into the container. It was quite an easy job because the rocket had already been disassembled into three main parts. The empty tanks of the fuel and oxidizer were the largest but lightest pieces and were placed in the back of the container.

Next to them, the cone of the rocket that contained the payload and the warhead was anchored with strong cotton belts to rings that were fixed on the walls of the container.

Finally, the heaviest parts, the rocket engine and nozzle were placed near the door of the container. Large metal barrels and special vessels that contained the fuel and the oxidizer were arranged along the walls of the container and were secured to them with metal chains.

The parts of the portable launcher were placed in a disorderly fashion where there was some free space. Raymond made sure that all the nuts and bolts and all the tools needed for assembling the launch pad and rocket were also packed in the two toolboxes that were placed in the truck's cabin behind the driver's seat.

The detonators and sensitive components were placed in a small metal box with soft foam padding and the box also was placed in the cabin. The truck itself had an external winch that was needed to move the heavy parts and properly position them for assembly.

Major Aswadi called Murad and gave him last minute instructions about the safe route and the method of communication between headquarters and the truck. He verified that Murad understood his directions by making him repeat everything in the presence of Raymond and the driver. He reminded them that Murad was in charge of the mission until they reached the designated launching spot and then Raymond would take over and make sure that the portable launch pad and rocket are correctly reassembled and pointed at the target.

He shook hands with each of the three men and wished them luck, reminding them they had three days to make the long journey to the designated spot near the Jordanian border with Iraq and to set up the rocket.

The process of loading the second rocket was repeated under the supervision of Kasim and the Major. This truck had a larger cabin to accommodate the Major, who was naturally in command of the mission, Kasim, Afrin, the driver,

Suleiman, and Raymond's second in command, Abbas, who would supervise assembling the rocket.

Kasim tried to enquire what his role in the mission was but the Major enigmatically said he would find out soon enough. Kasim suggested they leave Afrin behind in the relative safety of Al Raqqah, but she objected strongly and said she wanted to be with him at the great moment of their triumph. The Major liked her response and applauded her resolve.

Once it was dark, the two trucks set out together and followed the highway toward Deir Az-Zur that was ninety miles to the southeast along the meandering Euphrates River.

Normally, with a fast car in daylight, the trip should have taken less than two hours. But the trucks were travelling without using their head beams to avoid being spotted and targeted by unmanned drones and followed the escort the Major had promised at a pace of 40 miles per hour.

It was close to midnight when the two trucks separated from each other. Raymond's truck headed southwest to Iraq and the other truck with Kasim and the Major continued to follow the escort jeep to the northeast, toward the Kurdish controlled territory and Iran.

***

Unbeknownst to them, the ten Israeli commando fighters dropped out of their plane just south of Al Raqqah almost at the exact moment the two trucks separated from each other.

Had they arrived on the scene a few hours earlier they would have caught sight of the two trucks following the escort jeep at the junction of highway 6 that leads to the center of Al Raqqah and highway 4 that follows the Euphrates River to Deir Az Zur and beyond.

The Israelis assembled quickly near their commander, Ilani, and after verifying that they were all present and well, he led the way on foot to the road junction. There were only a few houses near the junction so Ilani was not too worried about being seen or heard.

Just in case he sent two of his soldiers to the west on highway 4 to stop and divert all traffic heading to the junction. With the rest of his force he formed a roadblock near the junction. The first car arrived a few minutes after they set up the roadblock. It was an old Nissan sedan driven by an old man with his family and they waved it through without even questioning the driver.

Traffic at that time of night was irregular and sparse so they waited patiently until two Toyota jeeps with ISIS fighters arrived. The drivers of the jeeps were barely awake and the troops in the cabin and the back were fast asleep. Ilani approached the first jeep and motioned to the driver to open the window while Sergeant Kogan stepped up to the window of the second jeep.

Without a word, each drew his silenced pistol and with a few quick shots disposed of the ISIS fighters in the vehicles. The other Israelis opened the doors and removed the bodies of the dead ISIS men and after verifying that they were indeed dead dragged the bodies to a ditch by the side of the road. They covered them with some vegetation that also grew in the ditch just so they don't stick out to people using the road.

Ilani decided to diverge from the original plan that called for three jeeps and loaded his troops on the two jeeps they had just commandeered. Under the direction of Yossi, they headed north toward the center of Al Raqqah. After crossing the bridge over the Euphrates River, they turned east along the same avenue that he had taken a few days earlier.

Within minutes they arrived at the walled complex, and according to plan they drove past it and stopped to let Yossi and Kogan off. The two men backtracked until they reached the gate where a bored soldier was having a smoke while listening on a small portable radio to a song that sounded like an endless lamentation. Yossi silently approached him and cut his throat before he could utter a word.

Kogan opened the gate a fraction and slid through it. He heard some sounds from the kitchen in the small cottage to the left of the gate and peeped through the window. He saw a second ISIS soldier brewing a pot of coffee, probably for his buddy and himself. Kogan tapped on the window and when the soldier came close to see what was going on shot him in the face with his silenced pistol. The sound of the muffled pistol was not heard above the lamentation from the radio.

The two Israelis checked to verify that no other guards were around and opened the gates for the jeep with Ilani to enter the complex. The trampled vegetable garden could be clearly seen in the jeep's headlights. The Israelis realized immediately what had happened – the rockets and bomb had flown the coop. Just to make sure, Yossi led Ilani and Captain Porat to the secret trap door.

No one was around and Ilani's worst fear was materialized

– they had risked ten of the best fighters from 'The Unit' in a wild goose chase.

He deliberated whether to carry on with the plan and blow the place up to create a diversion but decided that a quiet get away to the north to meet the friendly Kurds that were waiting for them was a better idea. He summoned his troops, told them they had arrived too late, and asked Yossi to lead the way to the north out of Al Raqqah.

**

The next morning the bodies of the six ISIS fighters were discovered in the ditch near the junction and two more bodies at the walled complex. General Ismail didn't doubt that it was an operation carried out by the Israelis.

He was furious and called for a nationwide manhunt for the two missing jeeps and the Israelis that hijacked them. He correctly suspected it was directly related to the rockets and atomic bomb and was glad they had gotten away safely a few hours before the attack. He started a witch hunt to seek out the renegade in his own headquarters.

After torturing quite a few people and going as far as executing some others no trace of a traitor was found. The manhunt didn't yield anything either as the Israelis were already out of the area controlled by ISIS. The general sent a short radio message to the Major warning him that the mission might have been compromised but ordered him to continue with it. The Major didn't bother to inform Raymond in the other truck about this setback.

***

Raymond's truck followed the escort and Kasim's truck along the south bank of the winding Euphrates River. Before reaching Deir Az Zur the escort and Kasim's truck turned to the northeast and Raymond continued to the town where they refueled and stocked up with some food and drinking water.

This part of the journey was in territory largely controlled by ISIS and its supporters. They continued along the riverbank for another hundred miles until they approached Ramadi. They turned west before reaching the city that had become the site of heavy fighting between the retreating ISIS forces and the Iraqi army with its allies. They turned on highway 1 that occasionally overlapped with highway 10 and headed due west.

The journey now was through areas that were mostly desolate, dry and practically uninhabited. Before reaching the Iraq-Jordan border crossing station at Rutba they turned due south on a dirt road that led to their designated launch spot somewhere near the Umm Chamain depression.

The trip had taken them almost 48 hours because they avoided travelling along the sparsely used roads at night where their truck with its heat signature would surely draw unwanted attention. Murad and Selim, the driver, kept asking Raymond what was so important about their cargo.

Raymond honestly said he wasn't sure what exactly the rocket's payload contained. He didn't say it was possible they were sitting just a couple feet from a plutonium warhead.

When they continued to badger him with their questions he clammed up and muttered that they should ask Major Aswadi. The mood in the cabin was not very friendly when they reached the designated spot and Raymond gave his approval that the soil was suitable for the launch pad.

They used the truck's crane to unload the cargo and started setting up the launcher and reassembling the rocket. The set of tools Raymond had packed in the shipping container before leaving Al Raqqah contained everything they needed and under his guidance the two other men completed the construction of the launch pad in less than two hours.

The rocket's engine and nozzle were first placed on the launch pad and the body of the rocket with the empty fuel tanks was connected to the engine with a set of nuts and bolts.

Placing the cone with the payload and warhead on top of the rocket was a difficult task for three men even with the winch but was carried out perfectly. Murad was worried that using the winch, that required running the truck's motor, would create a distinct thermal image so that part of the setting up was done after the sun had heated the desert floor.

Finally, the fuel was pumped from the metal drums into the rocket's fuel tank. Selim and Murad donned protective clothing and thick rubber gloves and used a self-contained breathing apparatus to transfer the fuming nitric acid oxidizer from the special container vessels to the rocket.

Raymond supervised the whole operation and when he was satisfied that everything was in order, he did a final check of the launch pad, the rocket, and the guidance system. He asked Murad to double-check his calculations, but Murad said he was much better with a rifle than with a computer and said he trusted Raymond. He added that, after all, Raymond was the famous 'Rocket Man' and the man who modified the rocket.

He then contacted the Major and said they were ready and waiting for the launch signal. The Major repeated his instructions that the launch was to take place one hour after sunrise and reminded Murad to set the timer a few hours before dawn and get away from the area.

***

The other truck followed its escort van along highway 4 but just before reaching the town of Deir Az Zur the small convoy headed northeast on highway 7 to Al Suwar. They continued in the same direction almost all the way to the city of Kamishli that was about one hundred and ninety miles away. Normally this part of the journey should have taken less than four hours, but they were travelling slowly in order not to jangle the precious cargo in the shipping container.

The escort van cleared the way through the roadblocks that were placed along the highway, so the truck was not searched even once. They turned on highway M4 heading almost due east crossing the old border post between Syria and Iraq and making their way toward Mosul and Erbil. The on-going battles between ISIS forces and the Iraqi army for control of these key cities made travelling through that area dangerous. Therefore, they travelled on secondary roads that circumvented the fighting.

Major Aswadi smiled to himself when he recalled the photos of the ISIS bulldozer mowing down the signs that separated the two countries. The image and the leader proudly announcing 'Kaser al-hudud' (the breaking of the borders) and the end of the colonial era with the 1916 Sykes-Picot agreement came to his mind. He felt that these borders were artificially created with total disregard of the ethnic, linguistic, and religious beliefs of the people by drawing a straight line on a map by European diplomats who had never set foot in the Middle East.

As they moved further east, the number of roadblocks increased. Kurd fighters seemed to be everywhere, but the Major was good as his word that safe-passage had been arranged for the small convoy. Several gold coins changed hands and they were waved through and in some cases even given an escort of Kurd militia. Crossing the border between Iraq and Iran in the part of the region that was controlled by Kurds was not even a formality as there were no real border posts. The Kurds saw this area as the heart of their future independent state or at least as their own autonomous region.

The Major's original plan was to reach the vicinity of Hamedan but due to an unexpected shift in the political alliances in the region, he had to amend the plan. Apparently, the Mullahs that governed the Islamic Republic of Iran had allowed the Russian air force to use the large base in Hamedan to launch its heavy bombers against ISIS forces in Syria.

Forgotten were the slogans shouted against 'the Lesser Satan' as the Russian atheistic, communist regime was called by the mobs in Tehran. The Major spoke to Kasim, "I just got word from headquarters that we need to stay as far away from Hamedan as possible because the Shiite dogs in Tehran are cooperating with the Russian infidels and allowed them to use their Hamedan base against our fighters. They have increased security in the whole region, and we cannot risk being stopped."

He consulted Google Earth map and added, "We'll divert to a small village called Bahar and set-up our launch pad over there. We can bypass the village and get closer to the mountains that will provide us with some additional cover."

Kasim also looked at the map and considered the Major's suggestion. He had a better idea and said, "There are too many other villages near Bahar. I suggest we travel a little further south of the highway, toward the mountain range near Cheshmeh Qasaban. This will increase the distance from Tehran only by a few miles but will be more secluded. I hope that the rocket can fly this far."

The Major replied, "As always, we trust in Allah for helping us do His work." This did not call for an answer or further discussion.

The two men fell silent and contemplated the effect of this change in their plans when a roar of jet engines broke the silence. Kasim searched for the source of the terrifying noise and when he looked up toward the clear sky, he saw a flight of four jet fighters and two huge planes climbing steeply.

The Major also looked at them and cursed the Russians and their Tupolev Tu-22M3 bombers and Sukhoi-34 strike fighters. However, his words were drowned by the earsplitting rumble of the powerful jet engines.

***

The escort van remained on the paved road while the truck took a dirt road that led toward the mountain range south of the highway. Once the truck passed through the tiny village of Cheshmeh Qasaban, there were a few narrow dirt roads that were barely wide enough to accommodate the truck. As far as they could see, the area was unpopulated.

The Major was quite pleased with the location but Kasim worried they wouldn't be able to get away after the rocket was launched. He felt that although there was no one in sight, a stray shepherd may come across their path to investigate what they were doing there.

He quietly said to the Major, "How can we avoid being captured after we launch the rocket? If we are caught and interrogated, then the entire plan will fail. If the Iranians know that ISIS is responsible, then they won't blame the Israelis–"

The Major interrupted his speech before the others could hear him. He said, "There will so much pandemonium that no one will be able to organize a search for us. Don't worry about the consequences just focus on the mission."

The scientist was no fool. He knew what the Major was implying, and he called Afrin aside and in a whisper said, "I fear the Major is going to kill us all after the rocket is fired. Dead men don't talk."

Afrin was terrified. "I don't mind dying for the cause. Dying fighting is not being shot like a dog by a man from our side. I also wonder how he will avoid us all being captured. Will he kill himself or does he have an escape route?"

Kasim had deliberated the same question. "Let's try to find out while we work on the construction of the launch pad and reassembling the rocket. We have several hours of work ahead of us perhaps we'll be able to gather what he is really up to."

CHAPTER 22

Mossad headquarters, Tel-Aviv

The news about the failure of the raid on the workshop at Al Raqqah hit David like a ton of bricks.

Everything had worked perfectly per the plan: the raiding party did its job without suffering any casualties and without getting into a firefight. They commandeered the vehicles, reached the walled compound, entered the clandestine workshop that was hidden under the vegetable garden and got back to safety unscathed.

Unfortunately, they were just a few hours late and could only find evidence that two trucks got away with rockets and were probably heading westward to get closer to Israel to launch their deadly warheads. This naturally reminded him of his miscalculation regarding the farm near Stavern and amplified his frustration.

He had no choice but to call Eugene Powers again and request the United States to increase its surveillance on the highways leading west from Al Raqqah. There were two parts of the pending conversation he abhorred: first, admitting the failure of 'The Unit' to destroy the rockets and the atomic warhead, and second, to do some serious begging for help without even being able to pinpoint the target or the region from which the rocket may be launched.

There was another reason he felt bad about the phone call and that is he remembered every single word of his previous conversation with Eugene. Especially Eugene's reprimand, 'How come you didn't alert the Dutch authorities and tell us about it? This is not how friends treat one another.'

In hindsight, he wished he had told the German or Dutch intelligence services about the farm near Stavern and stopped the ISIS plot before it got out of hand. He considered handing the Mossad Chief his resignation but knew that Shimony would never accept it, especially if there was still a chance to save Israel from an atomic attack.

He postponed the conversation with Eugene for as long as he could but finally had to make the call and request his help. He got a secure line. "Eugene, I have some bad news."

Eugene had anticipated this call, as the US satellites had transmitted every detail of the Israeli raid on Al Raqqah and knew about the failure. After all, he had managed to get the National Reconnaissance Office to enhance its coverage of Al Raqqah after David's last call. The NRO that was one of the largest US intelligence gathering agencies and regularly provides imagery intelligence as well as measurement and signature intelligence to other bodies in the intelligence community. Most of the NRO information is obtained by satellites.

When he received David's call, he played dumb. "David, good to hear from. What do you mean by 'bad news?'"

David told him about the raid and that at least two rockets were on their way to unknown destinations and that one of them probably had an atomic warhead. Eugene listened patiently, knowing full well that these rockets could not hit the US mainland.

"David, what do you want us to do? Do you want our satellites to track every truck in Syria that is carrying a shipping container and heading west? Although that's possible in principle, we cannot see what's inside the containers without stopping the trucks and searching them. Help us to help you by providing more specific information."

David had expected such a rational reply, but his frustration was getting the better of him and he said, "We have to do some risk analysis and try to limit the search area. I'll summon Mossad's analysts and discuss the problem with them and then get back to you. Could you just raise an alarm that a rocket with an atomic bomb may be headed toward Israel and get the NRO to look closely at irregularities on the highways that lead west from Al Raqqah."

Eugene replied, "If I were you, I wouldn't rule out that they may not head directly west because of the fighting in that area. I'll expand the search area to also cover other possibilities, but I do need feedback from your analysts."

David thanked him and hung up. He then went to Shimony's office, burst into a meeting that was being held there and asked for the Chief's urgent attention. This type of behavior was unheard of in Mossad, certainly in the Chief's office.

When Shimony saw the look on David's face, he asked him to wait outside for a few minutes while he concluded the topic being discussed at the meeting.

***

David waited for everyone to leave Shimony's office and then told him about his conversation with Eugene and his urgent need to get Mossad's top analysts to come up with useful ideas. Shimony heard him out patiently and said, "David, I understand that you feel a personal responsibility for not stopping these ISIS people already in Germany. But you had your reasons and they appeared to be valid at the time. First, I am giving you top priority on this matter and permission to pull the top analysts from whatever they are doing now and hold a brainstorming session with them. Second, let's take some defensive measures immediately. We have the most advanced anti-missile defense system in the world. Iron Dome systems are currently deployed to avert threats from the south from Hamas short range rockets in Gaza and from the Hezbollah short and medium range rockets from the north. We are also keeping an eye on long-range ballistic rockets from Iran and have our Arrow missiles ready to launch against them and knock them out even before the re-enter the atmosphere. So, I will get the Prime Minister and Minister of Defense to sign an order that will deploy a couple Arrow and Iron Dome batteries to ward off threats from Syrian territory in the northeast. In addition, although I am not sure this is necessary, I'll request one additional battery to defend against rockets fired from Iraq in the east. I hope this will provide some kind of insurance in case we fail to nip this threat in the bud."

David felt the Chief had given him everything he needed

and thanked him.

Shimony nodded and said, "Don't waste any more time – get on with the brainstorming meeting and keep me informed. If you need anything else don't come breaking down my door." He smiled. "Just tell my aide you need to see me urgently. I'll make sure he puts you right through. Now, go."

***

The brainstorming session was not very fruitful, as often happens when a bunch of opinionated people meet. The open minds and the fresh ideas that David had hoped for were not forthcoming in the room.

The only noteworthy part of the meeting was a long, and quite boring, presentation of the geo-political situation in the Middle East since the so-called 'Arab Spring' had begun on December 18th, 2010, when a young Tunisian, Mohamed Bouazizi, set himself on fire.

A wave of protests swept the Arab world resulting in the toppling of several regimes throughout Western and North Africa, the Middle East, and the Arab Peninsula. This was one of the most substantial examples of the 'butterfly effect' where a small, apparently insignificant event causes large global repercussions.

Some of the participants were daydreaming or even nodding off when the speaker came to the point that had some relevance to the purpose of the meeting. He said, "The Islamic State and concept of the New Caliphate have replaced the nationalistic movements. People in Syria, for example, were no longer interested only in changing Bashar Assad's government that relied on his Alawite sect. Some rebel groups, if this is the proper term for the armed militias, wanted to open a war on all Shiites, others wanted to align themselves with the West, yet others were supporters of communism, and then, of course, there were the Kurds that want an independent state or at least a large degree of self-rule. Each group had its external supporters from across the border. Assad initially gained the support of Iran and its Hezbollah lackeys in Lebanon fighting these militias. When ISIS also attacked his regime then Assad suddenly had open support from the Russians and less direct support from the West. The West supported the militias that opposed ISIS, Turkey supported all sides that were willing to fight the Kurds, Iraq was in shambles and different parts of the population and governments had their favorite militias that gained help from them. The government in Lebanon was helpless to do anything because Hezbollah threatened to topple it if it intervened. Egypt and the Saudi rulers have troubles of their own fighting against rising forces that swore allegiance to ISIS and carried out local terrorist acts. Jordan sent some air force jets and pilots to fight ISIS mainly with the hope of stopping the flood of Syrian refugees that tried to escape the carnage in Syria."

David barely waited for him to finish speaking before he said, "How does all this reflect on our problem, please focus?"

The speaker didn't like to be cut short, but replied, "This turmoil has formed many new and strange alliances that may be relevant. For example, the Kurds are busy fighting ISIS to death in parts of Syria that are near the border with Turkey, but in Turkey both these groups are against the Ankara government that alternately holds one of them responsible for terrorist acts. The same happens with Iran that supports Assad in his fight against ISIS but is also persecuting the Kurds that seek autonomy in Iran. So, the Kurds in Iran are willing to turn a blind eye on ISIS if it attacks Iranian targets. Egypt is cooperating with its former enemy Israel to curb ISIS activity in Sinai that is aimed at Egyptian troops and the tourist industry in the region. The Saudis hate Assad, Iran, and all Shiites but is involved in fighting ISIS that is Assad's worst enemy. Many other anomalies of this type exist in the 'New Middle East' that is the term still used by some diehard optimists to describe the current situation. In conclusion, never before in the Middle East have so many former enemies and former friends continually shifted alliances. So, David, your ISIS terrorists may now be working together with our friends, like the Kurds and the Turks to launch a strike at Israel or may be planning an assault on our enemies."

David thanked the speaker while the audience fell quiet trying to fathom the meaning of the political analysis they had just heard. The problem with academics, David thought, was they always had to present all the facets of the situation. This enabled everyone to draw the conclusions that were in line with his, or her, preconceived opinion.

There were too many facts that could be interpreted in too many ways, and too many shades of gray. Men of action, on the other hand, saw things as black or white – are you with us or against us. David let the discussion go on for another 15 minutes and when no useful insights were put forth, he adjourned the meeting.

***

David called Eugene and asked him if he had any new information on the whereabouts of the two trucks. Eugene said, "I have some bad news. Apparently the NRO is now focusing its attention on the Hamedan air base in Iran and cannot divert more resources to follow trucks. The US intelligence community is greatly concerned by the cooperation between Iran and Russia and the agreement that allows Russian bombers and fighter jets to use Iranian bases to launch attacks on ISIS and other anti-Assad groups in Syria. These air raids put American 'advisors' that are in fact members of the US special forces at risk. There already have been incidents that Syrian and Russian raids have barely missed the Americans and their allies. David, I hope you understand that this is the prime concern of the administration, because public opinion tends to turn against the President and his party members after unpopular wars that result in American casualties flown home in coffins wrapped with the flag."

David fell silent for such a long time that Eugene worried he had been disconnected. Finally, David said, "This is very disappointing because we are worried about what is going on near our borders not about things that happen over a thousand kilometers away. I would like to update you that we had a meeting with our experts and analysts, and it didn't lead to anything useful. They just carried on and on about the turmoil in the Middle East, as if anyone who reads a newspaper or watches the news on TV is not aware of the chaos in the region."

He concluded by repeating the adage. "Israel will do whatever it takes to guarantee the security of its citizens and its borders."

CHAPTER 23

Umm Chamain depression

Raymond, Murad, and Selim were exhausted. The task of constructing the launch pads and reassembling the rocket and its warhead were physically demanding.

The refueling with kerosene and nitric acid was also an unpleasant job, especially as they had to don protective clothing in the heat of the desert. Raymond kept thinking that this was not a task for three men, especially when one of them was in his sixties. He felt his heart was pounding from the combination of excitement, physical exertion, and fatigue and needed a rest to recuperate before making the final adjustments to the rocket.

Before darkness fell and the desert cooled, they had the main meal of the day. Murad surprised his two colleagues by pulling a bottle of fine cognac out of his backpack and proposing a toast to the success of their mission.

Raymond didn't expect such a gesture from one of ISIS's most faithful officers but was glad to allow the alcohol to dull his anxiety. As he sipped the liquor he asked, "Murad, how do we get away after the launch?"

Murad smiled. "Well, I have another pleasant surprise, not

just the cognac. We have a timer to allow us to fire the rocket autonomously. I have set it to go off just after dawn tomorrow. We will ditch the container here next to the launch pad, and travel with the unburdened truck back to the highway and head east toward Baghdad. We'll travel at night because we'll be going in the 'wrong' direction as far as anyone looking for suspects and as we have no cargo we are not worried about roadblocks."

Raymond wondered what would happen if there is some technical hitch and the rocket doesn't take off but said nothing. He had expected to die after the launch and here he was being given a chance to live.

It was Selim who opened his mouth. "How will we know if our mission was effective? If we fail and return to our headquarters, we'll surely be held responsible for the failure..." He didn't need to complete the sentence.

Murad responded, "We are bound to hear about the success of an attack on Tel-Aviv – it will be in the headlines everywhere. If we hear nothing along the way, we'll think of some way to save ourselves."

Raymond and Selim nodded and when Murad said, "Let's pray" they all got up and spread their prayer mats on the hard sand facing Mecca.

Near Cheshmeh Qasaban

The weather had suddenly turned as it often does in the mountain area. A light drizzle replaced the heat of the day and the humidity was very high.

Kasim and Afrin sat quietly together holding hands under an improvised shelter that consisted of a nylon sheet tied to the side of the shipping container. They preferred this barely adequate protection against the drizzle over the complete shelter afforded in the confined and stuffy container.

This type of public display of affection was frowned upon by Muslims everywhere and especially by ISIS radical fanatics, but Major Aswadi turned a blind eye on the couple. He knew this may well be their last chance to be together in this world and didn't doubt that in the world to come they would be separated – Kasim would get a seat at the feet of Mohammad while Afrin would be placed at the service of many other men. At times, he hoped to be one of those men, but he was now focused on the job at hand.

The launch pad had been constructed and the rocket was reassembled, fueled, and aimed in the direction of Tehran. Major Aswadi was the only person that knew for sure the atomic warhead was safely placed in the cone of their rocket while the rocket that was to be launched at Tel-Aviv was equipped with a standard warhead with five hundred and fifty pounds of conventional explosives.

His main concern was that their truck and shipping container would be detected from the air by a plane taking off or coming to land at Hamedan air base and he welcomed the cloud cover and drizzle that would provide his little group with some concealment.

NRO headquarters, Chantilly, Virginia

David didn't know that the United States NRO agency had dramatically increased its surveillance of the area because of the unwelcome (from the US point of view) Russian presence at Hamedan air base.

He was not aware of the new hyperspectral capabilities of the satellites that included high-resolution visible and infra-red imaging as well as long wavelength probes that could see through clouds and rain. Advanced new algorithms were added to the satellite's software package as part of the top-secret artificial intelligence unit that could automatically spot any anomalies.

The flickering red light and audible ringing alerted the operator at NRO headquarters in Chantilly, Virginia, that something unusual had been detected. The operator, Abigail Hill, a young lieutenant on loan from the air force, picked up the direct line to the Director of the NRO. "Sir, the satellite has identified an anomaly about twenty miles from the Hamedan air force base. At present, the nature of this anomaly is not clear, but it looks as if a large object has suddenly appeared in the middle of nowhere. I am calling you directly only because of the special instruction we received to immediately report anything unusual in that area."

The Director responded, "Keep it under close observation Lieutenant Hill and try to find out more about this and call me as soon as you have more details."

He then called both his bosses – the Director of National Intelligence and the Secretary of Defense to inform them of this development.

Abigail Hill had been raised in New Mexico where the appearance of 'strange' objects was regularly reported from the 1947 crash of UFOs and aliens near Roswell to the present day where people, drugs, and merchandize are regularly smuggled from Mexico along the Rio Grande Valley.

She understood what outwardly appeared to be an 'anomaly' always had a very logical explanation and was determined to discover what was going on in the remote area near Cheshmeh Qasaban. Based on the instruction of the NRO Director, she called for a special reconnaissance mission by a drone that patrolled the Iraq-Iran border area on the Iraqi side.

The drone, one of the HALE models (high altitude, long endurance), flew at an altitude of five miles and due to its low radar signature was almost impossible to detect. The drone's flight path was altered, and it headed due east toward the area where the suspect activity had been observed.

The drone's operator, sitting in an air-conditioned basement somewhere in Nevada, thousands of miles away from Iran, was pleased with the break from the boring routine of flying in circles around Sulaimaniyah in the Kurd controlled area and back-and-forth along the Iraq-Iran border. He was talking to Lt. Hill on a secure line and she explicitly described what she wanted – a clearer picture of the strange objects her satellite imagery had provided.

The problem was that the reconnaissance drones were built mainly for endurance so they could stay in the air for several hours, or even a few days, and not for speed. The drone operator estimated it would take his drone at least two or three hours before it could reach the target area. Abigail was not happy with the answer to her question but there was nothing she could do. She explained that she needed the information as soon as possible and the drone operator promised her he would do his best.

She then considered other options, but none were available on such short notice. She sent a brief update to the Director and he passed it up the line all the way up to the President of the United States.

***

Meanwhile on the ground, preparations for the launch were coming to an end under the supervision of Abbas, Raymond's chief assistant and an experienced rocketeer.

Major Aswadi explained to his small team that a timer had been prepared and he was setting it to send the launch command one hour after sunrise. He explained this would make it more difficult to pinpoint the exact location of the launch spot because at night, or in the dark, its thermal signature would stand out like sore thumb.

He added that this will give them ample time to get far away from the launch spot and offer an opportunity to evade being captured. Kasim was glad to hear this but the glance he exchanged with Afrin showed that neither of them fully trusted the Major.

The Major continued and said the cloud cover and drizzle also improved the odds of getting away safely.

CHAPTER 24

Mossad Headquarters, Tel-Aviv

Late at night David Avivi received an urgent call from Haim Shimony. The Mossad Chief summoned him to his office as new information had just arrived from a contact in Al Raqqah.

Despite the late hour, most of the senior staff members were still at work because of the state of special alert that had been declared by Shimony, when news the rockets had left Al Raqqah, was still in effect.

David walked rapidly through the corridor that separated his office from the Chief. When he entered, he saw that Shimony was holding a printed message in his hand. He said, "Haim, what's going on?"

Shimony looked up, his face ashen, and said, "I have already notified the Prime Minister of the imminent attack and he ordered the senior government employees and the elected politicians to stay away from the population centers in Tel-Aviv, Jerusalem, and Haifa." He paused before continuing, "I hope the PM has also warned the opposition members about this."

David smiled politely as he was aware of the tension and

mistrust between the PM and Mossad Chief. Shimony added, "Those on the A-list were given a choice of either going to the specially constructed underground shelter near Jerusalem or staying with their families somewhere in the countryside. Most had opted for this second choice."

David didn't need to ask what was supposed to take place – the expression on the Chief's face was enough. However, he wanted to know where the information had come from. "How reliable is the source?"

Shimony replied, "Our contact in Al Raqqah just sent a message the entire leadership of ISIS has vacated their headquarters in a hurry and were headed south toward Al Kawn. Apparently, there is a hilly area dissected by ravines and dry riverbeds where they had prepared a make-shift camp that will serve as a hideaway and shelter in case of a catastrophic attack on Al Raqqah."

Israeli intelligence had known of this secret refuge but while ISIS was winning on the ground the analysts believed it would never actually be used. David immediately understood the ramifications of the move. "So, we assume they are now expecting the retaliation from our forces and moving there. This doesn't make sense because they are defenseless and vulnerable over there. We can bomb the place and make one big plateau out of it without any concern about public opinion. After all, who cares about the death of a few hundred ISIS terrorists and some stray animals – human snakes and scorpions. I would have thought they would try to hide in a large city amongst civilians who we would hesitate to bomb. Something doesn't add up. I suspect the leaders are sending the rank and file, the disposable warriors, and would-be martyrs to these godforsaken hills while they go into hiding somewhere else. I wouldn't bother sending our planes to that area. I would concentrate our efforts of our defensive systems to avert the looming rocket attack as well as intensify our efforts to locate the launching spot. We can later exact our wrath on the real leaders of ISIS and the planners of the attack."

Haim Shimony considered David's words and for a long moment didn't say anything. Finally, he replied, "This is more of a political decision than a matter of Mossad's responsibility. I'll give the Prime Minister all the information regarding the situation and let him decide what to do and when to do it. By the way, he has preferred to go to the underground shelter with his family – which is against the rules, of course – because I believe his wife insisted."

David said he'd give Eugene another call just to make sure there was no new data from the search for the missing rockets.

Eugene picked up the phone before the first ring ended, after all it was still early afternoon in Washington, DC. He said, "David, I was just about to call you. Our NRO has detected some unusual activity in Iran, not far from the Hamedan air base. I would normally not bother to share this with you because it is so far from your borders, but the preliminary imagery information suggests this could be what you are looking for. Anyway, as we speak a reconnaissance drone is on its way there to get detailed information. The weather in the area is quite bad which is a mixed blessing – it will be harder to get good images, but the drone has a better chance of remaining undetected."

David wondered if this was related to the impending ISIS attack against his country and said, "I am not sure this has anything to do with us but please try to get more specific information. Can you get another round of satellite imagery of the areas on our eastern borders with Syria and Jordan?" Then as afterthought he added, "Perhaps also of Iraq's border with Jordan."

Eugene was surprised at the last request and said, "Why are you worried about Iraq?"

David replied, "We have some experience with Iraqi rockets fired at Israel in the 1991 Gulf War. I wonder if ISIS feels that getting into Jordan with the rockets may be too risky and they would settle for the second-best option – the western border of Iraq."

Eugene said, "Well, I'll see what we can do and get back to you."

Umm Chamain depression

Raymond Mashal, the 'Rocket Man,' took one last look at his latest and perhaps last ever, creation.

On the one hand, he was proud of what he had done – taken an old, outmoded rocket, modified it and increased its range and payload capability, modernized its guidance system and prepared it for a strike that will go down as a turning point in the history of the Arab nations. And he had done this feat almost single-handedly and under duress.

On the other hand, he had produced a death machine – a means for delivering a device that can kill, murder actually, tens of thousands of innocent civilians. This monstrosity of which he was a vital part may well put him in the pages of history as the 'Dreadful Rocket Man.'

The fact that his work was carried out under a threat of death would not release him from the responsibility. Raymond wondered if this is how Colonel Tibbets, the pilot of the B-29 bomber, felt before dropping the first atomic bomb on Hiroshima.

Murad looked at him and sensed his contemplative mood. He was also having some scruples about the act they were about to perform but kept his thoughts to himself. Selim, the driver, was jumping up and down impatiently and didn't seem to have a worry in the world. Raymond wondered if it was an effect of the alcohol, or perhaps of some dope he had smoked, or simply the young driver's reaction to what was happening.

Murad set the timer that would launch the rocket at Tel-Aviv, some two hundred and fifty miles away, one hour after dawn. Then the three of them got into the cabin of the truck and took off along the dirt road that led back to the highway. When they reached it, they turned east and headed toward Baghdad away from the Jordanian border and far away from Tel-Aviv.

The hills near Cheshmeh Qasaban

Major Aswadi looked at the small group that silently stared back him. He told them all to get in the truck and then walked around the back of the truck to look at the launch pad upon which the rocket was positioned.

He contemplated the scene for a long moment, then checked the setting of the timer one last time. He glanced at the shipping container to remain at the site and climbed in the truck's cabin and asked them all to pray to Allah for the success of their mission.

The truck made its way slowly back to the main road. When they passed through the main street of Cheshmeh Qasaban, the only paved street in the tiny village, a few stray dogs ran after the truck barking loudly. None of the residents accosted them or asked what they were doing there in the middle of the night – they had learned the hard way to mind their own business.

Kasim wondered if the small village would still exist when the government in Tehran discovered that the rocket with the atomic bomb was launched from there.

The escort van was still waiting on the main road and the two vehicles headed back west trying to get across the border back to Syria before the launch and before all hell broke loose.

Afrin's hand crawled across the narrow space that separated her from Kasim, and she squeezed his hand. He understood she felt relief that they were back on the way to safety, to a place where the Major wouldn't make them 'disappear.'

NRO headquarters, Chantilly, Virginia

The phone on Lt. Abigail Hill's desk rang. She had been waiting intently for the call and quickly picked it up.

The drone operator was on the line. "I am patching you live into the imagery sent from the drone."

Abigail looked at the blurred image and couldn't make out any recognizable objects. She said, "Please tell me what I am looking at."

The drone operator responded, "Wait a minute while I focus the camera. It is raining lightly over the area and the drizzle is interfering with the photography. I'll switch another wavelength and try to improve the clarity."

Abigail looked closely at the new images and excitedly said, "Now I can see an elongated object standing next to something that looks like a large box."

The drone operator replied, "Based on the reflection I am picking up; the large box is a metallic object and judging by its size it could well be a shipping container. The elongated object that looks like a huge tube is probably a rocket of some sort. As it is almost perpendicular to the ground it is difficult to tell exactly what kind of rocket it is but looks as if it is about ready to be launched."

Abigail had reached the same conclusion. "Could you take the drone down to a lower altitude to get a closer look near ground level? This will help us identify the rocket."

The drone operator said, "Are you sure you want to do this? I have standing orders to avoid being shot down on Iranian soil–"

Abigail cut him off. "It is within my special authority for this mission, in a case of national security, to take such calculated risks. I am giving you a direct order to fly the drone at a low altitude as close to the suspect objects as you can and get us some definitive evidence of what's out there."

The drone operator didn't care for her tone and even less for her terse order but had to obey. "Aye, Lt. Hill, but remember it's your responsibility. I'll need about 10 minutes to descend almost to the ground level and do a fly by near the object. Let's hope there are no anti-aircraft systems in the area. I'll try to approach from the south-east and get away as quickly as I can back to the safety of Syrian air space." The last words were pronounced with some irony.

Abigail was consoled that her order would be carried out and ignored the tone. "Call me when you get close. I'll update the Director. And thanks."

***

She called the NRO Director and updated him. Before she could complete her report, she got a 'call waiting' tone and apologized that she had to hang up with the Director and take the call from the drone operator.

"Lt. Hill, look at this beautiful image of the rocket."

She studied the image noting that it didn't look like any rocket the Iranians had. In fact, it looked more like the out-dated Scud B or Al Hussein rockets that the Iraqi army had, but there were obviously some modifications that changed its appearance.

She thanked the drone operator and wished him luck in returning the drone safely to its base. She called the Director again and told him about her conclusions.

The Director passed the information up the chain of command. The National Security advisor and the Secretary of Defense agreed that they should tell the President about the developing situation and agreed to meet in his office an hour later.

Based on the information that had been forwarded from the NNSA, the National Nuclear Security Administration, they couldn't rule out the rocket could be equipped with an atomic warhead. The National Security advisor suggested they tell the NNSA about the rocket and the information received by Eugene, who was the duty officer at NNSA operations center.

Eugene thought he should share this latest information with Mossad and called David. It was just past midnight in Tel-Aviv and David was trying to get some sleep on a cot in his office. He became wide awake when he heard Eugene's voice.

Eugene said, "I think we have found your rocket in Iran far away from your borders. We have excellent images that show it is probably a modified Scud B and there is no way that it can reach Tel-Aviv."

By now David's mind was working in turbo mode. "Eugene, if this is the rocket that ISIS built then it must be part of an intricate plot. Are they doing this as a diversion and plan some other attack on Israel? I wonder what they are up to."

Eugene thought that David was being a bit paranoid but, considering the ramifications of an atomic blast anywhere in the world and especially in the tumultuous Middle East, he said, "David, I agree that we must search for some ulterior motive here. I'll be in touch as soon as anything comes up."

CHAPTER 25

Mossad Headquarters, Tel-Aviv

David thanked Eugene and then walked into Mossad's operations center and asked the duty officer to display a map of the region on the large flat screen.

He zoomed in and marked the spot where the drone had located the shipping container and rocket. The terrain in the area looked like many other places in the Middle East with nothing exceptional or outstanding.

He zoomed out until he could see Tehran in the east and Tel-Aviv in the west. Cheshmeh Qasaban was about halfway between Baghdad and Tehran but Tel-Aviv was much further away, about nine hundred and fifty miles. He zoomed in again and did something he was taught during his physics studies at the Technion in Haifa – a thought-experiment (the original term used by Einstein was Gedankenexperiment). This was not much more than a fancy name for a 'what if' analysis of different scenarios but can serve as a powerful tool for analysis of fuzzy situations fraught with uncertainty.

What if a rocket with an atomic warhead was fired from the vicinity of the Hamedan air base toward Baghdad? The Iraqis would surely blame the Mullahs' regime of Iran. The world would be in awe because of the number of casualties and because the Iranians had grossly violated the nuclear deal they had signed in Vienna in 2015. The tens of thousands of victims would get added to the hundreds of thousands killed in the ongoing civil wars in Iraq and Syria, but the West and Russia would be less shocked by the fact that once again Muslims were killed by Muslims and look at this atrocity as just another tribal war on a larger scale.

After the nuclear strike, Iraq would surely disintegrate into three parts: Shiite Muslims in the south will unify with Iran, Sunni Muslims in the center will seek revenge, and Kurds in the north will seize the opportunity and declare an independent Kurdish state that will unite all Kurds from Syria, Turkey, Iran, and Iraq. These developments would hardly be favorable to ISIS because it would lose its grip on its remaining territories.

David then thought about the implications of a nuclear attack on Tehran causing tens of thousands of Iranian casualties, probably even upward of a hundred thousand considering the population density of Tehran. He figured that even though it would soon be known that the rocket was launched from inside Iran, the regime will automatically blame Israel and try to strike back with all its might in retaliation.

It would start by firing a few dozen long-range rockets at select targets in Israel and would soon be joined by a salvo of thousands of primitive short-range rockets launched from Gaza by Hamas and by a large barrage of tens of thousands of rockets fired indiscriminately at Israel by Hezbollah in the north. Israel would even the score, of course, destroying everything in the region but would suffer so much damage that it would have a great difficulty rising from the ashes. This could better serve ISIS, thought David, even more so than launching the atomic bomb at Tel-Aviv.

He called Shimony and told him about the conclusions of his thought-experiment and said they should send a warning to the Iranians. The Chief heard him out patiently but then asked the inevitable question, "What if you are wrong and Tel-Aviv is hit by an atomic bomb?"

David knew the gamble he suggested was huge. "We would do everything within our power to intercept any rocket fired at us. We have our three-tiered anti-missile defense systems at the state of highest alert. I suggest we warn them to expect an attempt to fire a rocket at Tel-Aviv just before dawn or soon after the sun rises. That is the preferred time for such a surprise attack."

Shimony then said, "We have another problem. Even if we forewarn Iran that Tehran may be the target of an attack by ISIS, they will either treat this as an Israeli ruse to prevent a counterattack or as a bluff. If you are right, David, and the attack is planned for dawn they won't have enough time to reach the launch area and destroy the rocket."

David replied, "If they act immediately on our information, they can send planes from Hamedan base and get there in a few minutes. They have several ground attack fighter jets – Russian made Sukhoi Su-24 and Su-25 as well as their own HESA Azarakhsh light attack aircraft. They can also ask the Russian air force to scramble some of the fighter jets from the same base. They don't have to score a direct hit – it's enough to blow the rocket off its launch pad. I believe they can do it even in the dark and the rain."

Shimony was skeptical if they could convince the Iranians to bomb their own territory based on a warning sent from Mossad in the middle of the night. He said, "Even if we persuade the Americans to deliver the information and warning, I doubt the Iranians will do anything before daylight. Perhaps we can exploit the renewed close relations between Russia and Iran – but we need to share the information with the Russians, and I have my doubts if they will pass it on to the Iranians in time."

David was frustrated. "So, what do we do? Do we sit still and wait for the catastrophe to obliterate most of the Middle East?"

Shimony smiled for the first time. "No, we do the job ourselves."

Seeing David's expression, he added, "You know the old Talmudic motto attributed to Rabbi Hillel the Elder who lived in the first century BC. Hillel says, *If I am not for myself, who will be for me? But if I am only for myself, who am I? If not now, when?* David was familiar with the quote from 'Ethics of the fathers, 1:14' and he nodded while Shimony continued, "David, we have the strongest air force in the region, the best pilots in the world and some of the most advanced aircraft, thanks to our American allies. We have just received the first shipment of F-35 stealth multirole fighters that the Americans call Lightning II, but we call Adir, meaning Great in Hebrew."

David's mouth fell open. "Do you seriously intend to send our most valuable planes on a mission that will take them one thousand miles through hostile territory without any planning, little practice, and even less combat experience? Why don't we ask the Americans to do this job?"

Shimony responded, "It's the only solution. The Americans need weeks, if not months, to run such an operation. I'll get the PM's permission while you get the Commander of the Air Force. Make sure that he puts his best F-35 pilots on alert and gets them ready to take off within the hour. Also, get him to prepare for mid-air refueling or else the planes won't be able to return to Israel."

David replied, "Haim, even our great air force needs time to plan operations. For an air raid that far from our borders we usually go through a series of preparations – intelligence gathering, coordination with the air force headquarters and operations section, flight crew briefing, assessment of vulnerable points, emergency planning, and so on."

Shimony said, "This is not a normal situation. There is no time to work according to standard operation procedures. Go, David, go."

***

The Prime Minister didn't like to feel manipulated by his underlings, especially by Haim Shimony. He loathed the man but due to his popularity couldn't afford to replace him without good cause. Now, he saw such an opportunity – if the mission of destroying the rocket hundreds of miles beyond enemy lines would turn out to be successful, as he hoped, then he would claim credit for authorizing it.

If, on the other hand, planes were lost and pilots were killed or taken alive as prisoners then he would claim he had been misled or even deceived by the Mossad Chief and that would give him ample chance to replace him with one of the few people he trusted. So, for the PM the decision to approve the mission was easy – it was a win-win situation.

He only made a statement for the protocol. "Shimony, make sure all our people return safely." Haim nodded and didn't bother to reply.

David Avivi called the Commander of the Air Force, General Yotam Lahav, and arranged to meet him at the airfield that served the F-35 squadron. There were only a handful of planes that were operational, as some served for training and most of the others had not yet left the Lockheed factory assembly line.

First, David briefed General Lahav and explained the situation, emphasizing they had no time to implement the standard operation procedures. Lahav understood the dire situation and immediately asked the squadron commander, Colonel Ehud, and the three most experienced F-35 pilots to join them.

The operations and air force intelligence officers were also called in. The attack plan was simple – see the target and destroy it. The complicated part was getting there without being detected and then getting back safely. The pilots had to contend with flying one thousand miles over enemy territory, including through parts of Iran that were heavily defended by the most modern anti-aircraft systems in the Russian arsenal that were sold to the Iranians.

Then they would have to rendezvous with their tankers for midair refueling, also over enemy territory. The fighters would be practically invisible on radar, but the tankers had a huge radar-signature so the refueling would have to take place as far away from Iran as possible and over an area in which there was a blind spot in the radar coverage. They would be most vulnerable at the time of the refueling so would have to do it quickly.

General Lahav asked, "David, we are worried about the Americans. First, their surveillance systems are sure to pick us up even as we take off and then follow us all the way to the target. Have they been notified of the plan and have they given their approval? Second, after the attack they may claim we used the F-35 for aggressive purposes and stop the delivery of the rest of the planes."

David expected these two questions. "We'll notify the Americans but not seek their consent because if we wait for that we are sure to be too late. So, we'll also give them the option of plausible denial – they can say that they couldn't stop us. Regarding your other question – our success would surely boost the sales of the F-35 planes and benefit the American aircraft industry that is having financial problems. If we fail, then it is likely Israel will no longer need these aircraft nor be able to afford them. General, please get your people to do the planning and show me what you had done in one hour. Considering the distance and flight time to the target, you'll have to take off in less than two hours."

***

An hour later General Lahav interrupted David's phone call with Eugene and signaled that the pilots were ready for the final briefing.

David said, "Eugene, I have to go now. As I told you, Israel cannot and will not sit still while its security and very existence are threatened. Please make sure your people do not interfere and refrain from any action or even too much unusual communication traffic." He hung up and followed the General.

The four pilots selected for the mission were sitting in the first row of seats in the small auditorium that served for briefing the air crews before missions and debriefing them after their return to base.

The squadron's intelligence officer was tracing the flight path on the map that was projected on the large screen and describing the threats from the defensive systems they had to avoid on their way.

Then the operations officer took the stage and explained in detail what they had to do when they reached the target. Finally, General Lahav stepped up to the podium and highlighted the importance of the mission for the survival of Israel and asked if there were any questions.

Colonel Ehud looked at his three wingmen with a somber face and saw that they all understood the responsibility that was placed upon their shoulders. The pilots and crews of the tanker planes were already assembled outside the auditorium and waiting for their briefing.

Ehud rose and led his men to the room where their flight pressure suits, helmets, and survival kits were hanging.

Within minutes, they were all suited up. Each pilot made sure that everything was in place and comfortably arranged and the foursome headed to the hangar where four F-35 planes were ready.

Every pilot walked around his plane and did a final check and then was helped up the ladder into the cockpit by the chief of the ground crew. After a thorough check of the cockpit, each pilot gave the thumbs-up sign.

The ground crew moved around the plane, removed the pins that secured the air-to-air missiles and the air-to-ground munitions as well as the defensive systems. A member of the ground crew stepped to the front of the plane and held up the pins with their attached red ribbons so the pilot could see that all systems were now armed.

The roar of the engines shattered the silence of the night. Without any word, radio-silence was strictly obeyed, the four F-35 fighters taxied to the runway and took off. Within minutes they headed east in a small formation of two pairs.

They switched off their navigation lights as soon as they crossed the Israeli border to the east. The flight path they followed was practically the most direct route from their base to Cheshmeh Qasaban, although they did wriggle a little to avoid some areas with aerial defensive systems.

Near Cheshmeh Qasaban

Colonel Ehud was all alone in the cockpit of his F-35 fighter. He had no one to talk to or to share his concerns and thoughts with. He missed the presence of another crewman in the cockpit like the good old days when he flew F-15I fighters.

He liked the F-35 and its exceptional capabilities, on a mission like this the stealth features were essential, but still would have liked someone else in the cockpit. When they reached the border with Iran, he switched his navigation lights on and off three times as a signal to his wingmen to ditch their external fuel tanks and further reduce the planes radar signature.

As they approached the target area, Ehud was totally focused on his mission and ignored his need to urinate. He couldn't see his wingmen and they couldn't see him but was sure they were in their designated positions – his number two on his left and a little behind him, numbers three and four on his right and further back.

Still maintaining radio-silence, he switched on his navigation lights and headed toward the target that was clearly depicted on his screen. He released his two guided bombs and turned back west to circle around the target.

His wingman came in and discharged his two bombs. Then plane number three delivered a couple of cluster bombs that spread hundreds of little bomblets all over the area.

This was considered by the Dublin Convention on Cluster Munitions as a prohibited weapon, mainly because many of the bomblets failed to detonate and remained on the ground posing a hazard to people in the vicinity.

The fourth plane ejected several flares that lit up the scene and enabled Colonel Ehud to see the results of their bomb run. To his horror, he saw that the while the shipping container had been blown to smithereens the rocket still appeared to be standing upright on its launch pad. There was a good chance it had been punctured and rendered useless by the bomblets, but Ehud couldn't take this chance.

He rolled over and strafed the rocket that thanks to the flares was now clearly visible to the naked eye. He was rewarded by a huge explosion that indicated the rocket's fuel tanks had been ignited. His worst fear didn't materialize – there was no nuclear explosion.

Colonel Ehud keyed his microphone three times without saying a word. The three clicks were picked up by several listening stations but only in one place, in Tel-Aviv, the meaning was understood – the mission was successfully accomplished.

The cheering was cut short by General Lahav. "Great. Now let's cross our fingers that they return safely. Their rendezvous with the tanker for refueling is due in twenty minutes over Turkish airspace. I hope our government has coordinated this because we want to avoid another conflict with the Turkish government."

David said. "We have arranged that. The Turks were reluctant at first until we convinced them that by this heroic act, we have averted an all-out war, perhaps a nuclear war, in the region and they stand to benefit from this."

General Lahav said, "I hope they don't get too enthusiastic and try to shoot down our planes like they did with the Russian jet fighter a while ago. If they try to do so, Colonel Ehud has strict orders to prevent this by all necessary means. As you may well know, Ehud is the best fighter pilot this nation has ever produced and the result of aerial combat with Turkish jet fighters is a foregone conclusion."

David saw that General Lahav's small stature had increased by 5 inches as he spoke. He didn't want to spoil the jubilant mood so refrained from speaking.

NRO Headquarters, Chantilly, Virginia

"Wow, what a display of fireworks," cried Lt. Abigail Hill as she watched the images sent from the satellite that was surveying the site near Cheshmeh Qasaban.

Everybody in the operations room rushed to see what she was so excited about, but she was already on the phone to the Director describing what she had just seen.

The Director had been given a heads-up from the NNSA about the impending Israeli strike, so he coolly thanked Abigail for the phone call and told her to make sure the news didn't leave the operations room.

The Director reported to his bosses that the Israeli strike had been launched and was probably successful. This was passed up the chain of command to the President who said, "Publicly we'll claim ignorance, but I want to award the Presidential Medal of Freedom to the Israelis who did this in a private ceremony."

Eugene wanted to call David to congratulate him on a job perfectly carried out but decided to postpone his call until the dust, literally and figuratively, settled.

Umm Chamain depression, one hour after dawn

A few excessively inquisitive snakes and scorpions that wandered too closely to the strange object that appeared in their midst were scorched by the huge plume of fire that bolted out of the rocket's nozzle as it ignited. It was just after dawn when the night predators were crawling into their hiding places to escape the day's heat and the creatures that were active in the daylight were just waking for another day of searching for food and moisture.

The rocket rose majestically gaining speed and altitude as it headed west on its 250 mile journey to Tel-Aviv. Its warhead contained 550 pounds of conventional explosives, not an atomic bomb, yet it had the potential to cause severe damage.

The noisy launch was not heard by any human ear but was immediately detected by the radar and surveillance systems of the Jordanians, Israelis, Americans, and everyone else that had assets in the area. The Israeli anti-missile defense systems calculated the rocket's trajectory and when it turned out that it was aimed at Tel-Aviv, two intermediate range rockets were launched to intercept it.

Raymond's improved rocket was quite primitive despite the modifications he introduced and had no maneuverability, so it was easy prey for the Israeli anti-missile rockets.

The first one exploded close to the tail end of Raymond's rocket and the stabilizing fins were sheared off by the explosion diverting the rocket off its original course and turning it into nothing more than a rock hurtling through the air.

The second Israeli rocket self-destructed once its target had disappeared.

CHAPTER 26

The aftermath

The residents of the Palestinian city of Ramallah were shocked by the explosion of the warhead in the cone of Raymond's rocket.

Aerial and ground photography taken a few hours after the explosion showed that it scored a direct hit on the headquarters and administrative center of the Palestinian Authority known as the Mukataa.

The president of the Palestinian Authority was buried under the rubble and died instantly. Cynics later said that his advanced age and fragile health would have done the same within a year or two.

Fortunately for the Palestinian people most of the corrupt leadership joined the president on his way to heaven, or perhaps to hell. After a period of civil strife, a new government was elected, one that was willing to live side-by-side in peace with Israel.

The prosperity brought to both sides by the peace accords was in sharp contrast to what was happening all over the Middle East.

***

In many capital cities, including Paris, Amsterdam, London, Brussels, and Moscow, the aggressive act by Israel was publicly condemned.

The Israeli ambassador in each country was summoned to the local foreign ministry and reprimanded. As soon as the reporters and press left the room, however, each and every foreign minister walked straight up to the ambassador and shook his hand.

At the headquarters of the International Atomic Energy Agency, the IAEA in Vienna, the Israeli representative received a warm embrace from the Secretary General of the organization. After all, she was an elegant petite woman whose outwardly gentle and soft-spoken appearance belied her keen mind and tough character.

***

Tehran's initial reaction was to threaten Israel for its blatant disregard of international agreements and the violation of Iranian sovereignty. Mass demonstrations in the streets of Tehran followed with the mob shouting 'death to Israel' and adding 'death to America' because that was the way to protest in a 'spontaneous' rally.

However, after teams from the Atomic Energy Organization of Iran (AEOI) collected samples of soil from the site and the debris near Cheshmeh Qasaban, where the rocket was destroyed, the attitude changed. The fact that plutonium was found scattered all over the ground was bad enough and the analysis of its isotopic composition indicated that it originated from the missing shipment of spent fuel.

The government in Tehran found an indirect pathway to thank the Israelis for their enterprise and it looked like the dawn of a new age in the tense relations between Tel-Aviv and Tehran.

***

The regimes of the moderate Arab states that were also threatened by ISIS were greatly relieved when the plot was foiled. They didn't know any details but understood that a daring strike by Israel had prevented a large war in the region that could have toppled their regimes. The death blow to the radical Islam was like a breath of fresh air to these Sunni regimes. Once the Palestinian problem was resolved – and the indications from the new Palestinian Authority were favorable – they could publicly establish normal diplomatic and trade relations with the Jewish State.

***

The leadership of ISIS couldn't return to Al Raqqah because it was now surrounded by the Kurd fighters, the Turkish army, and Bashar Assad's Syrian troops.

The male residents celebrated their release from the terror of ISIS by shaving their beards while the women burned the Chadors they were forced to wear.

The festivities were occasionally interrupted by a suicide car bomb or a booby trap going off, but the general feeling was that the price for freedom from the Islamic fanatics had been high but well worth it.

The dream of the New Caliphate was not dead even though ISIS wasn't in control of any territory in what used to be Iraq or Syria. It was still alive in the hearts of the hardcore factions of ISIS in parts of the Middle East, Africa, and Europe.

In the popular press, this situation was compared to a malignant cancer growth that had spread to other parts of the body. Surgery and radiotherapy are no longer effective to eradicate the disease, and although temporarily under control it may erupt again.

Dr. Raymond Mashal the 'Rocket Man' made his way safely back to Baghdad where he returned to his second career as a science teacher in a high school, under an assumed name, of course.

None of his colleagues or students understand why he keeps humming the song Rocket Man to himself, but have not had the heart to point out he is always a bit off tune.

Dr. Kasim and Mrs. Afrin Walid returned to Germany and are gainfully employed in a nuclear research center. They had to fabricate a completely fictional CV to get their jobs but as they passed the proficiency tests with flying colors, they were accepted. Their new names do not have any resemblance to their old names.

***

In Tel-Aviv there was a mood for celebration among the small number of people who knew the seriousness of the threat that had been averted. The printed press and media reporters had hinted that some exceptional operation by Mossad and the Israeli air force had taken place during the last twenty-four hours.

As they were not aware of the exact details of the threat or the preventive strike that Israel had launched, the correspondents felt free to circulate rumors and provide speculation.

One newspaper that was owned by a foreign supporter of the Prime Minister praised the PM for his foresight, courage, and determination in saving Israel from a new holocaust.

On the other hand, another newspaper gave credit to the brave pilots of the F-35 squadron and claimed the air force ignored the warning of the PM and carried out the daring strike in the heart of the territory of Israel's worst enemy.

The TV channels delivered endless programs of 'talking heads' with self-proclaimed experts on military issues, on nuclear and conventional terror, on Middle East policies, and on the political scene arguing with one another. The true facts were still considered a state secret, but this did not stop the experts from 'explaining' the facts to the public.

A modest ceremony was held at the air force base from which the planes had taken off. The PM and Chief of Staff of the Israeli Defense Forces awarded badges of merit to all four F-35 pilots as well as to the crews of tankers that refueled the jets over Turkish air space and the operators of the anti-missile battery that shot down Raymond's rocket.

General Lahav was given a solemn promise by the PM that

he would be first in line to be the next Chief of Staff.

Another little ceremony had taken place at Mossad head-quarters. The PM had ambiguous feelings about acknowledging Shimony's role in the operation. He was glad the operation was a resounding success and that it opened a window of opportunity to make peace with the Palestinians and their new leadership as well as amend relations with Iran and the moderates of the Arab world.

On the other hand, this meant that it would be practically impossible to replace Shimony with one of his men. But the PM was a great orator and delivered one of his best speeches, in which he commended Shimony for following his directive. The small audience that included the Mossad agents that knew the history of the operation and the details listened to the self-accolade with straight faces.

David Avivi returned to Amsterdam for a well-deserved vacation. Anika was waiting for him at the Schiphol airport terminal and whisked him off to a small hotel in the German Black Forest region where they spent the days hiking and exploring trails through the dense trees and the nights exploring each other's fantasies.

ACKNOWLEDGEMENTS

In this book, and my other books, **Mission Achemist, Mission Renegade, Mission Patriot, Mission Senator, Mission Menace** and **Mission Tango,** I have tried to imagine the unimaginable. Fortunately, these are works of fiction and hopefully they will remain so.

First, and foremost, I would like to thank you for reading this book. I hope you enjoyed it despite the scientific jargon that I have minimized.

I dearly appreciate your comments, so please send them to: Charlie.Wolfe.author@gmail.com

I would be especially grateful if you would post a review on Amazon, where you purchased this book.

This book would not have been possible without the help of Dr. Wikipedia and Professor Google and Magister Google Earth. I also found a wealth of information in scientific articles and books. However, any misinterpretation of the technical and geographical information from those sources is my own responsibility.

I should point out that Scud rockets, like all rockets propelled by liquid fuel, consist of four main parts: the payload, the fuel, the oxidizer, and the rocket engine. The 'Rocket Man' could do little to redesign the payload, managed to slightly increase the amount of fuel and oxidizer, and focused on the rocket engine. He did this by improving the combustion chamber in which the fuel and oxidizer are mixed and ignited and by designing a better nozzle through which the hot combustion gases are ejected, thus providing propulsion.

Of course, as this is a work of fiction, it is hard to believe that a lone scientist with limited access to technology could do better than the experienced Russian rocket scientists that designed the Scud.

According to the literature, plutonium can be extracted from irradiated nuclear fuel of commercial reactors. In principle, it can be used for making a nuclear device, and there are reports that it has been done in practice. However, there are serious doubts whether such a device would work. So, don't rush to try it at home.

It is unnecessary to declare that this book is a work of fiction and any resemblance to real events or people is not to be understood as anything but a coincidence. I apologize in advance in case any person feels offended by the plot. Some of the fictional characters have been inspired by exceptional young people I had come across in my career, but none exist.

Special thanks are due to Glenda Sacks Jaffe who meticulously edited this book.

Finally, I am grateful to my family and friends who read the manuscript and enabled me to improve the text thanks to their astute comments.